MW01493593

THE PICTURE
KILLS

IAN BULL

STORY MERCHANT BOOKS
LOS ANGELES • 2014

PRAISE FOR *THE PICTURE KILLS*
BOOK 1 IN THE QUINTANA ADVENTURES

"The settings are stellar and richly detailed. We're gripped from start to finish...pacing is spectacular, and story excels. Characters are multi-dimensional, and settings gleam."

—Writer's Digest National Book Competition

"A thrilling page-turner with real literary value...combines the international intrigue of Lee Child, the procedural know-how of Michael Connelly and, yes, the Hollywood insider's expertise of Jackie Collins, with a plot that takes the reader on a Bond-like adventure across the globe."

—Amazon reviewer

"The book comes together in a shocking, hair-raising climax that only later will the reader realize had been set up by the author chapters in advance."

—Amazon reviewer

"Steve Quintana is...a new thriller hero who's human, prone to mistakes, frailty, and self-doubt, yet with Scot Harvath power, Angus MacGyver ingenuity, and Ethan Hunt resilience that makes him ripe for a continuing literary series."

—Amazon reviewer

PRAISE FOR *SIX PASSENGERS, FIVE PARACHUTES*
BOOK II IN THE QUINTANA ADVENTURES

"The author has a stellar instinct for crafting interactions between characters...fabulous foreboding and panic...an engaging read and, in Steven, a character who could live on the big screen."

—Writer's Digest National Book Competition

"The adventures of Steve Quintana are as compelling as ever...with the action moving at breakneck speed. Bull's work is up there with Connelly, Cussler, and Patterson when it comes to creating an intense, exciting thrill ride full of technical expertise, whether it's Hollywood, espionage, or travel. And he has the guts to take his lead character into situations that you will have to read to believe."

—Amazon reviewer

"This book picks up where the first book left off, with Steven Quintana trying to track down the people who funded the kidnapping of Julia Travers in the first book. The twists are incredible. In the first book, Steven struggled to rescue Julia. In the sequel, it's Julia who must save Steven!"

—Amazon reviewer

The Picture Kills

Copyright © 2014 by Ian Bull. All rights reserved. Revised Edition 2020.

No part of this book may be reproduced or transmitted in any form or by any means, electronic or mechanical, including photocopying, recording, or by any information storage and retrieval system, without the express written permission of the author.

www.quintanaadventures.com
www.CaliforniaBull.com

Twitter: @IanBull3
Instagram: #CaliforniaBull, #CaliforniaNoirBooks

ISBN-13: 978-0-9904216-6-5

Story Merchant Books
400 S. Burnside Avenue #11B
Los Angeles, CA 90036
www.storymerchantbooks.com

THE PICTURE
KILLS

Dear Ina,
This is the
first in a trilogy.
I hope you like
them!

Donald

IAN BULL

To my wife, Robin and my daughter, Lily.
And to my grandfather, John Raynard, who used to sit
outside his silver trailer on Hollywood Beach, Florida,
reading thrillers. I wish he could have read this one.

THE PICTURE
KILLS

CHAPTER 1

STEVEN

Day 1: Thursday Morning

Whenever I sleep, the same dream haunts me. People move through my camera lens and freeze as the shutter clicks. The rebel soldiers gather around the village fire—click. A frightened mother holds a baby—click. The German tourist lies in the dirt, a rifle to his neck—click.

But the rebel leader stays in the shadows. My mission is to snap a photo of his face. I need the boy from the pigpen to lure the leader toward the light of the fire, but the boy stands by his mother, hiding in her skirts.

The rebel leader notices the boy and calls him over. The boy is the only remaining male from the village.

"¿Dónde están los otros hombres?" he asks the boy. *Where are the other men?*

The boy shakes his head like he doesn't understand…then steps closer to the fire. The leader repeats the question. The boy shakes his head again and takes another step closer to the flames. The rebel leader strides into the light and grabs the boy's arm. Something falls from the boy's pocket—the coffee candy from the MRE ration I gave him. The leader grabs it from the ground and shakes it in the boy's face.

"Americanos? Dónde están?" he asks. *Where are they?*

The other rebels grab their rifles and aim in four different directions.

The kid glances at us, lying in the mud in the dark, then points at us in the pigpen. The leader looks, and his face lands in my frame. He's tall, dark, bearded, with a Roman nose, and a streak of premature white in his long black curly hair—click. El Sádico. The Sadist.

People have wanted a photo of him for years, and I just got the perfect close-up.

Then he shoots the boy in the chest. The boy falls to the ground, dead.

The other rifles swing toward us and spit fire—

I bolt awake.

Same dream, every night, for five years.

My shoulder aches and my sheets are twisted and damp. Sleep won't come again, so I climb out of my sofa bed, open the glass sliding door and step out on the patio overlooking Tivoli Cove in Malibu, California. My hand rubs the scar behind my right shoulder out of habit.

It's predawn, but there's enough light to surf. My damp wetsuit smells like rotting seaweed, and tugging it on is a chore. But then I grab my board, dart down the wooden steps and across the cold sand, and I'm in the Pacific Ocean.

I paddle out. Tivoli Cove has a dozen houses on a sheltered beach that curves away from the coast road, ending at a rocky point that creates a slow wave that breaks left back to shore. I'm the only surfer out there at dawn in the middle of the week, which suits me fine. There's no jockeying for the wave, and no small talk to endure. Catching my first wave, I crouch low on my board and trail my fingers in the moving wall of glassy water.

After ten waves, I rest on my board and watch a pelican hovering above the swells. She tucks in her wings and dive bombs down into the water and comes up ten feet from me with a flopping fish in her oversized beak. It makes me grin. The Malibu morning show is better than any movie. The ocean is my only friend, and her vastness dilutes any memories that the night throws my way.

The twinge of pain in my shoulder is my signal to stop. The last wave of the morning is a three-footer that pushes me into shore right in front of the wooden stairs to my patio. I take off my ankle leash, gather my board and climb back up, then rinse off the salt water with the hose.

The stabbing pain returns as I tug the wetsuit down. All that shoulder rotation grinds down the bone in its socket. My doc at the VA says to quit surfing, but I want to feel the pain. It's a penance, like when I was ten years old in San Francisco and doing my catechism at St. Cecilia's.

I step inside, close up the sofa bed, pull on jeans and a sweatshirt, and then step into the kitchenette and turn on the coffee maker. Four steps total, wall to wall. Home is a bachelor apartment in the bottom of an empty decaying beach house, and the walls are covered with wine and beer stains from years of Pepperdine undergrad parties that the previous renters hosted. My neighbors love me in comparison—the quiet vet with his cameras. My stay in LA was supposed to be temporary, so I never painted. That was five years ago.

I grab my Nikon and step back onto the vast deck. It's much bigger than the inside, and the reason it's a great place to live. A low flying seagull rides an air current just ahead of a foamy green wave, backlit by morning light. My hand pulls focus on the long lens as it lands inside my frame – click. A good photo.

My cell phone rings: Offices of *Celebrity Exposed*.

"This is Quinn."

"It's Larry. How's my favorite shutterbug?"

"Do you have a job for me?"

"Julia Travers is going to a movie premiere. Be here by nine," he says, and hangs up.

Time for my day job.

I down my coffee, pull on my leather jacket, grab my camera and dart up my staircase to the street level. I start my Kawasaki and I slide into morning rush hour traffic on Pacific Coast Highway, headed into Los Angeles.

CHAPTER 2

JULIA

I step out of the guest house dressed in my white dobok, ready for my tae kwon do lesson. I'm 5'10", so the martial arts outfits for women are too small for me. The best alternative is the outfit for teenage boys, which is then too big.

Will Becker emerges from his mansion in a T-shirt and yoga pants so tight he can't raise an arm or leg in the air, but he does look immaculate.

"Will, you look like an ad right out of GQ."

"I try to look good, even when I don't feel good."

"Me, I'm trying to look like a marshmallow with a belt in the middle."

Will laughs, which is a good sign. He doesn't want to do this.

I rub his back. "Thank you for indulging me. You'll feel better once you warm up."

We walk out on the lawn beside the infinity pool and greet Carlos—our tae kwon do instructor. We bow to each other, and Carlos flashes me a smile as his head dips. I can't help smiling back. It's a beautiful day, he's a beautiful man, and this is the highlight of my week.

"Let's begin by stretching."

Carlos gets serious. We face him and mirror his movements, reaching our arms over our heads.

Carlos always comes to the mansion—Will Becker's mansion, not mine. I've been living in Will's guest cottage for three months since someone broke into the garage of my security building and threw a brick with a love note through my car windshield. The paparazzi were already following me whenever I went out, and the brick was proof that my home wasn't safe anymore either. Will's estate has high walls and security cameras, so when he offered me his guest house, I jumped at it.

"Shoulders. Small circles, arms straight, like a bird," Carlos says.

Will touches my outstretched flapping arm with his.

"You're the wind beneath my wings."

"Stop it."

We giggle, which Carlos doesn't appreciate. I can relax, act silly and be myself in here. Outside these walls, the pushy photographers and brick-throwing crazies surround me. That's when fear overwhelms me and I morph into a hissing cat.

"I believe I can fly…I believe I can touch the sky," Will sings.

"Be serious. I need this."

"Not when you're safe in here with me."

My therapist has diagnosed me as "hyper-vigilant," perceiving every passing cloud as a threat. All I know is that taking this class makes me feel better.

"Let's move to runner's stretch."

Carlos turns around and steps into a lunge. Will and I admire his taut bum cheeks in full stretch, then glance at each other.

"You're right, I am feeling better," Will says.

I met Will on the set of his film *Driftwood*, which was his stab at serious drama after his last two action movies tanked. Scarlett Johansson was the female lead, and I played her younger sister. Will was once the number three box office star in the world, and he says that one good movie will put him on top again. *Driftwood* tanked, unfortunately for Will, but I got good reviews and more work. We also became friends…and possible lovers according to the tabloids.

Carlos leads us through our katas—a series of punches and kicks. After thirty minutes I'm covered with sweat, but Will's outfit is still as smooth as his hair. He doesn't like to move if he's not being paid.

"Who's ready to spar?"

"You fight your imaginary bad guys, Julia, I need a break." Will puts on a warm-up jacket and sits at a patio table under a cascade of red and orange bougainvillea. His personal assistant Derek, a handsome fit man in his fifties, comes out of the house carrying a tray with lemonade, glasses and towels. Will grabs a towel from him and pats away his nonexistent perspiration.

Carlos and I bow and take our stances. Carlos shouts, then kicks and advances. Fear rushes through me, but I resist the urge to flee. Retreating in step with him, I turn on my heel and surprise him with a mule kick to his thigh and knock him back.

Take that, handsome. I can handle you. I can handle anybody.

Now I advance, punching and kicking, and Carlos must retreat ten yards as he blocks. My fear turns into anger—anger at Carlos for trying to scare me, at Will for dismissing my fear, and at the photographers who make money from my fear.

"She's making you look bad, Carlos."

Carlos aims a kick that creases the air in front of my nose, which shocks me. He could have busted my face open if he had wanted, and my fear comes back. I advance with kicks of my own, but they all miss. Carlos yanks the lapels of my dobok and sweeps my feet out from under me, sending me skidding across the grass.

"You have to stay balanced, especially when you're using your weaker side."

"I'm not a lefty, my kicks aren't strong on that side yet."

He helps me up, then flicks back his long black hair and flashes that smile for the second time. "I can show you some more moves at the studio if you like."

Will stands up fast. "Thank you, Carlos, Derek will show you out."

Carlos bows to each of us. "Until next week."

Derek escorts him across the grass back towards the house. My stomach aches. Carlos glances back at me, then heads inside the mansion on his way to the front door. Bye bye, bum cheeks.

"You're too intense out there, Rambolina."

Will tosses me a towel. I untie my long blonde hair and wipe off the sweat.

"Kicking him, or flirting with him?"

"Both."

"Why do you care if he hits on me?"

"I'm just looking out for you, Julia. You can't be dating the help. You must choose the right company."

This is the trade-off living with Will; I feel safe, but he micromanages my life. He flashes me his headshot smile and runs a hand through his curly brown hair. He always turns on the charm when he wants something.

"Julia, that leads me to ask again: are we going to the premiere tonight or not?"

I shrug and sip a lemonade to avoid answering. It's the third time he's asked this morning, so I can't dodge him much longer.

His eyes plead. "It's huge that you got invited. It's the biggest movie of the summer."

Will didn't get invited, which says a lot about the state of his career. I feel bad enough to want to help him, but not bad enough to want to go. Even with all my tae kwon do training, going to a public event terrifies me.

"It's just a movie, Will. It's not that big a deal."

Will peeks over his shoulder to make sure Derek is still inside. "How will people suspect we're dating unless they see us together?"

"Is that really why I'm living here? I'm the beard?"

His eyes soften. "Not fair. This arrangement could help both of our careers—if the hype is big enough," he says.

"I don't know. I get burned by paparazzi every time I go out on the town."

That's partly my fault. My breakout role was in *The Grand Scheme of Things* playing Stella, Susan Sarandon's bitchy daughter, so now the tabloids insist I'm as bitchy as my most famous character. I'm not, but when a paparazzo shoves a camera in my face, fear hits me, and I overreact. Now they're like dogs when they see me, harassing the cat until she hisses. They snap their photos, and I look like the out-of-control bitch from that movie.

"Three tabloid covers are good, Julia. You weigh publicity, you don't read it."

"*Celebrity Exposed?*" I ask. "Please. That magazine is embarrassing. Did you see the covers? In one, I'm shouting at the guy, in another I'm tripping with a drink in my hand and my boob is falling out of my dress, and for the last one he caught me on 'the walk of shame' at six in the morning leaving Colin's hotel room."

"A night with Colin Farrell is a good thing. It didn't hurt your career."

"The same scumbag photographer took all three pictures."

Just thinking about him makes my pulse race. Before this paparazzo came on the scene, I could still go out with my best friend

9

Trishelle, who is also my manager. Now, even with secret plans, evasive driving and clothing changes, he still finds us. Not right away, either. He waits, and just when it feels safe he surprises us, and he snaps a photo of me freaking out.

"This is what I wish I could do to him." I high kick the bougainvillea bush behind Will and send orange flowers flying.

"Whoa, don't get aggro on my flowers, otherwise I might start believing you're an out-of-control bitch myself."

"Sorry. I don't know how to do the fame thing."

"Let me help. I can teach you how to control the roller coaster ride."

He takes my hand and steers me to the edge of his lawn and the edge of his property, next to a steep hill overlooking all of Los Angeles. The air is clean, and the sky is a perfect blue.

"Look how far you've come, in just a few years. Relax."

"But how does he find me? He must be an expert. Or he has a team chasing me." My eyes scan the Hollywood hills. They may be watching me right now.

Will sees my dancing eyes and makes me look at the view again.

"Julia, I think there's something you're not telling me."

Glancing back at the house, I catch Derek looking at us from the kitchen window. He steps back. They planned this talk, I bet.

"What do you mean?"

"I think you have another problem a lot of actors get. I think you have a stalker."

He nailed it: that's the other reason I now must live behind high walls. My body shivers from a sudden cold sweat. Will takes off his warm-up jacket and wraps it around my shoulders.

"Who is he? Ex-boyfriend? Or someone you worked with?"

My leg muscles quiver in my cotton pants. "Both. We lived together in New York, and then in the Bahamas."

"The Bahamas? You're full of surprises, Julia."

It feels good to say it out loud.

"When was your last encounter with him?" His face is kind. He's listening. How much is safe to share? No one knows the whole story, not my parents, and not even Trishelle.

"Just after the Colin Farrell fiasco. I hadn't heard from him in years. A note saying he still loved me appeared in my dressing room on a closed set, on a studio lot with security."

Will shrugs. He's not that impressed. I want to tell him about the flowers he sent to my condo, but hold back.

"What's your greatest fear about him?"

"That he's watching me. That he's behind the paparazzo who's taking my photos. And the brick. That he's pulling all the strings and will swoop back in and ruin my life."

"Sounds like a powerful guy."

"He is, and he didn't like it when I left him."

"And he popped back into your life just when you started making a name for yourself, right?"

"Pretty much. My face getting plastered all over the tabloids didn't help."

"Guess what? I'm powerful too, and together we can play this game better than him, or anyone."

"How?"

"Just let me manage everything for you, for six months."

"Are you asking to be my manager? Because Trishelle has that job."

"Let me handle your publicity first. Trishelle is a loyal friend, bless her heart, but she can barely handle a press junket."

Our eyes lock, and he smiles that smile of his. He's making this about him again and creating an "arrangement." I cross my arms and give him my laser stare.

"Okay, what's the first thing you'd do as my publicist?"

"You like animals, right? Make appearances at animal shelters for two months straight, and people will stop calling you Stella. And that brick through your windshield? It's not too late to feed the tabloids the police report and get some sympathy press. They could even send over a photographer to document how we live."

"Anything else?"

"Start dating me officially. I'll even give you a ring and ask you to marry me."

"Please. Derek deserves better."

"Derek understands how it works. When you're ready to move out, I'll break off the engagement and your heartbreak will make the cover of *People* magazine."

"You are good."

He raises an eyebrow. "I've done this before."

I remember reading about his other heartbreaking romances with young actresses whom "he left," who then went on to greater success. Maybe he's right.

"Now let's go to the premiere. Please, Julia? This is about both of us."

"What if that photographer is there?"

"There are fifty paparazzi out there on any given day. They all look the same."

"I know which one he is. I remember faces."

"Just relax and let me cover you with the protective Becker bubble."

"Okay...I'll call Trishelle and tell her that we're on for tonight, but she comes too. And it has to be super low key."

CHAPTER 3

STEVEN

Day 1: Thursday Morning

I arrive in the lobby of *Celebrity Exposed* by 9:00 a.m. The offices have dark blue walls, egg-shaped lights and chrome furniture, like the inside of futuristic spaceship. The place didn't look this slick five years ago when I first met Larry. My photos helped him build this high-tech lobby where he now likes to make me wait.

Robin, the blonde receptionist with the pierced eyebrow looks up at me. "Mr. Naythons is in a meeting." She knows my name, but she always acts like it's my first time there. It'd be silly to call her on it; she'd just pretend she doesn't remember me, which is typical for Hollywood where almost everybody is a nobody. I smile and take a seat.

Larry strides out wearing a tight tailored black suit with a bright pink shirt and no tie, sporting a Bluetooth in his ear. He's trim and fit from all his P90X workouts, and he's proud of his Italian model looks. It's a little showy, but hey, it works for him. No one's noticing me in my leather jacket, jeans and sweatshirt, that's for sure.

"Hello, Steven," he says with a handshake, "I know, I look like a dork with this Bluetooth, but when you're on the phone all day it's best to keep moving. My phone app says I'm averaging three miles a day."

"That's great."

"You should try it. Come on back." He motions for me to follow him.

Larry leads me past the framed editions of *Celebrity Exposed* that line the hallways.

"Yours…yours…that one was yours…yours again." He taps them as we walk.

We pass through a rabbit warren of cubicles filled with computers and ringing phones.

"Minimize those porn sites! Editor coming through!"

His staff of young twenty-somethings all laugh as we pass. His personal assistant Anna hands him a mug of coffee, and we step inside his glass-walled office in the center of the insanity. Everyone will see us, but no one will hear us. Larry likes to be watched.

He finds an envelope in his desk and tosses it to me. There's a fat check inside.

"Still planning to retire at forty?"

"Sooner." I put the envelope in my jacket.

Larry checks his iPhone and then stands up and starts pacing behind his glass desk while maintaining eye contact with me, which is distracting and weird.

"You'll retire faster if you work for me exclusively. We can write up a contract today. You get all my tips, and I get exclusive first rights for four weeks. We'd then split ownership of the actual photos."

"I like working for myself."

"Why? You're in Hollywood now, you've got to trust people. Success here is based on friendships." He smiles.

Larry isn't serious about being my friend. We've never even had a beer together, but we've made each other a lot of money and that passes for friendship here.

"I consider this job temporary."

"You said that five years ago."

"What's the tip you called about?"

"The premiere tonight is for *The Extreme Zone* at the Egyptian Theatre. I just got confirmation a second ago that your favorite moneymaker will be there. No one knows she's coming except me…and now you."

"What's the angle?"

Larry stops pacing and looks at his iPhone. He must have hit some milestone, because he grins and sits down.

"She's dating Will Becker but she wants to keep it private."

"That action movie guy?"

"The action movie guy from four summers ago. They'll be coming together."

"So to keep their affair on the down low, they're going to a gigantic movie premiere where I'll take a photo of them kissing, and they will become outraged?"

"I'd be happy with that."

My job is absurd but lucrative. Plus no one's shooting at me, which is a bonus.

"But there's one twist. The tip is not from her people, it's from his. She may not be ready for a big public display of affection, but he wants one."

"So how is this supposed to go down then?"

"They will be in one of fifty black limos with no set arrival time. They'll rush down the red carpet and just before they head inside he'll stop and hold her hand. Maybe kiss her."

"So you want me in last position behind the barricade on the red carpet before they duck inside. That's easy."

Larry wags his finger, reprimanding me for such an obvious idea.

"I want more than that from you. I want you to make it special. Exclusive. That's why I pay you the big bucks."

I lean back and ponder the situation. Creating something anonymous is best. I need to locate, track and isolate them, all without them realizing that they're being led into my camera frame. Then I snap their photos and disappear, and no one gets hurt.

"If I pull something off, are they going to play ball?"

"They'd better. I pay Becker good money for his tips."

"I'll get it. They won't even know I'm there."

"She did try to run you over the last time you snapped her photo though, right?"

"She never came close. When she left Colin Farrell's house, I stayed back and used a long lens from down the street. She came out with Medusa hair and carrying high heels, and she didn't know I was snapping pictures until she got into her car. Then she spotted me in the street and gunned the car at me, but it was easy to jump clear."

"She's got an anger issue, Steven. Sit down with one of my writers and I'll put your story on the cover: 'Photographer Leaps Clear of Angry Speeding Starlet.'"

"She doesn't know who I am. It's better that way."

Larry opens his door for me. "Fine. Go work your magic," he says.

I leave the tree-lined streets and clean air of Beverly Hills and drive past downtown to industrial South Santa Fe Avenue, where it's all blazing hot asphalt and cement and the only breeze comes from the eighteen wheelers zooming by. I pull my Kawasaki up to a huge warehouse the size of a city block. Behind the roll-up doors are sixty limousines on three floors, but the only clue from the street about what's inside is one tiny sign over a gated door: *Allied Limousine*. I push the doorbell and they buzz me in.

The front office looks like a tiny post office from the 1950s, with a wooden counter and high frosted glass around the one receptionist window. Only the roar of the cars and the constant whirr of the freight elevators give any clue to what's going on upstairs. Behind the counter is an attractive African American woman with tight cornrows and a colorful dashiki summer dress. She looks me up and down.

"Can I help you?"

"Can you tell Malik that Steven Quinn is here to see him?"

She buzzes Malik and then gives me the thousand-yard stare. I play it cool and look the other way, then catch myself in the mirror. My black hair is a little messy from my helmet, but I look tan and in shape. My biker look may not be chic enough for Beverly Hills, but that's not where I hang.

When I glance back at the receptionist, she's still staring. Maybe she approves. I haven't had a date in a long time, and I've done okay with African American women, so why not give it a shot? "I haven't seen you here before. What's your name?"

She just keeps staring, which is answer enough. I rock on my heels in awkward silence while the limos rumble above us. A gate closes and feet pound down the long steep wooden staircase from the second floor. Malik appears, wearing a crisp white shirt tucked into black chinos, and sporting the high and tight haircut from his former life as a Marine.

"I'll be back in an hour." He waves at the receptionist and steers me outside.

"Embarrassed to be seen with me?"

"Always. You can buy me lunch, I'm hungry."

We hit the local Wienerschnitzel where Malik wolfs down two Chicago Dogs while I sip a Diet Coke. He wipes away the mustard from the corner of his mouth, throws down the napkin on his tray and gestures that he is ready to hear my request.

"Is Allied handling *The Extreme Zone* premiere tonight?"

"Yes."

"I want Julia Travers to arrive in a white limousine," I peel off three one hundred dollar bills.

Malik takes the money, then answers. "Certain things are just better when they're black—leather jackets, women, coffee and limousines. And movie stars always insist on black."

"Julia Travers is suddenly a movie star?"

"Yes, she is, and you helped make that happen. And I get abuse from managers whenever I send over a white limo. What do I say when that shit rains down on me?"

"Tell them it's hip. White is the new black."

"I'll let you know how that line works." He flicks his fingers that he needs more cash. I peel off three more one hundred dollar bills before his fingers stop moving.

"White it is." He pockets the money, but then stares at me.

"What?" I ask. "Spit it out."

"I wouldn't normally tell you this, but you did serve with honor—even if you Ranger types are all nuts."

"Rangers lead the way in that category too."

Malik leans across the orange Formica table. "You're not the first person to ask about Julia Travers's limo. Some tall Latin guy came by and paid me to put a bouquet of roses inside."

"Maybe she has a stalker."

"No, he was all business. Military too, at some point. I could tell. He acted like he was a stone-cold badass."

"One of your Semper Fi buddies?"

"Please. He was South American something. Packing heat, too. It was one of those small and slim 9mm handguns, but I still saw it."

"How many hundies did you make him fork over?"

Malik stands up. "The same as you. Just thought you should know."

CHAPTER 4

Day 1: Thursday Afternoon

My blush Armani mini dress still fits, but it's a little tight over my tummy. My mid-section is sporting some pizza pounds, but not enough to need Spanx. I pop my Tiffany diamond stud earrings in, add a matching bracelet, then run a brush through my blonde hair. We're good to go.

People say that I look like 1930s movie star Carole Lombard, especially gussied up like this. Put a wave in my hair, and I could be her double. I like the comparison because she was funny, and I think I'm suited for comedy too, even though my current reputation won't allow it. My first roles were comic; maybe my luck will change and I'll get another chance to prove myself.

I leave the guest cottage and walk into the house and meet Will in the mansion's entranceway. He looks handsome in designer jeans and a purple shirt.

"Why do you have a high heel on one foot and a flat on another?"

"So you can tell me which is better. It's one of your jobs."

I lift one foot up, then the other.

"Go with the flat. More girlish and fun."

"I like it." I toss the heels aside and put on the other flat.

A car honks outside and my heart skips a beat.

Will exhales. "Limo's here. We're on."

This feels exciting. I get to go out with Trishelle again, maybe have some fun….

We step out the front door and Will gasps, grabbing his chest. Parked in his circular driveway is a long white limo with tiny flashing lights rolling across the bottom trim. I bite the inside of my mouth to keep from laughing.

Trishelle pops out of the front passenger side and rushes over to Will, who is blinking away tears.

"Come on, Will, it's not as bad as you think."

"You mean it's not really a cheesy white stretch limo?"

"The guy at the limo company told me that 'white is the new black.'"

"Trishelle, it's WHITE! I am not Dolly Parton going to the Country Music Awards. I'm Will Becker going to the premiere of an action movie."

"I apologize. But you two said you weren't going, and then you said you were going, and then you weren't, and now you are again. By the time I called them back this is all that Allied had left. And I won't call a new limo company we haven't used before, especially on the day of the event."

Will clenches his fists and paces on his cobblestone driveway. He's having a full OCD freak-out and doesn't realize how funny he looks. Trishelle and I trade glances and fight to keep straight faces.

"If your career will be ruined if we show up in this, let's not go."

"Fine by me," Trishelle chimes. "I heard it's not that great anyway."

"You two don't get it. We have to go."

Trishelle shoots me a look as my eyes narrow to slits. Something is up.

"Why? Is someone expecting us?"

"I arranged for a photographer to be in last position on the red carpet to grab our first PDA photos together. But there can't be any photos of us coming out of a white limo."

"What's a PDA?" I ask.

"Public Display of Affection," Trishelle says.

"What kind of display do you expect from me, Will? And when were you going to tell me?"

"I thought we could hold hands. Maybe kiss."

"You arranged a red carpet kissing shot?" Trishelle asks. "She told us both that she wants it low key. That means you just walk inside."

"Julia asked ME to help her change her image, and this is the first step."

"I'm her manager, not you."

Will and Trishelle step toward each other, lean in, fingers pointing.

"I've been doing this for years. You have no clue."

"You have no right!" Trishelle says.

I shout over them. "Stop! You're the only two friends I have! Figure it out!"

Trishelle flips back her brown hair and puts her fists on her hips. She's a big girl with Jessica Rabbit curves, and I can tell she's ready to punch out this action hero.

Trishelle puts her hands up. "Fine. I did my job. I got everyone invited. You figure out how to make your photo work. And we're not changing limos."

Will sighs and looks at the driver, who stands ramrod straight by the open passenger door.

"What's your name?"

"My name is John, Mr. Becker."

"John, how well do you know the Egyptian Theatre?"

"Like the back of my hand, Sir."

"I want you to get us to the rear entrance without anyone seeing us. There's a parking lot there. I'll call security and tell them we're coming through the back."

"So no red carpet kiss, right?"

"We'll wait for the after party. I'll bring the photographer inside for five minutes. How's that for a compromise?"

"And I tell the photographer exactly how to shoot it."

"You got it. I'll call and arrange it all from the car."

I want to tell him to never make plans like this without consulting me again, but I am still his house guest, so I can't push him too much.

"Let's go then," is all I say.

"Let me turn on the party lights for you," John says, and he reaches inside the door and flicks a switch, lighting up the back passenger area with flashing LEDs that run along the trim of every window. With the seats facing in, it's like the VIP room in a disco. Will shakes his head, disgusted.

We slide in, and John closes the door. I can't see him slide into the driver's seat through the smoked glass in front, but the limo rolls forward and soon we're headed down the hill toward Hollywood Boulevard.

Will pulls out a bottle of champagne from the fridge and looks for glasses on the narrow bar hugging the side window, but a small bouquet of roses blocks his view.

"The roses are a nice touch, but I can't find a glass around here." He spots something in the bouquet and stops. "Hey, there's a note."

My body levitates trying to get away from the bouquet. Trishelle hits the electric button and lowers the smoked glass separating us from John in the front seat.

"How did those flowers get in here?"

His eyes widen, and he sputters when he spots them. "I didn't check the back when I got the car. The privacy glass was up, and the lights were off."

"Thank you, John." Trishelle hits the button and raises the window between us and the front seat. "That's the last time we can use Allied."

"Are you sure they're from him?"

I put on my sunglasses and look out the window. "Go ahead, read the note. I know what it says already."

Will tugs the note off the bouquet and reads:

"Julia...we were together at your start and we're meant to be together now. Love always, Xander."

Will slides the note back inside the envelope. "It's not that threatening. Who's Xander?"

"Xander Constantinou," Trishelle says.

Will's eyes widen. "I've read about him on The Huffington Post. Your stalker is a Greek millionaire?"

"Billionaire," Trishelle says.

"You're dodging a billionaire? If a homeless guy follows you, that's a stalker, Julia. A billionaire who follows you is just persistent. I say go for it, girl, even if he's ugly."

Trishelle jumps in. "He's actually kind of handsome. Plus he owns estates around the world. He even has his own island."

I widen my eyes at her and she tones down the gushing.

"But he is a little intense," she adds.

"Scary is more like it. I don't want to see him again. Ever."

Will pulls a rose from the bouquet and sniffs it.

"Well, I think every billionaire deserves a second chance. He could even steal you away from me. That would be a good story."

I take off my sunglasses and look directly at Will. "I'm not some prize for two rich men to steal back and forth. That's why I'm not with him anymore."

There's an awkward silence. We all look out our windows.

Will pouts. "I hope you're not putting me in the same category as him." He has a way of making the drama about him.

"I'm sorry, I didn't mean it that way."

They actually do share some of the same qualities—talent, ambition and childish narcissism—and I ended up living with each of them. What does that say about me?

"The truth is, we're supposed to be friends, we live together, yet you've never shared anything about this man with me."

Trishelle leans in. "Me either. Even I don't know everything."

"Because I'm ashamed that it even happened, okay?"

"We deserve to know, Julia. What if he breaks into my house next and leaves flowers in my kitchen? Or worse?"

I exhale slowly. He's right; if I'm living in his house because I'm afraid of Xander, then Will deserves to know.

"Five years ago, Trishelle and I were living in New York. I was trying to make it as an actress and Trishelle was the manager of Le Centrale restaurant, where Xander Constantinou would go all the time. I met him one night and he swept me off my feet. I moved into his place after two weeks."

"I wish I hadn't introduced you," Trishelle says.

"It's not your fault, I was naive. He told me to drop my agent and let him handle my career. His first step would be to produce a movie with me as the lead. I only had three years acting experience, but he said that he'd transform me into a star."

"And you believed him?" Will asks.

"Yes, because he did it. He bought an award-winning script, he hired a director and a top line producer and cast actors. We shot half the movie in New York, and the second half was supposed to be shot in the Bahamas."

"He bankrolled a movie for you? He must have really loved you."

"But then he halted the movie," Trishelle says.

"So that's when you were living in the Bahamas?" Will asks.

"Yes, I ended up at his estate, waiting for production to start up again, but it never did. And when I complained, he'd disappear for weeks."

"Gone with other women?" Will asks.

"Other women whom he kept in his different homes around the world. Some called themselves singers and he'd produce their albums, some called themselves fashion designers and he'd fund their clothing lines. I was his 'actress,' but the movie was his way of toying with me. So I decided to leave."

"I bet that felt good," Will says.

"Except I couldn't. I had no cash or credit cards, he had my passport, and his staff wasn't about to help me escape."

"But you got away somehow," Will says.

"It took an act of God, but I did it."

"And you made it on your own without him," Will says.

"Except he's been pissed ever since. Or obsessed."

"Because you're the one who got away," Trishelle says.

Will hits the button, opens the window and tosses the bouquet into the street.

"Well, this is our night and he can't ruin it. You're in the Becker bubble now."

He pops the champagne and pours a glass and raises it to Trishelle and me, which infuses me with a tiny bit of confidence.

Trishelle leans in. "We can still cancel, you know."

"I promised him," I whisper back. "And I can't live my life afraid all the time."

CHAPTER 5

STEVEN

Day 1: Thursday Afternoon

I ease my motorcycle between the limos and town cars already backed up on Hollywood Boulevard. They are heading to the Egyptian Theatre; a restored movie palace originally built in the 1920s as an Art Deco version of an Egyptian temple. Turning klieg lights flank the red carpet leading into the theater, while news crews and photographers cluster behind metal barricades. Limos pull up and spit out their movie stars. The crowd yells, and the late afternoon light blows up brighter as the flashbulbs explode for the arriving celebrity. The Hollywood machine is in full gear.

There are only black cars in line. I make a right on Las Palmas and head to the back of the theater. A high fence surrounds the rear parking lot. That is where the after party will be. They've stretched thick muslin painted with fake hieroglyphics around the inside of the fence to keep the prying commoners from staring at the elite guests who will spill from the back of the theater once the movie ends.

I drive my motorcycle on the sidewalk and peek through a space in the muslin. Caterers arrange fake palm trees around the outside of a white tent in the middle of the asphalt. It will feel just like Egypt, until you look down at the fake rug under your feet and remember you're really in an oil-stained parking lot.

I turn on the walkie-talkie strapped to my belt, and slide the earbud under my helmet and into my ear. I find walkie chatter immediately. On channel one, event coordinators argue about the guest list…catering is on two, and security is on three. I click my walkie.

"Security, what's your twenty? The rear parking lot gate is open, do you copy?"

Security guards in dark suits and sunglasses appear around the back gate. Five total—all of them twenty pounds overweight with fake tans. Not too scary. They touch their earbuds.

"Gate is locked. Do you copy on three? Copy?" one guy asks into his walkie.

"Copy. Thanks, guys."

The five guards look around, searching for me. I recognize two of them as regulars on Tom Kittredge's team, which gives me confidence. Tom is a former cop who now runs a security company that handles big Hollywood events, but he's better at schmoozing celebrities like Will Becker than running actual security. Tom likes to escort the celebrities from their limos himself, steering them by the elbow and putting his palm up in front of the cameras and raising his voice. It's a personal touch that makes for good drama and gets him in the photos too, which raises his profile. It's also easy to breach his security; he's so busy hogging the spotlight he doesn't notice me getting close with my camera.

I roll back into traffic, dodging the angry commuters zooming through side streets trying to avoid the congestion on Hollywood Boulevard. I drive a zigzag pattern for a few blocks, waiting for her to appear–and she does. A white limo is coming up Las Palmas from Sunset Boulevard.

My plan is working so far. They hate the limo, so they're coming in the back. Find, follow and isolate, while keeping them unaware of me.

I park my bike in the back of an apartment building on Selma Avenue. I take off my helmet and leather jacket, and secure my small Nikon under my armpit. I open my motorcycle case and pull out my own dark suit jacket and put it on, hiding the camera. This leaves my hands free, but with one tug on the elastic strap the camera will go right up to my eye. My leather fits in the case, my helmet gets locked to the bike. My own pair of dark glasses completes the look. Tom Kittridge would hire me in a second.

Now things get serious—sort of. When I did reconnaissance, I'd stay hidden for days in war zones while people hunted for me. That was risky. In Hollywood, Only a third of my training comes into play, I never feel in danger, and when a good plan starts kicking in, it's the same feeling as when I'm in the ocean—it's a zone with no thoughts, no worry, and no regrets. It's just harmless pictures.

A homeless man pushing an overloaded shopping cart greets me on the sidewalk. Gary is African American, middle-aged, with a patchy beard and dirty skin, wearing thick canvas pants and a padded army jacket. He's ready for cold weather even though it's mid-May.

"Gary! You're right on time."

"Can you spare any change?"

"It's me, Steven. I'm hiring you, remember?" I slide a hundred dollar bill into his hand.

"You always look different."

He pushes his cart down the street, waving for me to follow. When we reach the back corner of the Egyptian Theatre parking lot, Gary pulls a thick wool blanket from his cart and tosses it over the top of the fence, covering the barbed wire. I jump into his cart and use the blanket to vault over the fence and land between two catering vans, then unhook Gary's blanket from the barbed wire and toss it back to him.

"Thanks, Gary." He's already rolling away.

A bit of white limo flashes past a gap in the fence. Switching my walkie back to channel three, I stride up to the security guards still gathered at the back gate.

"Becker is in a white limo, gentlemen! Let's open the gate!"

The five former halfbacks stiffen when they hear my voice and fall into place.

"Who's in a white limo again?" one of them asks.

"Mr. Will Becker."

They all nod, impressed.

"Where's Tom, doesn't he escort all the celebs?"

"He's on the red carpet and says to just get the limo inside."

One guard opens the gate and waves at the driver to pull in. Once all four wheels are through, the guards pull the gate closed, and the driver gets out and rushes around to open the door. Julia's brunette girlfriend pops out first and glances around, which means Julia's inside. The other security guys move close to the car and create a gauntlet. Since I'm one of them, I just join their line at the end.

Julia's friend looks around. "Where's Tom? He always escorts us."

A big blond guy rushes up to the car door. It's Tom, right on cue. "I'm here! Tighten the line guys, we're on."

The girlfriend motions that it's safe. Will Becker and Julia Travers emerge like scared gophers and peek around.

"It's Will Becker, I can see him!" a voice shouts from the other side of the fence. The muslin blocks their view, but the fans can peek through where it's tied to the fence posts.

"And there's that Stella bitch!"

A dozen people hold their cameras over the top of the fence and click randomly, hoping to get something worthwhile.

The line of men moves forward. I pull the camera out from under my arm and snap photos of Julia and Will holding hands. He whispers "thank you" in her ear, and he kisses her cheek. Not exactly passionate, but I get ten photos in five seconds, then slide my camera back under my arm. If I leave now I can be over the fence in thirty seconds, but there's no cover shot yet. Maybe something special will happen.

Then Julia spots me.

"Hey!" she yells and points, "You're that photographer!"

Everyone looks at me and freezes.

Julia strides past the line of guards. "You're not supposed to be here. Give me your camera."

"Sorry, I'm using it." I snap three photos of her angry face just before a guard grabs for my camera. It's easy to duck him and back away.

Will runs up. In the microsecond that we make eye contact, I raise my eyebrows, asking, *what now?* We're both getting paid for this, but this is his show.

Will puts his hand up at the security team. "Back off! I'll handle this guy!"

Tom and his confused guards freeze in obedience. That's rule number one: obey the celebrity.

Will runs at me, screaming and kicking martial arts style.

I snap a good shot of his foot swinging past right the camera, but then he kicks me hard in the chest with his other foot. Shit, he's serious. I drop, plant my hands on the ground, sweep my heel fast and knock his feet out from under him. Will hits the pavement hard, and the fake Persian rug doesn't do much to soften his landing. He stares up at me while I snap his picture.

"Why the fuck are you here?"

"Larry said you wanted drama."

He moaning face fills my frame. "I told Larry to wait until the after party."

"Who's Larry? Does he work for Xander too?"

Julia catches me with a perfect roundhouse kick that slams the camera back into my face. My left canine shatters as a flash of white pain shoots through my skull. The taste of blood and metal floods my mouth. The tooth is gone for sure.

"Will you guys get his camera, please?' She points at the guards surrounding her.

The frozen guards realize it's not a movie. They come back to life and rush forward.

I sprint toward the back of the theater, jump and hit the wall with one foot, then grab the bottom of the fire escape and swing my legs up. My heel hooks on the metal ledge of the first landing, and I pull myself over the railing. I'm lucky none of the security guys can jump that high.

I spit blood, wipe my mouth on my sleeve and climb the metal staircase. She knows my face. How did that happen? Either she's phenomenal, or I'm losing my edge.

Voices chatter through my earpiece, grabbing my attention.

"Seal all the exits and head up the stairwell. I don't want him coming down."

I climb the last ten rungs and jump down onto the roof. The theater has arching cement buttresses, unseen from the street, which hold up the fake Egyptian facade. I dart between them to the front of the building, creep to the edge and peek over.

Madness swells below. Metal barricades hold back a sea of screaming fans, photographers and video cameras. A red carpet cuts through the middle of the pressing humanity. It's a calm bridge along which VIPs stroll, and then pause to be bathed in explosions of white light.

Shouts come from behind me. Two guards are already on the roof and running.

I step on the ledge, turn, and balance my toes on the edge, like I'm prepping to do a back flip off a diving board. Instead I just step back, fall, and grab the lip of the building on the way down. My legs swing out and brace against two cement columns. The fake carvings stick out enough for me to find spots for my hands and feet, and I climb down into the sea of people.

I push through the crowd and vault over the barricade onto the red carpet, which is the only clear route out of this place. Everyone screams and snaps photos of a nearly naked Katy Perry in a sheer dress standing ten feet away, so no one notices me. I walk back down the carpet and get to the curb just as a black Lincoln Town Car pulls up. My hand grabs the door handle.

"Welcome to *The Extreme Zone*," I say as Bruce Willis steps out.

"Thanks." He points at my mouth. "Do you know you're bleeding?"

"Yeah, I lost a tooth. Can I get your photo and then use your car to go to the emergency room?"

"No problem." He and his girlfriend strike a friendly pose, and I snap their picture.

I hop into their car and shut the door.

"What's the deal?" the driver asks.

"Just drive." I toss a hundred dollar bill into the front seat.

He pulls away just as the guards rush up. I sink low in the seat and do my best not to bleed all over the leather interior.

This is a signal for me to cash out.

It's surfing and taking photos of seagulls from now on.

CHAPTER 6

JULIA

Day 1: Thursday Night

We stay in the theater manager's office for an hour until the movie is half over, and then leave out the back in the same white limo. We don't speak for the whole trip back to Will's place; instead, Will spends his time clenching his fists and glaring at me through his pain. He hurts now, but when the photos come out he'll really be miserable.

I know how you feel, Will. Welcome to my world.

I lean forward, but he puts up his hand to stop me from speaking. Trishelle sniffs with disdain, but when she opens her mouth I put my hand on her leg to stop her. That's enough for tonight.

By the time we get to his house, Will's lower back is so sore he can't move, but neither of us offer him assistance. Derek rushes out and helps Will out of the car. Trishelle and I watch through the limo's open windows.

"Sorry I ruined your photo op. Maybe it won't be so bad," I say.

"It'll be bad." He tries to smile, but he looks sad. "Let me know where you end up. I'll send you your stuff tomorrow."

"Will? You arranged the brick through my windshield, didn't you?"

He stops on the steps, shrugs and smiles, but doesn't answer.

"How many tips did you sell to the tabloids about me? That's how the photographer would find me, right?"

Again he shrugs and smiles but doesn't answer.

"Did you tip them before I went out with Colin Farrell?"

"I need to go inside, my back is killing me." He hobbles through the door.

That's enough of an answer for me. "Are you working with Xander too?"

"Just the brick and the tabloid tips. Don't get too paranoid. The whole world isn't out to get you."

He slams the door, and I know we'll never speak again.

John gets out and holds the door. "Where to, Miss Travers?"

"The Montage in Beverly Hills," Trishelle says. "It's discreet."

I slide back in. Soon the limo rolls back down into the dark canyon.

"How bad will this end up being?"

Trishelle sighs. "The photos will be bad. Becker will also say terrible things about you, which won't help."

"I blew it again."

Trishelle laughs. "Hey, I LOVED it. That kick to that photographer's face was awesome. Will and he deserve each other. Who cares how bad the photos are?"

That's why I love her.

When we arrive at the Montage Hotel, we walk through the lobby and down a carpeted hallway, turn right and exit the hotel. Then we walk alongside the outdoor patio to Beverly Boulevard and hail a taxi. Nothing against our driver John, but that's standard operating procedure for me now.

"The El Rey Theater on Wilshire Boulevard, please," Trishelle tells the driver.

"You think it's safe?"

"Just pretend we're back in New York. We're anonymous again."

The El Rey Theater is a funky old movie house that now hosts music shows, and eight hundred people can fit on the ballroom floor in front of the stage, with tables along the side.

We exit the taxi, weave through the crowd, and pass through the front doors. As we enter the main hall, a waiter gestures for us to follow, and he leads ups to an open table.

Trishelle smiles. "I used to date the manager Ricky." Trishelle makes things happen. This is just her magic, and I've been benefitting since we were in high school.

Soon we are drinking Patron tequila shots and talking to two hipster men in their twenties, while *Rebecca and her Car Thieves* blast out their alternative rock from the stage. The music is great, but so loud we have to speak into each other's ears to be heard.

"My name's Brad. You look familiar to me."

"I've heard that line before. Is that the best you can do?"

Brad works as an audio engineer at a recording studio. He's a handsome blend of two races—Asian and Caucasian maybe—and he's wearing a tight T-shirt with the Da Vinci man printed on the front, only he's playing guitar.

He stares at me. "I'm serious. Did we go to high school together?"

"I'm a few years older than you, but it's sweet that you think that."

Trishelle looks up from flirting with her own young suitor, and we make eye contact. She flashes me the "thumbs up" sign and raises her eyebrows at me. However, she's not asking me if everything is "all good." That is our way of asking if Brad is a jackass. We have a series of hand signals that we flash to each other when men hit on us in the clubs. The "A-OK" sign means I like him, and "thumbs-up" means he's horrible so please rescue me. Trishelle's "thumbs-up" means she's assuming he's a jerk.

I flash the "A-OK" sign to her, then touch my nose once, which means he's okay, but I want to leave in an hour.

Brad tells me about the home recording studio that he's building, and his energy is infectious. I remember being that excited about my future when I first came to Los Angeles, which was only five years ago. The floor is full of attractive young people wearing tight dresses and tight jeans, girls with messy hair done just so, and the hipster men with trim beards. They laugh, dance, and touch, their lives carefree.

Scary Hollywood is gone, and what's left is vast Los Angeles, where no one knows me and I can feel alive and wonderful, for as long as it lasts.

An hour later, Trishelle hangs up her cell phone and nods at me, which means the taxi is outside. Rebecca is in the middle of a song, so I shout in Brad's ear, "Kiss me like I'm your high school girlfriend."

He smiles, leans in and gives me a perfect long kiss. He lingers, with just the right amount of softness and pressure. He breaks away.

"You're a good kisser and very sweet.But I have to go."

"Can I give you my number?"

"I'm from out of town."

"You're one of those girls who likes to kiss and dash."

"Guilty as charged."

He sticks out his bottom lip in a pretend pout.

"Thank you for helping me forget." I give him a final peck.

Then we are out the doors and back in a taxi again. I lean back. It's been months since a man kissed me, and Brad lingers in my mind until Trishelle interrupts me with a reality check.

"The paparazzi will descend on my place tomorrow once the photos from the premiere come out and people know you're not living with Will anymore. I'm putting you someplace quiet for three days until your movie starts in Chicago—L'Ermitage."

L'Ermitage is a small four-star hotel in Beverly Hills nestled in the trees on fast moving Burton Avenue, so people don't spot it. There are no shops nearby, so there's hardly any foot traffic either, which means gawkers and paparazzi stand out like circus clowns if they're in front, and they certainly won't get into the lobby.

Inside there are bright flowers everywhere, but the decor is spare and elegant with dark, plush furniture and low light. The mood is so sedate that everyone ends up whispering, guests and staff included.

Trishelle helps me check in. My hair is a mess and we smell like cigarettes and booze, yet the woman behind the desk gives me a welcoming smile and says less than twenty words to check me in. After all the excitement, I feel like I'm on a church retreat.

"Enjoy your stay with us at L'Ermitage," she says, and hands me the room keys.

We get through the door into the suite; I walk past the couch, the TV and the dark wood table and collapse on the huge white bed. The comforter is covered with zillion count thread cotton and stuffed with so much softness it's like being on a cloud.

Trishelle climbs next to me on the bed and gives me a hug. "Will was such a puppet master. I wish I'd seen it."

"I'm just glad you're here." I hug her back, my only real friend.

"I asked the hotel to hire an extra security guy to watch you tonight so don't be surprised by your bill tomorrow."

She tosses back her brown hair and props herself on her elbow to look at me. The curve of her breasts down to her ample hip is like a ski slope, and I feel scrawny next to her. Inexperienced too. Despite my success, she's still more at ease in the world than me.

"Thanks for taking me out. That's exactly what I needed."

"We take good care of each other," Trishelle says.

She's right. We met in high school, two misfits who only had each other. We have our passions, however, and we moved together to New York to pursue them. Hers is managing restaurants. Mine is acting. Drama was the only class where I excelled, and I'm still the most relaxed and most like myself when I'm pretending to be another person. And we fill each other's gaps. I would never have been brave enough to explore New York if Trishelle hadn't dragged me out, and Trishelle would have slept through alarms and lost every job if I hadn't gotten her out of bed and made her coffee.

"Do you think I'm 'hyper-vigilant'?"

"Hyper-what?" Trishelle asks.

"Like I'm always on edge, thinking that the world is out to get me. Like that photographer, or Xander stalking me."

"You were right to be suspicious, except it was Will who was messing with you."

She's right. I'm not even hyper-vigilant about the right people.

"Once we got to the club you were fine. I just think that you're so stressed you can't have fun."

She's right about that too, but with Will and his photographer gone, that might change. But those flowers still found their way into the limo. Xander Constantinou is the one remaining "unknown" in all this.

"How crazy is Xander, do you think?"

"I don't know, he wasn't my boyfriend. But his notes don't seem that wacko, especially after the way you left him."

"I had to. It was the only way I could have gotten away."

"Have you spoken to him since the break up?"

"Why would I? Things ended horribly."

"But you don't talk to any of your ex-boyfriends. You probably won't talk to Will again, either."

She's right yet again, which bugs me. I turn on the bed and face the window.

"We can't all be friends with our exes, like you."

"It's not like I'm buddies with them. Some of them were real pigs. I just stay in touch. That way, the drama fades and whatever power they had over me fades with it. We end up laughing over drinks and I wonder what the fuss was all about."

"I'm not good at normal talk." I turn back to face her. "That's why I act—I never have to worry about what to say next because it's right there on the paper."

She pokes me. "You seemed fine with that boy Brad."

"Because I was pretending to be from out of town. Not myself."

"With Will, the photographer, even Xander—as long as you're scared or angry about what they've done, they own a piece of you."

"Xander is different. It was such a crazy experience."

"Crazier than that premiere? That was pretty wild."

"He's stalking me, Trishelle. That's wrong."

"Then end it. You're not some twenty-two-year-old from Thunder Bay, Ontario anymore. You're Julia Travers now. You left him years ago and hit the Hollywood jackpot on your own. You have status here, more than he does. Whatever power he had over you is gone. But you may not feel that unless you see him," she says.

"You mean confront him?"

"Not at all. But if he appears in front of you, just relax. Listen to his speeches, blah blah blah, and see him for what he is. He's just another man, Julia. They live and they die, and they come and they go."

Trishelle is right. Cold sweats with quivering legs is no way to go through life.

She strokes my hair. "Want me to spend the night? I'll spoon you."

We laugh. It's been so long since anyone, man or woman, has spooned me that the idea is too hilarious, and laughing makes me feel better.

"No thanks. I want to prove to myself that I can be here alone."

"I'll be downstairs at 8:00 a.m. to check on you." She kisses me goodbye and jumps off the bed.

I fall asleep in my clothes, then bolt awake in a sweat two hours later. My body is still in "fight or flight" mode from the premiere. I turn on the TV just as a review for *The Extreme Zone* comes on the late news. I click it off just as fast.

I put on some hotel slippers and head down to the lounge. There's a security guard in the lobby. Is he the one they hired for me. We trade nods. Should I introduce myself, so he knows to keep an eye on me?

I shake my head. Stop it. Live like a normal person for once.

Soon I'm sitting on a couch, drinking a glass of cabernet. It's a cool and foggy spring night and there's a cozy fire going.

It'll be a day before the photos are in print, but they're probably already online. Screw it, it's not worth thinking about them. Trishelle will figure out how to handle it, that's her job. I'm going to sleep in, order room service and do nothing but rest.

I have to gather my strength. Get my wits back. Eat right. Stretch. Prepare. Saturday morning I leave for Chicago. I have a movie to do. It will be hard work and long hours, but it's controlled. I know how to act. I'm always good on set, and I have to stay that way. I have to be a pro again, not let this shit bother me. I have to nail it.

"Rough night?" The voice is familiar.

It's Xander. He hasn't changed much in five years. He's twenty pounds overweight but he still could pass for a fifty-year-old Anthony Quinn with dyed black hair.

The cold sweats come instantly. Bad sign. My eyes look for the guard, but he's gone.

"Long time no see, my dear." He sits down next to me and smiles. "You used to leap up and hug me when I returned to you after being apart. I guess things have changed."

My legs shake, but I fight it. Trishelle is right, these feelings just prove that he still has power over me. The only way to make that feeling disappear is to face him.

"You're persistent, Xander. I will give you that."

"Persistence is a building block of success. It's how you get what you want."

Standing behind him is a man I've never seen before; tall, olive skin, short dark hair slicked back, with one thick streak of shock white hair sweeping off his forehead. He's handsome, but his face is harsh.

"Did you get my flowers?"

My eyes meet his. "I did. They were quite a surprise."

"I'm glad you liked them."

That's not what I said, but I don't contradict him. His friend circles behind the couch which scares me. Where's that guard?

"At least no hurricane can interrupt us here in Beverly Hills. You do get earthquakes, but a temblor seems unlikely." Xander stares at me, then laughs. "So no sneaking away this time."

What would Trishelle say right now? I sip my wine and search my mind for a clever response, but find nothing. Screw facing my fears, my skin is too wet and clammy. The guard finally walks back in the foyer. I wave at him and start to stand up.

"If you want to talk, call Trishelle. She will book a time after I get back from Chicago."

Xander's tall friend with the harsh face sits down next to me on the other side, pinning me on the couch between the two of them. The guard should be in front of me by now, where did he go?

"The guard works for me, by the way."

My legs want to run, but they each grab a knee. My gut says scream, but my mouth can't. What is happening?

I won't let you leave without a proper good-bye this time. Now be a good actress and follow my directions."

The room tilts.

CHAPTER 7

STEVEN

Day 3: Saturday Afternoon

L arry stands behind his desk in his glass cube office at *Celebrity Exposed*, leafing through today's edition of his tabloid and admiring my latest photos: Will kissing Julia's cheek…Julia screaming…Will attacking…Will lying on the ground.

I sit up in the chair across from him and inhale deeply. The cool air stabs at the exposed nerve of my shattered tooth.

"Tooth hurt?"

"Like hell."

"She keeps it real. That's why she's a good actor."

"Any feedback?"

"They both love them."

"She didn't seem too happy at the time.".

"If she didn't want her picture taken, then why didn't she just get back in the limo? Actors always want an audience."

Larry tosses an envelope across the desk at me. Inside will be a bonus check.

"Remember, they get paid too. We were all in it together."

It's still odd, though. My antennae are up and telling me that something is different about this one—but then again, maybe the exposed nerve of my shattered tooth is shooting confusing signals up into my grey matter.

"Do you see yourself doing this much longer, Steven?"

"Nope. I think it may be time to stop."

"I don't blame you, you've made a lot of money working for me. But I have one more job. Enough to push you over the top."

"How much?" I ask.

"One hundred thousand."

"For one photo?"

The pain in my tooth fades as my hearing improves. It's amazing how relative your pain becomes when you are presented with a different goal. That's the story of my last five years in Hollywood—the right photo at the right price, and you can forget anything.

"Yup. If my tip is any good it should be easy. It'll be your last photo of Julia Travers too."

"Again? Doesn't she want to be off the radar for a while?"

"Seems Julia has gone AWOL from the set of her new comedy *No Time for Love*. Studio's furious."

"Even with her temper I thought she was smarter than that."

"She never even showed up. The rumor is that she ran back into the arms of her former lover, a Greek billionaire named Xander Constantinou."

"I know that name. He made his fortune in arms dealing. He used to be a middleman in US weapon sales to the Egyptian military."

"Wow, did you read that in a book? You surprise me, Steven."

My skin flushes. Larry considers me to be just a muscle head with a camera. Then again, I've never given him any personal information that would make him think anything different.

"What's she doing with him, anyway?"

"Why? Are you her older brother all of sudden?"

"It's just weird they would be together."

"He was Julia's sugar daddy when she was in New York, first trying to make it. He's produced a few movies, all schlocky stuff overseas. He did one with her that never got finished."

"So why is she going back to him now?"

"For love? For his money? Who cares? But the tip is from her this time. Maybe the whole thing is publicity for the movie she dumped in Chicago, and the studio arranged all this. All I know is that they're sneaking away to his island in the Bahamas, and we're the only ones who know."

My mental antennae tingle for an instant, but the signals are too mixed up to analyze. Gossip is not reliable fact, so it's impossible to figure out anyway.

Screw it, let them go to his island. I'll do this last job and then leave Los Angeles too. I'll drive north to Central California and find a place near the beach where I can get wet and forget.

"Where do I go?"

"His luxury yacht is docked at the Palm Beach Yacht Club. I booked you on the red-eye to Miami tonight."

"I have to get my tooth fixed."

"Sorry, you go tonight. You can get all new veneers when you get back."

"Thanks, Larry. If this works, this is our last job together."

"I figured. After a while, you just don't need the madness."

We both stand up and face each across his massive glass desk. He smiles, and I notice that he has no wrinkles on his forehead or eyes. His face is like crystal. He could be thirty-five or fifty-five, and he'll be here when he's seventy-five. He's just like his glass table; cool and smooth but sharp when he needs to be, and everything slides off because nothing penetrates.

He sticks out his hand and we shake. "Upload and e-mail me the photos tomorrow and I'll wire the money to your account Monday morning. No need to even come in."

I ride home and pack a small bag. The tooth will have to wait. As long as I don't drink anything too hot or too cold, chew food only on the right side of my mouth, rinse a lot, and take Advil every four hours, I'll be fine. Thinking about that final paycheck will help me put up with the pain.

The flight to Miami is empty. A shot of Jack Daniels eases the ache in my face, and I read eighty pages of a Lee Child book before falling asleep. The plane lands Miami on Sunday morning.

My taxi drop me off at the Palm Beach Yacht Club. Constantinou's yacht, *The Petrokolus*, is parked in a slip halfway down the first row of boats, directly across from a harbor restaurant called The Rusty Scupper. I eat breakfast there, pay my bill, then go to the bathroom where I rinse my mouth and pop four more Advil. Then I climb the back stairs to the roof, lie down on the gravel at the edge of the building overlooking the harbor, take out my camera and wait.

The Palm Beach marina is quiet late on a Sunday morning. Most sailors have already taken their boats out for the day. There are about three hundred slips in six different long wooden dock rows, and about half are empty. Only a few of the remaining yachts have people puttering on board. There's not one boat that's under fifty feet long—maybe they won't lease you a slip unless your boat's that big. A light breeze cools my face and makes the rigging in the sailboats clang against their metal masts.

One hour later, a black town car pulls into the parking lot. Six men get out and escort Julia Travers and her billionaire boyfriend through the metal gate, down the wooden walkway and onto the first raft of boat slips. They're holding hands. He's tall, in decent shape, with dark black hair. He's wearing a dark suit with a pink open shirt, a gold chain around his neck and red loafers with no socks. She's wearing a white and blue sailor outfit.

I snap photos, but don't have the killer shot yet. They disappear and appear between the white yachts, flanked by their guards, so it's hard to get a great angle.

Then everything falls into place. The guards slow down and Julia and her Greek friend stay in front—click. They walk up the gangplank to the yacht—click. The billionaire stops midway up and looks around, and Julia does the same—click. He touches Julia's ass and guides her the rest of the way up the gangplank and onto the boat—click. They stop and look out over the harbor—click. The guards gather behind them, but my eye stays on Julia and Constantinou. He kisses her on the cheek—click. That will be the cover. Then they disappear below decks.

The yacht starts its engines and slowly motors out of the marina and into the harbor—and off to his island, I presume.

My watch says I've been in Miami three hours. It was an easy gig. Anyone could have done it, but I'm glad Larry gave it to me.

Back at the airport I upload the photos to the *Celebrity Exposed* secure file transfer site, then catch the next flight back to Los Angeles. My bike is waiting for me at LAX. We cruise up the coast highway and I'm back at my apartment by 10:00 p.m.

I sleep well for the first time in weeks. The boy visits me once.

CHAPTER 8

JULIA

Day 4: Sunday Night

My eyes open. I blink. Where am I? I'm on a bed, but it's moving. I struggle to sit up. My brain is still cloudy, and it takes a moment to register what my eyes are seeing. I'm in a spacious suite bigger than my first apartment in New York, with varnished wood and brass everywhere. Ornate but tacky. The bed linen has little colored triangle flags and anchors on it. I look out the window. It's dark, water is passing by.

I'm on his yacht.

My last clear image is of him sitting down next to me at L'Ermitage. There was a man with him, tall with black hair and a streak of white like a skunk. He moved behind the couch as I looked for the guard. I sipped my wine and looked at Xander and tried to think of something clever to say. I got scared and tried to get up, but couldn't...

The skunk drugged me like a clueless party girl.

Trishelle, we were wrong. You don't meet with your stalker. When you get icky feelings that make you sweat and shake, that's your body being smarter than your brain. You're supposed to listen to your gut and run away.

Cloudy memories creep back. I was in a town car, then on a jet. I was so stoned, I couldn't remember how to scratch an itch on my face. I remember looking at my hands and feet, not knowing how they worked. I remember staring at people and seeing their mouths move, but hearing just mumbling.

A tall woman helped me go to the bathroom, then helped me wash my hands and drink water. She helped me undress and put me in bed and told me to sleep, and I did. She came in later and helped me dress in new clothes. My body obeyed, like a zombie.

I'm wearing a preppy boating outfit with gold trim and little gold anchors sewn on my blue pants and the epaulets of my white shirt. He dressed me up for his little boat trip, like a Barbie doll on the Good Ship Lollipop.

A memory comes back of him pushing me up the gangplank and trotting me around the top deck of the boat and telling me to smile. My brain was so stoned that some part of me was relieved that my legs and arms moved when someone asked.

Since then I've been sleeping, and this yacht has been rumbling along in the darkness, heading somewhere.

My mind fights to stay awake, but it can't. My body falls back on the bed, my eyes close, and sleep conquers me again.

CHAPTER 9

Day 5: Monday Morning

My dentist takes me first thing in the morning and caps my tooth. Getting home at noon, I check my account and find an extra $100,000 is there, giving me $600,000 total.

I sit down on the deck and stare at the ocean. I'm thirty-two and single, and live on less than thirty thousand dollars a year. I can live this way for another twenty years. Or I could drive away and start fresh somewhere…anywhere.

Why waste time? Driving north, I can be in San Luis Obispo in three hours.

My clothes, camera gear and laptop fit into two backpacks. It's everything of value that I own, and if life suits me up there, I won't even come back for the rest—hauling my stuff up north would cost more than it's worth. It's better to start fresh. My landlord can have it all when he comes by and discovers me gone. I climb the stairs one last time. I tie one backpack to the bike, slip the other one on my shoulders, and then slide into the stream of traffic. Once I top off my gas, I'll be gone forever.

I stop at the gas station at the bottom of Corral Canyon on Pacific Coast Highway. I fill up and go inside for gum and Red Bull. The latest edition of *Celebrity Exposed* is already on the racks, with the headline: "Julia Travers Runs Back to Billionaire's Love Nest."

One of my photos fills the entire cover. It's amazing that they transformed my work into a lead article and got it on the stands that fast. I took the photo around noon Sunday, and it's 3:00 p.m. on Monday afternoon. They must have had the entire issue written, prepped and ready to print Sunday night.

But seeing the photo blown up and ten inches tall and eight inches across sets my antennae tingling. Something is wrong.

Julia stands with her head too far forward, like she's ready to fall. Her back is stiff, her lips are pursed, and there are lines on her forehead. She looks confused. Scared.

I look closer at the chorus line of six men behind them on the yacht, the ones whom I ignored when my focus was on Julia and Constantinou. Three have their hands in their jackets as if they are carrying pistols.

I leaf through the magazine and find my other shots.

As Julia and Constantinou walk up the gangplank and then onto the boat, the Greek boyfriend is posing. When he kisses Julia, her body is too tense. In three of the photos, the tall man follows close behind Xander and Julia. As the couple stands at the top railing of the yacht, the tall man stands behind Julia, but he looks straight at the camera…like he knows I'm up there on the roof.

Looking closer, I notice a streak of white in his slicked back hair.

It's El Sádico. He looks different than how he looked in Colombia, but it's him.

My stomach sinks.

"What are you going to do?" the blond surfer guy behind the counter asks. He wears a knit cap and a Red Hot Chili Peppers shirt, and strokes his hipster goatee.

"What?"

"It's like you're frozen, dude. Do you want to buy it or not?"

"I'll buy three." I put twenty bucks on the counter, grab my gum and Red Bull and leave without waiting for change.

I start my bike up again and head back toward Los Angeles.

CHAPTER 10

JULIA

Day 5: Monday

My eyes open. For the first time in days, my mind feels clear and not drugged. I'm still in the tacky stateroom on his yacht, we're still moving, but now bright sunshine streams in through the windows. I am a long way from home. My stomach aches and I start to sweat, staining my cute little sailor suit.

I breathe slowly and close my eyes. Why didn't I listen to my gut? I should've run from Xander the moment he spoke to me.

I can handle this. I must handle this. It all comes down to his motivation. What does he want? He can have hundreds of women. Why me, and why now?

I'm crossing my fingers that it's twisted love that's driving him. This weird "vacation" he's taking me on will last a week, and then when we get back to shore, I'll run away and hide inside another gated mansion. Until then I must stay cool, and not get angry. There's no limo to jump in here. I must humor him, laugh at his jokes, play along and pretend to enjoy myself. I must be an actor.

I just hope I don't have to sleep with him. I'd rather jump overboard first.

The door swings open and a tall woman in her fifties sticks her head in.

"Hello. Who are you?"

"I'm Beatrice, Miss Julia. Don't you remember?" she asks in an English accent.

"You're my dental hygienist, right? I've been flossing, I swear."

She laughs. "There's that sense of humor Mr. Constantinou was talking about. I'm glad you're feeling better."

Beatrice walks into the stateroom and slides open a wooden panel revealing a closet. Inside are two dozen dresses in all colors—sundresses, skirts and even a gown.

"Mr. Constantinou asked me to get you a new wardrobe." She walks over to a varnished chest built into the cabin wall and pulls open the two top drawers.

"And here are shirts and workout clothes, and some new underthings. I got a little fancy, I hope you like them."

"I've never had a personal shopper before."

"We're nearing Eleuthera, if you'd like to join us on the back deck?"

"I'm allowed to leave my room?"

"Of course, dear. The yacht is completely safe."

She closes the door, and I walk to the closet. This Shirley Temple sailor suit is ridiculous. The clothes are all designer and brand new. I pick a yellow sundress and find wedge sandals at the bottom of the closet and a floppy sun hat on the shelf above.

Inside the chest of drawers are T-shirts, halter tops, and Capri pants. Silk blouses are all folded and tucked away neatly. The top drawer is full of underwear and lingerie. Push up bras, stockings, silk panties and G-strings, in raunchy styles and goofy colors that only a man would like.

"You jackass. I swear you'll wear these before I ever do."

I dress, comb my hair and step out of my stateroom. I pass the galley, go through the living room, and onto the back deck where the hot Bahamian sun is blazing. Showtime.

The water is turquoise, the island is green, and the sky is jet blue with billowing white clouds. My eyes blink, the world is so instantly brilliant. I smell jasmine mixed with salt water carried by the wind. The beauty slows my pounding heart.

The yacht is over a hundred feet long. I'm on the bottom floor on the back deck, and there are two more levels above me, with the top deck crowned with satellite and radar dishes. It looks like a sleek ocean liner, but smaller and stretched out for speed. There's very little plastic—the interior walls and the furniture are all polished wood and metal.

The crew works around me. There are six men, and two I recognize as bodyguards from my previous stay on Eleuthera. In their dark clothes and dark glasses, they look less like sailors and more like Mafia members who have been watching *Sopranos* reruns.

Xander descends from the deck above dressed all in white linen, with a broad white straw hat covering his jet black dyed hair. He looks the part of a yachting billionaire.

"Julia. You finally emerge." He kisses my cheek. "Have you been catching up on your sleep?"

"No, I was unconscious. You have to drug a girl to get a date now?"

He laughs, but he's irritated that I'm challenging his version of events.

"I hope crossing against the Gulf Stream wasn't too rough. We're on the Bahama Bank now, where it's shallow, warm and safe."

I resist the urge to argue with him. Instead, I look out on a sight I haven't seen in five years—the town of Governor's Harbour. We are three hundred yards off shore, which is far enough away to see the whole stretch of the town, but close enough to see the buildings in dozens of pastel colors. They line the oceanfront and rise in rows up a small hill to the top of the island. Xander's estate, French Leaves, is on the other side of that hill, on a beach overlooking the Atlantic.

"How is French Leaves?"

"It sustained a lot of damage in the hurricane, but it's been repaired."

The two-story coral cinderblock courthouse, painted bright pink, is still the centerpiece of the town. The island jail is in the basement of that building, which is where twenty people and I weathered Hurricane Ida. That was the day I ran away from Xander, hoping to never see him again. Best not to mention that part.

"Did you miss Eleuthera?"

"Let's just say I never expected to be back."

The tall man with the shock of white in his hair comes alongside me. He pushes his sunglasses into his hair, stares at me with dark brown eyes and nods.

"Julia, this is Rolando."

Yup, he's the asshole skunk who drugged my drink.

"Rolando will be taking special care of you from this point on. He is taking Beatrice's place, since Beatrice is going ashore to work at the estate with Etta."

"How is Etta?"

"There she is, on the pier," Xander says and points.

A short strong woman with black skin, wearing a red cotton dress and a big straw hat stands on the end of the long pier. She waves when she sees me, and I wave back.

When I spent four months at French Leaves, with Xander away most of the time, Etta was my only friend. A dedicated employee, she revealed the truth of my situation to me without saying a word. I'd grill her with questions, and her face would say it all. I gleaned the truth about the other women, the other estates, and how there was no chance of our movie ever getting finished.

"It will be great to see her. When are we going ashore?"

"We're not, darling," Xander laughs. "I don't want you sneaking away on me again."

I then remember the one thing Etta did say out loud to me, after the storm had passed and I stepped out of the cinder block jail to begin my new life without him.

"Stay hidden. Because he won't let you leave him this way."

I shiver at the memory and look back at the pier. In the distance I see Etta helping Beatrice onto the pier as the rubber Zodiac comes racing back.

"Where are we going then?"

"Someplace wonderful and remote, where there is no cell phone service and no Internet. There will be no temptations to stray from our work."

"Work?"

"Our movie. We're finally going to finish it."

The men secure the Zodiac. The engines engage and the yacht starts motoring away.

"Finish the movie? That's impossible."

"Impossible? I remember telling you that you'd be a famous actress one day, and you said that was impossible too. But I turned out to be right."

"It can't be done because I won't do it."

"When we arrive, I have a presentation that I'm sure will persuade you."

CHAPTER 11

STEVEN

Day 5: Monday Afternoon

I stand in the space age lobby of *Celebrity Exposed* for ten minutes waiting for Larry to appear. Robin, the punk blonde girl with the pierced eyebrow, rolls her eyes instead of making eye contact with me. Visitors and delivery men come and go through the glass doors, dropping and picking up packages, shaking hands and going back for meetings, yet they keep me waiting. Anna his secretary finally comes out instead.

"Steven! Larry's stuck in a meeting and can't break away. He says the money was wired right into your account, and he thanks you again. Okay?"

I come close. "I just wanted to thank him for all our work together. Will you let him know?"

"Yes, of course. All the best, Steven."

When Anna turns and heads back into the office, I follow behind her and dart right so she doesn't notice me. I zig zag through the cubicles and walk into Larry's glass cube. He's on the phone.

"I know for a fact that BMW provides monogrammed floor mats for free, so yes, I want them free."

He sees me and hangs up.

"Steven, what's up buddy? You got the money, right?"

"You're buying a BMW?"

"Excuse me?"

"Who paid you to set the whole thing up?"

"Paid?" He blinks like he's barely tolerating me.

"Who paid you to fake that article about Julia Travers? If you paid me 100k, you must have been paid a lot more."

Larry leans forward and points his finger at me. "How much people are paid here is none of your business. I run the magazine. You just take pictures."

"But I've taken enough pictures to know that the shoot was a setup and that she's in trouble."

"Why do you even care?" His voice reeks with disdain.

"Because you used me to do it."

"Used you? I just gave you the biggest payday of your life, you ungrateful Jarhead." He hisses through clenched teeth.

"A Jarhead is a Marine. I was in the Army."

Larry exhales sharply then glances up and away. He's either lying or hiding something, or both. For a guy who deals in secrets, he can't hide his own deception very well.

"I'm going to find out anyway. Just tell me."

He raises his voice in outrage. "That sounds like a threat."

"It's not a threat, it's a request. Or are you scared of whoever paid you?"

"It's none of your business, you paranoid psycho vet."

He leans over his table and sticks his finger in my face. "I made you! So don't come in here—"

I punch him in the sternum with bent knuckles, and he falls back in his chair.

It's the first time I've hit someone since leaving the Army. Add Julia's kick to my teeth, and I'm overdosing on human contact this week.

A noise makes me turn. Anna stands wide-eyed in the doorway, holding his coffee.

"Leave." I shut the door behind her.

Larry gasps, trying to get the wind back in his lungs. Security will be here in less than a minute. I lock the door, and as I close the vertical blinds to cover the glass walls, two reporters grin and flash me the thumbs-up sign.

"You think you're having a heart attack, but you just got the wind knocked out of you."

"I'm going to sue you..."

"Julia Travers was kidnapped, and you're involved. That's ten years in prison."

"She's having sex with a billionaire. It's a story."

I open the edition and show him the photos. "All these guys are packing guns. All for an actress? He's pushing her up the gangplank in this one. In this photo she's scared. Here the billionaire is posing for me, while this guy stares into my lens. They wanted me to take these pictures."

"Because they're people who want publicity."

"Who brought you the tip?"

Larry stays silent. Someone bangs on the door, shouting.

"Four guards are here with Tasers! Open this door before we break it down!"

I open the magazine and put it in front of Larry.

"When the police come to arrest me, I will tell the whole story, and the truth will end up in a different magazine and you won't get to keep your money."

Larry points at the tall guy with the dark glasses and the streak of white in his hair. "He paid me in cash, and said to hire my best photographer and send him to Miami, so I called you, you fuck."

"Thank you. Now where is he taking her?"

Larry holds his fist to his chest. "To his island. It's somewhere in the Bahamas. Read the article, you idiot."

"I needed to hear it from you, and who paid you for it."

"I'm calling the police—"

They kick the door again, and it bulges in on its hinges. I grab Larry by the collar and drag him in front of the door and stand to the side just as the guard kicks one more time. The door flies open, and a guard instinctively hits Larry with his Taser and Larry crumbles to the floor. Three more guys rush in, and I step through the open door and run.

I sprint for the fire exit. People applaud as I run past.

CHAPTER 12

JULIA

Day 5: Monday Afternoon

I push away a plate of bones from a roast chicken and dig into an enormous Caprese salad. The ship's dining room is empty except for me and Rolando. He sits on a stool by the door, staring at me with blank eyes, like a shark eyeing me from inside an aquarium. He scares me, but my belly is screaming, so I stuff my face while sneaking glances at him.

The yacht's carpeted dining room is on the middle deck, with four big booths facing outward so you can eat while staring at the water going by. Besides some utensils clanging from inside in the kitchen, there is no noise. I glance over my shoulder again and he's still ten yards away from me.

Xander is in some stateroom, managing his empire, or what's left of it. He can't be doing well if he's resorted to kidnapping me.

"Julia?"

I jump as Xander joins me in my booth.

"Are you ready for my presentation?"

"Do I have a choice?"

"It starts with this." He pulls out a small jewelry box and pushes it across the tabletop toward me.

I open it, and inside is a diamond Piaget watch, called Possession.

"Remember that watch?"

"You gave it to me as a gift."

The Possession. It's what I was to him before, and what he wants me to be again.

"You left it on the bathroom counter the afternoon you left." Put it on. It may jolt your memory about what happened that day."

I slip the watch on my wrist then stare at the passing waves. There is no land in sight, just the hypnotic roll of the blue-green sea. The sky is filled with vertical white clouds like bowling pins stretching as far as the eye can see. We sit in awkward silence. The last thing I want to do is talk about how I humiliated him.

"Late May has good weather," Xander says. "Not like September when hurricane season starts. Do you remember the day when Hurricane Ida hit?"

"Yes, I do—"

Xander interrupts. "I secured the construction site on Elysian Cay and then flew the seaplane to Eleuthera to get you to safety. And Trishelle too. She was visiting you then at French Leaves, remember?"

My stomach drops in an eerie yet familiar way. I forgot how he used to talk over me all the time, and despite the years apart we're right back where we left off, icky feelings included. To him, it's like no time has passed and I haven't changed at all.

"Yes, Trishelle was visiting—" He jumps in again.

"We rushed Trishelle to the airport for the last commercial flight back to Miami, but then you were in no hurry to get on the seaplane with me to Nassau."

From the corner of my eye I see him smiling.

"No, you wanted to stay and make love. Or so you said."

I glance behind us. Rolando is still there, listening and staring. I wonder how much of this he's been told.

"It didn't seem urgent. The ocean was like glass. It didn't seem a hurricane was coming at all," I say.

Xander moves closer. I keep staring forward out at the water, afraid to look at him.

"But you knew a storm was coming, and you made me think you wanted a thrill. You told me to take my little blue pill. We sipped champagne. Then we fell on the bed—"

He moves even closer now, his arm behind my back on the edge of the booth, his mouth so close to my ear he can whisper. He knows that I'm scared, which is the reaction he wants.

"We kissed. I remember finding your nipple through the fabric of your bra. Then just when we were about to make love—"

"I got up to go to the bathroom." I interrupt him this time. I swallow for courage and face him, so he knows I can look at him without flinching.

"And you didn't come out."

He stares, but I hold my gaze back at him.

What he leaves unsaid is how I shut the bathroom door but didn't lock it. The long frosted window opened easily. I was dressed in a cotton shirt and jeans, with five hundred dollars in my pocket that Trishelle had slipped me. I took the watch he'd given me off my wrist and left it on the counter.

I should have squeezed through the window and just left, but I was angry about what he'd put me through. I opened a drawer, found my lipstick and wrote on the mirror:

You lied to me and used me.

You called it love, but you don't know what love is.

I don't need you and I will make it without you.

71

I squeezed through the window and ran up the driveway and into the trees. Shouting started behind me, but the shouts soon faded. The trees hid me, and an hour later his seaplane fly away. By then the storm had come and I fought my way through the howling rain to the cinderblock courthouse. That was where all the locals went for shelter, including Etta and her family.

It took twelve hours for the hurricane to pass, and the next day I stepped outside into brilliant sun and the start of my new life—

—but now that past life is back. I am trapped on a boat with no land in sight.

"Earth to Julia." Xander taps my forearm to bring me back.

He smiles as if he knows my thoughts.

"You're such a success now. Any regrets?"

A few come to mind. Falling for him in the first place. Not trusting my gut in the hotel when he reappeared.

"Too few to mention."

"What about what you wrote on the mirror?"

In an instant that becomes my biggest regret of them all.

"Everything you wrote was wrong, and I need you to understand why. Once you do, maybe you'll appreciate why you're here and change your mind."

"Change my mind about what?"

"About our time together, about our movie project…and about me."

He touches my hand. His face softens and he smiles.

He truly seems hurt, which stuns me. I know that anger, obsession, and revenge are boiling in his brain, but is love part of that squirming mix too? My mind flashes back to the lingerie drawer and I cringe.

"For the first part of my presentation, I'll start with the last line you wrote: 'I don't need you and I'll make it without you,'" he says. "Who gave you your first break?"

"You did."

"That's right. I was the first to recognize and invest in your talent. I gave you your first real role. I gave you tools. On the job training from professionals."

"Yes, you did," I admit. He is right. Our time in New York prepping and shooting the movie was an education. Mostly it taught me that I could do it.

"So you didn't make it without me. In fact, I provided the all important first step for you to get to where you are today."

"If I'd gone back to Canada, you'd never have come after me. I'm here because I succeeded in Hollywood without you, and you can't stand it."

"And if I hadn't helped you, you'd have gone back to Canada anyway."

No matter what I say, he will chisel my answer until it fits his argument.

"What do you want from me?"

"I want you to acknowledge your debt and repay me by finishing the movie we started."

"That will never happen."

"When you see Elysian Cay, you'll change your mind. You'll love it so much you'll never want to leave."

CHAPTER 13

Day 5: Monday Night

I can't believe it. Julia Travers is in the in-flight movie to Miami, something called *Junk Conspiracy* where she plays a coat check girl who loses some ransom money. It's a small part, but she's in whole scenes with Brad Pitt and George Clooney, plus she's funny. It's the first movie I've seen her in and it makes me think of her differently.

The movie ends. "It's too bad," the middle-aged woman sitting next to me says. She's about sixty, with dyed blonde hair and tan skin. She wears a flowery blouse with black pants, and there's a charm bracelet on her wrist with tiny baby photos.

"What's too bad?"

She nods at the copy of *Celebrity Exposed* sitting in my lap. "Julia Travers, she's so talented, but her personal life is such a mess."

"You can't always believe what you read in these things."

"For her sake, I hope that's true." She peers at the magazine.

I smile and hand it to her.

"Thank you. I love the tabloids. They take my mind off things. It's kind of reassuring that the rich and beautiful are screwed up too, right? Worse than the rest of us sometimes."

As she leafs through the pages, I see my photos again, but now through the fresh eyes of a middle-aged white suburban housewife. She is my audience. Looking at pictures of the stars being humiliated helps her forget her troubles, just like I forgot mine when I took them.

She looks up at me, embarrassed. "I'm Maud."

"I'm Steven. On your way to see your grandkids?"

"You can tell? Am I that obvious?" She runs a hand through her hair.

"Just a guess."

"My daughter just had her second baby, my first granddaughter, and I'm going to help out—if she'll tolerate me. She and I fight, but I do love my grandkids. Where are you headed?"

"The Bahamas."

"Vacation?"

"To see an old friend, and I have some business that needs settling."

"Oh? You don't strike me as a businessman."

That's for sure. She saw me stuff two backpacks with all my worldly belongings into the overhead bin before I sat down.

"What do I strike you as?"

Maud looks at me and squints her eyes. "A police officer. A tired police officer."

That's funny. The police may be looking for me, but I suspect that Larry will hold his tongue.

"Nope."

"You're an actor then. You play cops on TV…or tough guys, right?"

"Exactly," I reply, so I don't have to say more.

"I knew I've seen you. You're like a young Charles Bronson. Not quite handsome but still attractive."

"If that's a compliment, I'll take it."

The jet engines hum over our awkward pause. She goes back to leafing through the tabloid and pauses at the photo of Julia and the billionaire on the gangplank.

"I read about them. He bought a script for her called *Betrayed in Paradise*."

Maud then holds up the magazine and reads from the page: "She plays a former New York police detective with a mysterious new husband who turns out to be a murderer."

She reads it with the authority of an expert, and then looks up at me. "They broke up five years ago halfway through filming, but now that they've fallen in love again they're finishing their movie together on his private island resort," she says with certainty.

"Do you believe that's true?"

"Sure. Everyone likes a good romance. And she's such a hothead, maybe it's good she's with an older man. He can calm her down."

She turns the page to another shot of them on the boat. Behind them is El Sádico with the streak of white in his black hair, and he's staring right into my lens like he knew I was there. What he doesn't know is that he has stared into my lens before.

"He's scary. It's like he's staring right out of the paper and right at us."

She's right; he is scary—the worst kind of scary, too. El Sádico's real name is Rolando Caballero, and he's not working for this billionaire because he's a filmmaker. You hire him because he's a killer, and soon he'll kill Julia Travers just like he killed the boy.

There's only one other person who would believe any of this— and that's the other Ranger who was in the pigpen with me that night, Sergeant Carl Webb, my team leader on the 5th Ranger

Regimental Reconnaissance Detachment. He lives on Long Island in the Bahamas now, and he's the reason I'm on this plane.

"You seem tired, you should get some rest."

My watch says it's 2:00 a.m. PST, three hours into a red-eye flight that will land in Miami in another three hours at 8:00 a.m. EST. She's right. Jammed up against the window with a spongy airline pillow, I close my eyes and manage to drift off.

The dream comes again, but this time Carl is in the dream with me.

We track five FARC rebels through the Colombian jungle and into an Arhuaco village. Carl crawls straight into the muck of the pigpen, and I follow, snuggling between sleeping pigs who grunt as they make room for us. Carl raises his weapon while I switch lenses and raise my camera. We are eighty feet away, but it's close enough to use my long lens.

Carl nudges my leg, and I glance over. His camo boonie hat is pulled down so low on his bald head that his face is barely visible, but his marble blue eyes still pierce into mine. He points at my eyes, then at his.

I'm your eyes, he's telling me, because once I put my face to the viewfinder my awareness narrows down to just what's in the frame. He lays his leg next to mine so we can communicate through kicks, like body-to-body Morse code.

I put my eye to the viewfinder and enter the zone.

The rebels make the kidnapped German tourist toss a log on the fire and stoke the flames, then tell him to lie on the ground. I can see through my telephoto lens that he has blond hair and one of the lenses of his glasses is broken. The rising fire improves the light, and I snap a perfect shot of him with a rifle to his neck—click.

Three Arhuaco women bring out bowls of rice and beans and clay mugs with water. The rebels sit at a table and eat. Two feel safe enough to pull off their boots, and I see that boot rot has blackened their feet—click. I get my group photo.

"¿Dónde están los hombres? Quiero que hablar con ellos," asks a lanky rebel with curly hair and a beard. *Where are your men? I want to talk with them.*

"En el pueblo de al lado, para la cosecha," answers a short dark woman with long black braids. *In the next village, for the harvest.*

"¿O tal vez escondidos en la obscuridad?" he asks. *Or maybe hiding in the dark?*

The other rebels laugh.

My senses are tingling. This bearded guy is the leader; maybe Caballero. The only intel we have is that he's tall, lean, and has a Roman nose and a streak of white in his hair. I still can't see him; he stays in the shadows and the heat from the fire blurs the infrared.

Webb taps my boot three times and puts his rifle down. That means he's transmitting our location from his GPS. I know Webb; he's afraid more rebels will show up, so he wants to turn in our info to the Colombians now and just disappear.

He taps me twice. That means we have two minutes.

A boy carrying a bucket enters the circle and stops. He must have stumbled out of bed for his pre-dawn chores and wandered into this. The rebel leader gestures from the shadows for the boy to bring the bucket close.

"¿Qué llevas ahí?" he asks. *What are you carrying?*

"Es basura para los cerdos," he answers. *Garbage scraps for the pigs.*

He motions for him to go ahead. We sink deeper into the muck. The boy walks up to the pigpen, opens the gate and steps under the sloping roof and into the dark. He dumps the scraps into the trough behind us...and inhales quickly.

Webb spins in the mud, yanks the kid down, covers his mouth with one hand and holds a knife to his throat with the other. The boy is maybe eleven. Webb nods to me that it's time to go.

I should whisper to the boy to lie down and count to a hundred so we can roll under the fence and be gone, but my gut says it's Caballero by the fire.

My leg taps his twice, telling him *two more minutes*. Webb grimaces but doesn't shake his head "no."

Webb holsters his knife and turns back to watch the rebels. The pigs grunt and eat their slop which covers any noise we make. I open a MRE packet of chocolate covered coffee beans and shake it under the boy's nose. He tries one and his eyes widen. I give him the whole packet.

"¿Odias a estos hombres?" I ask. *Do you hate these men?*

The boy nods.

"Ayúdame a acercar el lider mas al fuego," I say, patting my camera. *Help me. Get the one with the beard closer to the fire.*

Nodding, he hides the MRE packet in his shirt and leaves. Every hair on my neck stands on end as I slide back into place next to Webb. He is not happy, but I know he'll give me exactly two minutes.

The fire is bright now. One of the women puts a clear bottle on the table and the rebels "ahh" in appreciation. Homemade rum. They sip and pass the bottle, each of them wincing as it goes down. One spits a shower into the fire and the flames leap up and scare the German, which makes everyone laugh. The bright light illuminates more faces which I snap quickly—click. I have great close ups of everyone now, except the leader.

The leader notices the boy standing by his mother, half-protecting her and half-hiding in her skirts. He gestures for him to come close.

"¿Dónde están los otros hombres?" he asks the boy again. *Where are the other men?*

The boy shrugs like he doesn't understand, then steps closer to the fire. Good boy.

The leader asks again. The boy smiles and shakes his head and steps closer to the fire. The rebel leader grabs the boy's arm—and something falls from the boy's shirt—the MRE ration I gave him. The leader grabs it from the ground and shakes it in his face.

"¿Americanos? Dónde están?" he yelled. *Where are they?*

The other rebels hear him, grab their rifles and aim in four different directions.

Webb gestures with his fingers—mission blown, time to go.

The kid slowly lifts his finger and points at us in the pigpen. The leader looks toward us and for an instant I have his face in the frame, with his Roman nose and the streak of premature white in his long black curly hair—click—and I snap the first ever perfect close up of El Sádico.

Carl rises up on one knee behind a pig just as a flashlight beam lights up his face.

"Allá!"

They fire their weapons, hitting pigs but not us.

Then El Sádico shoots the boy in the chest. The boy falls to the ground, dead.

And I bolt awake.

The airplane bell chimes. The plane is descending into Miami.

"Did you get some good sleep?" Maud asks.

"A little."

"I hope you get some time off. You look like you need it."

"And I hope you have a great time with your family."

I look out the window and see the ground rising fast. We land with a jolt.

CHAPTER 14

JULIA

Day 6: Tuesday

The legs of my lounge chair sink into the pink sand at the water's edge. Tiny waves lap underneath me. I lean back in my black Prada bikini and sip a banana daiquiri. In front of me is a long wooden dock that stretches out into the water, where a black cigarette boat is tethered, and anchored farther out is Xander's yacht, *The Petrokolus*. Behind me is a vast estate that looks like a colonial sugar cane mansion from 1700s Jamaica. All is beautiful and serene.

Inside my head, I'm ready to explode.

I am on Elysian Cay, Xander's remote island estate in the Bahamas. It's a five-star luxury getaway so remote that there's no contact with the outside world, which makes it perfect for a vacation.

And perfect for keeping someone a prisoner.

"Hello, darling. Beautiful, isn't it?"

Xander walks down and stands next to the lounge chair. He looks tan and relaxed, his black hair combed straight back. He sticks his hands in his white linen pants which he's rolled up so he can walk ankle deep in the shallow water next to my chair.

I want to scream and attack him, but it would only make my situation worse.

"You've done an amazing job. The island is tremendous."

He pushes his sunglasses into his hair and sits on the end of the lounge chair. His cologne is strong; it's a mixture of lemon and sandalwood. I move my feet as far away from him as I can without levitating.

"Have you changed your mind?"

"No. I'll sit here forever before I finish that film."

"Then I must continue with my presentation. Let's discuss the second sentence you wrote: 'You called it love, but you don't know what love is.'"

"Must we do this?"

"I spent years thinking about it. All I ask for is five minutes."

I stare at the water to avoid answering.

"Look at the emblem at the top of each outward facing wall," he says, and then points up at the villa. "What do you see?"

I twist my body and look up at the villa. Just below the pitched roof is an ornate stone crest embedded in the stucco, and in the middle are the letters V and J.

"V and J?"

"Villa Julia. I built all this for you."

The same emblem with its interlocking V and J letters are embossed on the beach umbrellas. It's on the napkins and the towels, too.

"I don't understand."

"The summer you were on Eleuthera at French Leaves, lolling in the sun, where do you think I was? I was here, supervising construction of all this. For you."

"No, we went to Eleuthera to shoot the second half of our movie, but you stopped production. That's what happened."

Xander shakes his head, but keeps smiling. "You said you loved me. You said you wanted to share my life forever. But it turns out forever for you was three months."

This is his version. Once we arrived on Eleuthera, all talk of our movie stopped. Xander would leave me for weeks, but when he returned he'd smell of perfume and his pockets would have receipts from restaurants in Miami, Los Angeles and London. His phone would ring with different ringtones and he'd walk down to the beach to answer.

"You bragged about your island the first night we met. Whatever you were doing here wasn't for me."

"You doubt my passion? I bankrolled a movie for you. You don't think I would build a mansion in paradise for you?"

I pull my knees up on the lounge chair and cover my legs with my hands. We are far enough apart on the lounge chair that if he stood up it would tip backwards into the sand.

"Do you know why I stopped production? Because you weren't great in the New York scenes we shot. Good, but not great. I think even you know that."

My face flushes. His words sting, because the barbs have truth. I was a beginner who had the talent but not the chops.

"How do I tell the woman I love that she's not good enough? That was my challenge. I decided I wouldn't, until I had a plan. I decided to build you this and tailor it for filming and editing. We'd edit your scenes, you'd see your work, we'd refine your style, and then we'd shoot the second half of the film here and make it great. And why would I do that? Because I wanted to keep my promise to you and make you a star. Yet you say I don't know what love is."

"Please, I know about your other women."

"Are you shocked that a man like me would have other women in his life? Most of them pursued me. But I was getting rid of them, one by one."

"I was trapped on Eleuthera. Even when I could've gone back to Miami with Trishelle when the storm was coming, you said no. You said I had to get on the seaplane and go to Nassau with you."

That final afternoon is impossible to forget. Etta had convinced Xander to let Trishelle visit for a few days because I was so bored. Trishelle saw my dilemma and cured me of my romantic delusions. She told me that I was just another mistress, al-though the perks were tremendous. If I performed well and beat out my competition, he'd maybe reward me by finishing the movie someday. That was the unwritten arrangement. It might have been good for some women, but not for me. Luckily, Trishelle had five hundred dollars, and Hurricane Ida was on its way.

"I knew that if I could get away, you'd stop looking for me because of the storm and leave without me. And that's exactly what you did."

"And I thought you were dead. Until I read about your surprising success in Hollywood."

"And you can't stand it. That's why you're doing this."

We stare at each other. His weird frozen smile quivers.

"It did give me the drive to finish this place, and now to finish the movie." He leans forward and strokes my foot. "I had to show you that I do know what love is."

His harsh blue eyes match the color of the flat water in the distance behind him. He completely believes his story. He's spent five years convincing himself it was true, and now he demands that I agree. This is what narcissists and sociopaths do.

"I'm not doing it." I pull my leg away in disgust.

His face darkens. I pulled away too fast.

"My line producer says we can finish the whole project in seven shooting days. We're lucky you're so beautiful. The photos we shot of you yesterday show you haven't aged a day. Nathan, the new director, and David, the cinematographer, both think that the footage that we shot four years ago in New York will match just fine."

"Director and cinematographer?"

"They arrive by seaplane tomorrow, along with an entire film crew."

I can't help laughing. His eyes narrow.

"This movie will NEVER happen. Even if I agree to shoot it, my agent and lawyer will make sure every studio and distributor blocks its release."

"Julia, I understand how important you think you are now. But whether you come back to me or not, I will finish this movie. You admit that I invested in you, and I insist on getting a return on my investment."

Xander beckons to someone behind me. Rolando walks across the sand toward me, followed by two bodyguards from the yacht. Remi is an unshaven Frenchman who always smokes cigarettes, and Hans is a sunburned, muscle-bound Austrian. Both worked on Eleuthera.

Rolando hands Xander a paper, which Xander hands to me. It's the latest issue of *Celebrity Exposed* magazine, complete with photos of Xander and me boarding his yacht, under the headline: "Julia Travers Runs Back to Billionaire's Love Nest."

The banana daiquiri in my stomach curdles instantly and I almost throw up.

"That was published yesterday morning. And yesterday I also sent a copy of our original contract to your lawyer, your agent and the studio."

"Contract?"

"I'm exercising the option to restart production at any time, in first position before all other contracts, requiring you to abandon all prior commitments. Although they are upset, the studio executives have no choice but to agree."

My stomach tightens up even more.

"People will be looking for me. They'll know something's wrong."

"No one is looking for you. The world thinks you came here willingly. The studio is furious with you, which doesn't help your reputation after the madness at that movie premiere. The truth is, you probably need me to get your career back on track again."

My body rises off the chair, every fiber vibrating with anger. His bodyguards step closer.

Xander wags a finger. "Temper, temper."

"It'll never happen. I'm getting out of the sun before it ruins me."

Remi and Hans block me, forcing me back down on the lounge chair.

Xander stands up. "Sorry, darling, just a little longer in the sun. We need your skin a tad darker and your hair a touch lighter, to match the footage. And we need you four pounds heavier, so keep drinking those daiquiris."

Xander bends over to kiss my forehead. My hand slices at his face, but he backs away.

"Never try to kiss me. I hate you."

My fear is becoming anger again, which never works, but I can't help it.

"I will continue to try to persuade you, but if I can't then Rolando will. It's your choice." Xander walks away.

Remi and Hans stand on either side of my lounge chair, their black tennis shoes getting wet in the water, while four smiling waiters descend on the beach. One carries a table, another an umbrella, a third carries folding chairs, and the fourth has a large tray with food, drinks, towels, suntan oil and a script. They quickly assemble a shady spot for Rolando to sit and eat, and then they disappear again. Rolando picks up the suntan oil and a towel and walks over and stands above me.

"Flip on your stomach. You must tan your back now."

I throw my daiquiri at him, but he dodges it. He then takes out what looks like a toy pistol and sticks it against the bottom of my foot. He pulls the trigger—CLICK—

—and hundreds of volts of electricity burn into my skin. My legs contract so fast that my knees bang into my forehead. He does it again and the pain is so red hot that it lifts me off the lawn chair. He moves to taze me a third time, but I throw up my hands.

He holds up the stun gun to my face. "Hurts, doesn't it? Next time I will touch you in a much softer place."

It excites him. My anger flows out of me like water, leaving me with only my shivering cold fear again. I stare at my feet to avoid Rolando's eyes.

Rolando gets a new banana daiquiri from the tray and hands it to me.

"Drink it."

I sip, but Rolando tips the rim of the glass higher so I must guzzle it to keep it from spilling all over my face. He pulls the glass away and wipes my mouth like a baby, and I blink at him with cowed obedience. He motions to roll over on my stomach, which I do right away. All my muscles tighten when I can't see him, afraid of what he might do.

"The director said no tan lines either." He pulls the string from my bikini top so that the ties fall away.

Remi and Hans chuckle.

My anger returns, but this time I don't let them see it.

Rolando drops a script on the chair—*Betrayed in Paradise*.

"We start shooting tomorrow. Learn your lines."

"Yes, sir."

I want to throw the script far out into the water, but resist.

CHAPTER 15

STEVEN

Day 6: Tuesday

I arrive in the Bahamas late in the day, after too many hours traveling. The small prop plane coasts down the runway and stops at a cinderblock building with a tin roof baking in the sun—the main terminal of Deadman's Cay airport on Long Island. I'm the only arrival.

The pilot points for me to go inside the terminal while he gets my two bags out of the hold. I walk past two old Bahamian guys playing checkers. One gets up, follows me inside and hits a button on the wall, and a baggage belt roars to life. My bags come through the rubber straps and into view, like a miniature version of LAX airport.

"Need a taxi?"

"I don't know. How far away is Deadman's Cay?"

"Ten miles south. There are no buses."

"Enough said. Let's go."

It's strange to be in a country where they drive on the left-hand side of the road, but they also drive American cars with the steering wheel also on the left side. My brain keeps shouting that a head-on collision is coming my way. Maybe it is.

To keep from flinching, I stare out the taxi window at the blue water in the distance. Long Island is 360 miles southeast of Miami. It's eighty miles long and three miles wide, and the Tropic of Capricorn cuts through the top of it, so I'm officially in the tropics. It's the most scenic island in the Bahamas, with miles of rolling hills and beautiful beaches.

If that sounds like I got it off a website, I did. When I was in Nassau Airport, I found a bar with internet and did some research while waiting for my connecting flight.

I only know two other facts about the Bahamas. The first is that Elysian Cay, Xander Constantinou's island, is ninety-seven miles southwest of here, close to Cuba. The second is that Carl Webb lives somewhere around here. I just hope he'll see me.

I have Carl's mailing address and e-mail address, but nothing else. We traded Christmas cards two years ago and I sent him four e-mails telling him I was coming, but he's sent nothing back.

Ten minutes after leaving the airport, my driver turns off the island's main highway onto the road to Deadman's Cay, a small town overlooking a sheltered blue bay full of fishing boats. Brightly colored houses line the few streets that make up the town. A few kids play soccer on the school field, but everything else is quiet.

"Where to?"

"A bar called The Screw Pump."

"You sure, man?"

"Yeah, I'm sure. Why?"

"It's not for tourists. Don't you want to go to a hotel?"

"I'll start there, thanks."

He shakes his head, then drives down a road paved with crushed white limestone rock. It curves when we reach the water and runs alongside the bay. We reach a row of waterfront businesses built over the water and one has a sign hanging out front—The Screw Pump. I pay and get out onto an empty street.

"You sure you're okay here, man?"

"Yeah, I'm fine."

He shrugs and drives down the white street and turns the corner.

The pub starts on hard ground and spreads onto stilts over the blue water of the bay. It has only one entrance, which means it has only one exit too—unless I go out a window into the water. Reggae music flows out into the street.

I have my two backpacks with me. Maybe the driver was right. Maybe I should have checked into some hotel, stowed my bags and alerted people to my arrival before I entered the darkest bar on the island. I've seen worse, so I head inside.

My eyes adjust to the dark. Six men are laughing at the bar—three are white, and three are black. They look like happy fishermen in shorts, and T-shirts with sunburned skin, bleached hair and wide smiles...until they see me and fall silent. The bartender turns down the music and steps from behind the bar.

"Can I help you?"

"I'm looking for an army buddy. Carl Webb? He gave me this bar as his address."

"Never heard of him. Sure you got the right town?"

"The Screw Pump, Deadman's Cay, Long Island. I sent him a Christmas card here."

"That's real sweet. But like I said, there's no Carl here."

"He's a big tall bald guy?"

One of the fishermen turns on his stool.

"I've lived here my whole life and I've never seen him."

"If he ever shows up will you tell him that Steven Quinn...Steven Quintana is looking for him?"

"Don't you listen?" the bartender says. "He just said we've never heard of him."

When I step back outside, I almost walk into the same taxi that dropped me off. I pause a second, then open the back door, toss my packs inside and slide back in. The driver zooms off, leaving the pub in a cloud of white dust.

"You were confident I'd need a ride again."

"No place for tourists in that part of town. Where to, boss? Hotel?"

I'm winging it, and badly. Los Angeles has four million people and it's easy to hide among them, but this island has four thousand people tops, and they all know each other. My skull is way out in the breeze for the whole island to see.

"Take me to the main harbor. I need to rent a fishing boat."

"You like to fish, huh? I'll take you to the best fishing guide. He's excellent."

We drive around the edge of the bay to a marina. A long cement pier juts out into the water and fishing boats and pleasure yachts bob in their slips alongside. The driver turns the taxi down the narrow driveway that hugs the marina wall, passing market stalls selling painted conch shells and palm frond hats. Tourists flow between the boats and stalls, pausing to haggle with the locals. Everyone seems to be here, and my taxi driver honks at them all. Soon they're all staring into the taxi at me, the pushy jerk who is in such a hurry. So much for laying low.

He stops his taxi in front of a slip with a forty-foot fishing boat. There's a wooden sign bolted to a flagpole in the seawall—Captain Marcus Fishing Expeditions.

I get out and pay my second fare of the day. "You don't have to wait this time," I say as I hand him the money.

"Sure thing, boss. Enjoy your vacation."

He's already talking on his cell phone as he drives away. He spots me in his rearview mirror and waves.

"You interested in a fishing trip?"

A man steps off the stern of the boat and offers his hand. He's got a wide smile and nut brown skin so perfect I can't tell whether he's thirty or fifty. He wears a T-shirt, shorts and flip flops, but a white captain's hat that he wears sideways gives him some swagger.

"I am," I say, shaking his hand. "Are you Marcus?"

"Just like the sign says. Do you have our coupon from a hotel?"

"No. I asked my taxi driver to take me to the best guide."

"That's me. And the best fishing is far out from the island, man, off the bank in the Tongue of the Ocean. That's where you'll find shark, marlin, sailfish—"

"I'm more interested in fishing around the remote cays."

"Keys," he corrects me. "It's spelled c-a-y-s, but we say keys."

"I heard there was good bone fishing around Elysian Cay."

"Really now? And where did you hear that?"

"A fishing buddy of mine from Miami."

His smirk tells me that he thinks I'm full of it. He whistles, and a dozen heads turn. "Hey! This man wants me to take him to Elysian Cay!"

Every local person on the dock laughs.

"Your friend is a fool. There's no good fishing there."

"I'm willing to pay."

"No thanks." Marcus steps back onto his boat. I almost ask the next charter captain until I catch the evil eye coming at me from all the other fishermen in the marina.

It's time to leave. I follow the main road away from the marina, wearing one pack and carrying the other. I've got on a red long-sleeved T-shirt, jeans and sneakers and my sweat starts to pour in the late May heat.

After walking a few blocks, I notice six guys following behind me. One of them is Marcus. I walk faster, but they catch up. Two guys are behind me, two are parallel to me one street to my left, and the last two are one street over to my right. Two backpacks make it hard to move fast. This demonstrates good Situational Awareness, but my situation is not good.

I round a corner then dart into the first doorway. The door is unlocked and I go inside. When the three guys following me pass the window, I exit the building and double back.

I turn the corner and spot my taxi driver standing next to his car with a camera around his neck. Someone punches me in the face. I drop my pack and block the next punch, but all six guys are on me. They knock me to the ground and kick me in the head and stomach. The taxi driver leans in and snaps my photo. A kick to my kidneys shoots pain down both legs, and a kick to my head sets off an explosion of white light in my brain. It's been a while since I've gotten the shit kicked out of me, and I don't remember it being this painful.

CHAPTER 16

JULIA

Day 6: Tuesday Afternoon

I stand on the patio balcony outside my bedroom and look over the lush gardens of Xander's estate. It gives me a perfect view, looking north. Elysian Cay must be only ten miles long, and Xander's property hugs the southern end of the crescent shaped island. There's an airstrip just north of the estate, but beyond that the island is wild, with tall trees and low rolling hills until you reach a tall light beacon at the other end.

It's late afternoon and the light reflects silver against the small waves crashing on the sand shoals surrounding the island. The sand is just under the water, like giant swirls of yellow left by a painter. Past the shoals the water turns light blue, and then farther out the water is dark blue. It looks deep. I scan the horizon looking for the lights from a passing ship, but see nothing. This really is the middle of nowhere.

The film crew has arrived. Twenty people put up c-stands, pin colored gels to lights and pull electrical cables on the veranda below me. A dolly wheels up, and the assistant cameraman carefully mounts a camera in place on the dolly head.

Xander appears and two men rush over to meet him. He smiles and shakes their hands, then glances up and sees me looking down at them. He waves at me, a huge grin on his face. It's as if the torture episode with Rolando never happened.

"Julia!" he shouts. "This is Nathan Marshall, our director, and David Harkin, our cinematographer. I'll bring them upstairs to meet you."

They enter the mansion thirty feet below me, and twenty seconds later Rolando opens my door and they walk into my suite. Nathan and David stare at me with awkward grins, almost bowing. I'm like a princess receiving an audience.

Nathan seems young—definitely under thirty. He's skinny and wears Chuck Taylor Converse shoes, tight black jeans and an Atari T-shirt, and his black hair is spiked up with gel. He seems more like a musician than a director. David, the cinematographer, is about forty-five, heavy set with salt and pepper hair and beard. He looks the part of a DP, with his safari shirt and cargo pants.

Nathan speaks first. "Julia, I'm just so thrilled that you and Mr. Constantinou are allowing me to help you finish your film. I promise I will NOT fuck this up."

"And I promise to make you look wonderful," David says.

"Thank you," I say, without smiling.

They blink. I must seem like a bitch.

Nathan pulls out a dog-eared script from his back pocket and hands it to me. The inside is full of post-it notes, with scribblings in all the margins.

"I know this script is an award-winner, but I had some thoughts on making your character stronger."

He hands it to me. I leaf through it, but the words are just a blur. I swallow, trying to hide my nausea.

"Thank you, gentlemen. Julia must rest now," Xander says.

Nathan is confused by my reaction, and sulks out. David nods an apology and leaves right behind him. Rolando shuts the door.

"I'm not saying one line, even if your Frankenstein shocks me before every take."

Rolando grins. He'd like that.

"Come enjoy the view," Xander says, and steps out on the patio balcony.

Anything to get away from Rolando, so I follow Xander outside into the late afternoon sun. The salty wind rustles the trees and cools my skin.

Xander points at the film crew dashing around on the veranda below. "Since you still refuse to embrace this opportunity, I'll continue with the last part of my presentation."

"That's okay, give yourself a break."

"There's only one more sentence that you wrote on the mirror. The shortest and the first: 'You lied to me and you used me.'"

"You did. And you're using me now."

Xander puts up his hand. He paces along the balcony's edge, running his fingers along the cement trim.

"From your narrow perspective, relaxing on a beach in the Bahamas, I understand how you might think that way. But there is a larger truth that, you, a young naive actress, couldn't understand at the time."

He stops at the edge of the balcony where another tacky cement crest has been plastered into the stucco. His fingers trace the V and the J letters as he speaks.

"In the summer of 2008, I arrived on Eleuthera with the woman I loved, for whom I'd abandon all others. An expensive woman. After all, I was producing a movie and building a villa for her."

I sigh and shake my head, but he keeps going.

"Then the economy changed. Money evaporated overnight. Many of my businesses went under. Challenges arose that were larger than any movie or villa. Yet I soldiered on, so I could keep our dreams alive. Then a hurricane came that threatened to destroy both this island and Eleuthera. I went back to rescue you."

He smiles and opens his palms. His eyes moisten again. He really believes this story he has invented, and he's sticking to it.

"No matter how much I lose, I thought, at least I have her. She'll be patient. She'll wait for the physical and financial devastation to pass."

He stops pacing. His eyes bore into mine.

"But you didn't wait. Instead, you wrote those lies on the mirror and left, which proves that *you* were the one who used *me*."

"I was your prisoner. A possession. Just like I am now."

Xander bites his lip and shakes his head, amazed that I can't see the light he's bestowing upon me. "But I forgive you because I still love you. I'll give you my world. You'll be bigger than any star you could ever imagine. If you finish the movie."

My fists go on my hips. "Call my agent."

Xander snaps his fingers.

Rolando comes out on the balcony and speaks into his walkie-talkie. "Lead her off the ship and onto the dock.".

Xander points down at the beach. His yacht, *The Petrokolus*, was gone for much of the afternoon, but now it's back and parked alongside the long wooden dock. Remi and Hans escort a woman down the gangplank.

Although they are silhouettes in the bright light reflecting off the water, I know her walk.

It's Trishelle. My heart sinks.

"Why is she here?"

"I hired her as the publicist for our film. She's surprised that we're back together but considers the job a wonderful opportunity. She should, I'm paying her a fortune. She also understands that the project must stay secret, so no one knows that she's here, either."

"Trishelle will do whatever I ask. One word from me and she'll stop."

"I don't intend to use her as a publicist. I already have people for that."

"Then why is she here?"

"Because bad things will happen to her if your work is less than perfect."

Xander waves at her. Trishelle spots us up on the balcony and waves back.

"If you care about her, you should wave too."

I do.

"You're an odd pair, you two. But she's very loyal to you."

"I think she's the only real friend I've ever had."

"You can wait inside, Rolando."

Rolando leaves us. Xander steps closer.

"I anticipated everything before I brought you here and I'll stay several steps ahead of you. If you rebel, attempt sabotage, engage in any subterfuge, or if your acting is less than perfect, Rolando will have his way with her, then kill her."

"You're insane."

"No, I just don't give up. That's why I'm on top again. Even this will be a success."

"I'll never come back to you. I'll die first."

"My offer still stands. Because I know stranger things have happened. When the stakes are big enough, anything is possible."

CHAPTER 17

STEVEN

Day 6: Tuesday Afternoon

They kick me in the head a dozen times before my flailing hands catch a guy's foot. I twist hard and yank him to the ground. As he bounces off the asphalt, I rise up on my side, get some leverage and twist it until his ankle snaps. He screams.

I get my back against the car door and kick another guy in the groin, sending his testicles up into his throat. There are still five more attackers, and their kicks and punches rain down on me. At least my arms are covering my head now. My back is against the car, which protect my kidneys, but the pain is bad.

A whipping noise creases the air, followed by three cracks in a row, like bones breaking. Men howl as the kicking stops. I drop my arms and peek.

It's been a few years, but it's Carl. He's bald with a goatee, and very tan. He's whipping around a collapsing metal baton that looks like an old radio antennae, only thicker. He slams it against one guy's hand and the bones shatter. The final five guys limp away. My rescuer pulls out a pistol and aims it at the two guys I hurt still rolling on the ground.

"Run, run, run away, live to fight another day," Carl sings in a lullaby voice.

My friendly taxi driver opens his back door and the two men tumble into his backseat. As he drives away, he flips us the middle finger—and Carl shoots out his back window. The taxi swerves, then speeds off with broken glass flying everywhere.

Carl Webb looks at me for the first time in five years. He wasn't smiling the last time I saw him and he's not smiling now.

"Damn, Quintana, you suck at this. What the hell happened to you?"

"I guess I'm out of practice. Sorry."

"Hollywood has made you soft. Stupid too. The whole island knows you're here."

"Was I that bad?"

"When a plane lands with only one passenger and no hotel reservation, the word goes out pretty quick. And you asked to go to Elysian Cay? That spreads even faster."

"Asking about Elysian Cay is that bad?"

"It's private, owned by a one-percenter who's probably hired half these guys on the waterfront at some point. You'd have had better luck trying to go to Johnny Depp's island."

A motorcycle pulls up. It's the bartender from The Screw Pump. He hands me a towel.

"Say 'hi' to Tyler. He works for me sometimes."

I blow the last bit of red mucous out my nose. "Thanks, Tyler. Why didn't you say anything back at the bar?"

Carl answers for him. "The bar is my fake address, so when a stranger shows up and asks for me, they tip me off. I don't need any blasts from my past, know what I mean?"

They help me limp the six blocks back to The Screw Pump where Tyler pours me a rum on the rocks—something called Ole

Nassau. The alcohol burns, but I hold it in my cheeks until my mouth is numb. I swallow. It tastes like burnt vanilla. Not bad.

Tyler aims a flashlight at my face while Carl pulls away the bloody towels and examines my wounds.

"Did you get my e-mails?"

"I did, but I didn't know for sure that it was you, so I didn't answer them."

"Are you in some kind of trouble?"

"I should be asking you that question." Carl and Tyler examine the gash on my skull. "But I've had a few high profile cases in the last few months and it's best to live off the grid for a while."

"What kind of cases?"

"Corporate security. Energy company executives working in South America who get kidnapped. I work for a company that arranges the ransoms—sometimes a rescue. When we succeed, people get angry. People with a long reach and even longer memories."

"I want to hire you. That's why I'm here."

"Later. First we have to get you stitched up. Your scalp won't stop bleeding until we do."

Carl drives me short four blocks to Dr. Hassan, the island country doctor. His house and office is built out of limestone and coral rock painted blue, with wood trim painted bright orange. Inside his office, all the furniture and medical equipment is out of the 1960s, but it's white and clean.

Dr. Hassan is about fifty with grey hair and olive skin. He is Pakistani, but the certificates and photos around the office show he and his family have been doctors in the Bahamas for generations. He sterilizes me with a gallon of rubbing alcohol, and then sews up the cuts on my eyebrow and scalp. Twenty-five stitches in all.

"Scalp wounds always bleed a lot. Tough to sew up, too," he says, then looks at my pupils for the tenth time. "You are very bruised, but you don't seem to have a concussion. Just make sure your friends watch you."

"I will."

He hands me over-the-counter painkillers and an ice pack. "And no more alcohol for at least two days. Understand?"

When I try to pay him with a credit card, he waves for me to put my wallet away. "Mr. Webb and I have an understanding."

"Sounds like Carl. I bet he has understandings with a lot of people."

Dr. Hassan smiles. "Yes, valuable understandings."

Carl waits for me outside. "Let's go to my place."

My watch says it's seven p.m., the sun is setting and I've only been on the island about three hours.

Carl drives us back through town and onto a narrow solitary road that hugs the shoreline all the way over to the far side of the bay, where it dead ends against limestone cliffs. We reach a short row of five brightly colored two-story homes, all facing the water.

The houses are locked and shuttered, except the middle one. It's painted bright pink with blue trim, and music spills out of every open window. Carl parks, and then helps me limp out of the passenger side.

"We're home!"

A long-limbed girl with curly hair and freckled caramel skin rushes down the stairs and drapes her arms around him. She kisses him on the mouth.

"Cherie, meet Steven. Steven, meet Cherie." Carl grins with happiness. I offer my hand, which she takes but then pulls me close and kisses both my cheeks.

"You haven't changed, Sergeant Webb."

"You can call me Carl. I'm out of the Army."

They help me up the stairs and inside. It's a narrow colonial style house made of coral rock and painted wood, with breezes flowing through the open windows. Red, orange, and white bougainvillea creep in everywhere, while birds flit through the house. The sun seems to sit right on the horizon, filling the rooms with pink light that makes the varnished wood come alive.

Slow rotating fans cool soft leather and rattan furniture. The walls are decorated with mementos of a life lived around the world—photos from army days, a painting of Carl holding a gigantic sunfish and beer labels and traffic signs from different countries. Guitars and fishing rods are in every corner, and there's a beat up old piano against one wall.

Carl and Cherie steer me into the kitchen and onto a stool.

"Are you from the Bahamas?" I ask her.

"Guadeloupe. I am French."

"How far away is that?"

"I have been in this place a year," she says, smiling, not quite understanding me.

"You look so very bad," she adds, with a French singsong accent.

I see myself in an old "Red Stripe" bar mirror hanging on the wall. My head seems two times too large, and it's tipping back and forth on my neck like a bobble head doll. Carl comes close and looks in my eyes yet again.

"Your pupils are still the same size. Want to sleep?"

I nod.

He turns to Cherie and whispers something in French. She whispers back, in a tone of judgmental pity.

They steer me through an open door into a small dark room with a queen size bed. My two backpacks are already on the small dresser. Cherie pulls down the covers. I pull off my blood caked T-shirt, kick off my shoes, yank off my jeans and tumble into bed. As I close my eyes, I feel her kiss me on the forehead as Carl mutters something.

"Smart ass still hasn't learned," is all I understand, and then I am asleep.

CHAPTER 18

JULIA

Day 7: Wednesday Morning

I sit beside Xander on the main veranda and finish my breakfast of mango and conch ceviche. If this is my prison food, it's wonderful. However, it's impossible to enjoy my meal, or even enjoy being out of my room and in the sunlight—because surrounding us in a wide semicircle is the entire film crew, waiting for me to finish eating. It is bizarre having so many eyes staring at me.

Xander pours me another banana smoothie. "Be a good girl and drink. Two more pounds."

I sip. When I am out of my room, Xander or Rolando sit or stand next to me every moment of the day, so there is never a chance to misbehave. Escaping the island and the movie seem impossible, and if I don't act well, both on screen and off, Trishelle will die.

I sleep alone though, thank God. That gives me hope. I haven't taken Xander up on his offer to rekindle our romance, which means they lock me in my room with a guard outside. Sometimes it's Rolando, sometimes it's one of the others he's hired.

The film crew waits because they have questions and Xander insists that every decision be run past him. Now there is a backlog of requests, and he handles it all by making everyone stand in line in the hot sun.

"Why do you make them wait like this? It looks like a bread line."

"I'm paying them well. If they want to leave, they can."

"They're staring at me, but I'm not allowed to speak to them. It's bizarre."

"I told them it's one of your acting demands. To stay in character, you won't interact with the crew unless it's absolutely necessary."

"You think of everything."

He smiles. "Yes, I do."

He pours himself another cup of coffee and waves that Rolando may escort the next person to our table. It's Trishelle. She kisses me on the cheek, and then kisses Xander.

"I just finished the first press release. I'd love to send it to the trades today."

"Read it to us," Xander says, and puts his arm around my shoulder. I hate the feeling of his hand on my bare skin, but for her safety I must tolerate it.

Trishelle flips open her iPad and reads: "In the gamble of her career, Julia Travers is abandoning all other film roles to finish *Betrayed in Paradise*, a film she started five years ago with producer Xander Constantinou, on which she is co-producer. The star is confident that the film will become a thriller classic, á la *Basic Instinct*."

"Good movie comparison," Xander says.

Trishelle smiles and waits for me to respond, but I stay poker faced. She blinks, confused, and then taps her iPad and keeps going.

"Julia Travers plays Risa Baker, a former New York police detective on her honeymoon in the tropics. Her new marriage seems perfect until her ex-boyfriend, played by Trevor Pennington, arrives on the island with evidence that her mysterious new husband, played by Bernard St. Jacques, may be a murderer."

"We need to spice it up with something sexy," Xander says.

"We can take photos during the beach scenes and get some bikini coverage."

"Perfect. When you're done, give it to my secretary on a flash drive."

Trishelle nods, then shoots me a confused smile. "Is everything okay?"

"This is how I work, that's all."

I stay frozen behind my big Lady Gaga sunglasses. She finally turns and leaves. I ache for her, but sending her a signal now is too dangerous with Xander and Rolando right next to me.

Next in line is Trevor Pennington, the actor who plays my ex-boyfriend Mike. Rolando escorts him to the table along with Nathan, the director.

"Gentlemen?" Xander asks.

"If my first scene with Julia is tonight, I need to warm up with her." Trevor says.

"What do you mean, warm up?" Xander asks.

"I'd like to start with some sense memory exercises, then move on to some guided improvisation with Nathan—"

Nathan interrupts. "Rehearse. The actors need to rehearse."

"You can while Nathan is blocking the scene."

"Please, Julia," Nathan begs, interrupting Xander to plead his case directly to me. "Rehearsal is crucial, especially with Trevor and Bernard. You know that. They're already rehearsing without you."

"I would love to rehearse—" I say, until Xander interrupts.

"She's better in the moment. After blocking."

My co-star Trevor sniffs. "So the press about her is true then. She's too big to rehearse now."

"Exactly," Xander says.

"Well, I believe in doing good work. That's why I'm here."

"You're here because I paid for the veneers on your teeth, your new hair and liposuction so you'd look the same as you did five years ago."

Trevor falls quiet. Xander raises a finger at Nathan. "Keep your actors in line. And don't interrupt me again."

"Yes, sir."

"Watch this. I have a lesson for you."

Xander glances at the line of crew people. Everyone fans themselves and sprawls, looking like first class passengers whose flight is delayed. He spots the actor playing my murderous new husband, Bernard St. Jacques, flirting with Toni, the makeup girl.

"Bernard!" Xander yells, and waves for him to come over. Bernard strolls over, he is dressed in a white and blue seersucker suit with a straw hat and sandals.

"Yes, Mr. Constantinou?"

"Are you enjoying your time here?"

"But of course! I'm in paradise."

"Does it bother you that you have not spoken to Julia, who plays your new wife?"

"No, I'm just thankful to have this job."

Xander smiles and opens his arms. "Thank you, gentlemen. We'll shoot the first scene tonight," he says, and then gestures to Nathan that he can go.

Xander is performing. He needs everyone to see that he controls the movie, the crew, and most of all me, which is why he struts on

his stage. But he has one problem, which is also my opportunity—
I'm a better actor. I have to play to my strengths. I just have to figure
out how.

CHAPTER 19

Day 7: Wednesday Evening

The sound of laughter wakes me. I sit up and look in the dresser mirror. My face is still swollen but at least my head is the right size, and the pain has subsided to a dull throb. My body isn't screaming for more painkillers, but my bladder is about to explode. I use the guest bathroom, then turn on the shower and wash off days of sweat, dust and blood. The laughter comes again, even louder.

I pull on fresh clothes from my backpack and open the bedroom door. The living room is so crowded I have to turn sideways and squeeze between four people to exit the room. The fishermen from the bar all pat me on the back. I squeeze past Tyler the bartender, another ten men and women of different shapes, sizes and colors, all crowded into the living room and kitchen. Everyone is cooking, slicing, eating, dancing, laughing, arguing, drinking and kissing. Carl spots me from inside the kitchen and shouts.

"The prodigal protégé awakens from his slumber!"

On cue, everyone raises their glasses and shouts hello.

The clock on the wall says 6:00 p.m. I went to bed yesterday with the sunset, and now it's six in the evening the next day?

Someone sticks a beer in my hand just as a Bob Marley tune starts on the stereo. A petite black girl with green eyes and brown hair appears in front of me with a plate of food.

"Conch fritter?"

I take one and bite into the batter-fried gastropod. It's hot, greasy, chewy, spicy and delicious. Chased with a beer, it's even better. The doctor said no booze, but one beer won't kill me.

"My name is Nicole."

"I'm Steven. Do you always talk that way?"

"What way are you talking about?"

"In that sing-song way. It sounds like music."

Nicole smiles and shrugs. "It's how I speak. Want to help cook? We all chip in."

She leads me into the kitchen and we slice limes for the beers and dice tomatoes for the salsa. She shows me how to clean, batter and deep-fry conch meat, and I help grill fresh wahoo that Carl and his buddies caught this morning. After I walk three filets across the hot grill, Carl appears and grabs the tongs.

"I'll take over, buddy. You rest."

A chair on the front patio calls to me. My butt finds the cushion and my eyes take in the view. Just across the narrow street, the bay stretches like bathwater to the horizon where the setting sun lights up the clouds orange and red. There's a flash of green just as it drops into the water.

The party gets even bigger. Nicole pulls me into the living room and we dance. Later, Tyler plays guitar, and one of the Bahamian fishermen tells a story about how he fought off a shark when he fell out of a fishing boat. Cherie then calms us all down by singing French lullabies from the West Indies.

"She seems wonderful," I say to Carl.

"She's making me nervous. She says she wants a kid."

"Is that so bad?"

"I know what I want, and it's not that. Not yet, at least."

We sip our beers and stare at each other.

It's awkward, until he smiles. "What about you? Do you know what you want yet?"

"Not in the least."

"Yet you came here for a reason."

"Yes, I did."

"And you still create a hell of a commotion, my friend."

"For that I apologize yet again. But I need your help to fix a problem."

He finishes his beer, slamming the dead solider on the table. "Let's talk then. Get what you need to show me and meet me upstairs."

I go back into the guest bedroom and find my camera, pull out a copy of *Celebrity Exposed* and bring both upstairs.

Carl is on his bedroom balcony, caught in Cherie's loving grasp. She coos sweet French phrases in his ear in between kisses. He pecks her back, but she refuses to let go. "My love for you is bigger than the ocean, but I have to talk to my friend. Please, go downstairs and sing more. I want to hear your voice."

Carl dances with her a moment, then pries her arms from around his neck and steers her back inside. I sit in an easy cahir and take in the view of the harbor. The water is so dark and still that you can see stars and silver clouds reflected in it, lit up by the rising full moon. Carl returns and sits down in a chair opposite me, his face as calm and still as the water behind him.

"Is the water here always this calm?"

"It gets rough. There are no ocean swells on this side of the island and it's shallow for a long way out, so it just seems quiet. But when a storm comes, that shallow water chops up a lot worse than the deep water of the ocean, and there's no place for that turbulence to go. That's why people drown all the time trying to escape from Cuba. Fishermen, too. And when hurricanes come? Watch out."

"Sort of like you."

"I'm rough when I need to be."

Someone plugs in an electric guitar downstairs and strums three chords from a Nirvana song, and a cheer goes up.

"Do your neighbors get upset with the noise?"

"I don't have neighbors. I own all the houses on this block."

"All five of them?"

"After rescuing my sixth kidnapped oil company executive in Brazil, I felt my luck was running out, so I cashed in and bought these. I rent the other houses out to tourists and friends. We are at the far end of the bay and we're pushed up against the limestone cliffs behind us, so there's no reason to come out here unless you're a friend."

His street is on the one road heading back to town. Two Bahamians standing under a streetlight stop a man and woman who are walking toward the party. The Bahamians shake hands with the newcomers, share a laugh, and let them pass.

"Is someone watching from behind the house too?"

"Yup. Seems smart after what happened yesterday."

"Thanks again for that. And for this party. You got a nice setup here, Carl."

"What about your surf shack out in Central California that you wanted?"

"I was close. But then I had to come here."

"Had to?" His face turns serious. "When you showed up, it upset a lot of people."

"I was just asking questions."

"While you were passed out I asked some questions of my own. The one-percenter who owns Elysian Cay is a guy named Xander Constantinou, and half the men in town helped build his estate. Many still get paid. These islands don't make a lot of money, and when someone like him opens his wallet, the money buys a lot of loyalty."

"He has a woman on Elysian Cay. She's in trouble."

"Is she your girlfriend?"

"Believe it or not, we've never spoken."

Carl raises his eyebrows and laughs. "Still shy with girls? Okay, keep going."

"She's an actress. A movie star. I took her picture a dozen times for this tabloid paper, and I made good money." I nod at the copy on the table.

Carl turns the magazine toward him and looks at the cover.

"How much?"

"A hundred thousand dollars."

"Damn. Paparazzi work is good! How much does she get?"

"Nothing."

"Nothing? You get it all?" He is genuinely confused.

"She gets publicity and stays famous. My photos feed that."

"But she doesn't even know when you're there?"

"She spotted me twice. One time she tried to run me over with her car, the other time she kicked me in the face and knocked out a tooth."

"I don't blame her. Sounds like Hollywood is fun."

"Except now she's in trouble. I think she'll be killed, and Constantinou is using photos that I took of her to cover it all up. I can't allow that to happen again."

He raises his eyebrows and nods when I say the "again."

"Can you show me anything?"

I open the tabloid to the "Billionaire's Love Nest" photo spread and lay it in front of Carl. "Can you see going on in these photos?"

Carl brings a table lamp closer and leans over the magazine. "A good looking blonde, athletic, wearing sunglasses and some kind of sailor suit, is getting on a yacht with a middle-aged man who seems to be wealthy, fit, of European descent—perhaps Greek or Arab— and they are flanked by…bodyguards."

"Look closer." I point. "Look at that photo there and there."

Carl studies the photos carefully. "She's not happy, and the guys around her don't look friendly. They have guns."

"Exactly. She's being forced onto that yacht."

"Interesting." His tone is noncommittal.

"My antennae weren't up when I took the photo, but they are now. She's been kidnapped."

"Has she been declared missing?"

"Not yet."

"Has anyone said yet that they're worried about her?"

"No, but that's because Constantinou paid the magazine to write an article claiming she went with him willingly. They used my photos to sell that lie."

"Okay, let's say she's there against her will. It's not a prison. She's surrounded by luxury. What makes you think she needs to be rescued?"

I point at the picture of the guy with the sunglasses and black hair with the streak of white, looking right at the camera.

"Does he look familiar?"

"Nope." Carl shakes his head.

"That's Rolando Caballero, leader of FARC's 37th Front. The Sadist who shot the boy in the chest. He shaved his beard and cut and slicked back his hair, but that's him."

Carl strokes his goatee for a long time. If he is intrigued, he's not letting on.

"You found Caballero, after the entire Colombian military couldn't?"

"I took both photos. I've seen him close up through my lens. This is what I'm good at, it's my job to know this stuff. I know it's him."

Carl looks at me, then at the photo. He stares for a while before looking up. "Let's say it's him. What difference does that make?"

"This guy likes to kill. Do you remember the intel? Over six years, he kidnapped twelve Colombian politicians and businessmen for the FARC. He tortured them until the ransom money came, but still killed eight of them. The army finally chased him into the Sierra Nevada Mountains. He didn't hesitate when he killed the boy, and he won't hesitate with her."

"So why not go to the LAPD or the FBI or Interpol? Why come to me?"

"Proximity is destiny. If you weren't in the same country, I'd still be spinning my wheels talking to a detective in the Hollywood precinct right now, or in a conference room with Beverly Hills PD."

"And let me guess—your new profession doesn't get a lot of respect with those guys." He leafs through the pages.

"But yours does."

He closes the magazine. "Fine, I'll make some calls and check it out."

He leans back and gives me his icy stare. My bent knee moves up and down on the ball of my foot like a small piston.

"I sense you want something more?"

"Like I said, I want to hire you."

"To do what? Mount a gigantic rescue?"

"You rescue people for a living. Just name the price. One hundred thousand? Two? Three?"

He leans forward. Every worry line pops out on his face as he eyes me up and down. He finally speaks. "Not interested."

"Can I ask why?"

"Officially she hasn't been kidnapped. There's no demand for a ransom, or even concern from a family member. There's just you and your photos, and you don't even know her. With no evidence of a crime, it's not a rescue, it's an invasion. You can't hire me to break the law."

As he leans back in his rattan chair, I lean forward.

"The guy who killed that boy in Colombia and almost killed us, is less than a hundred miles from here. We have a chance to bring him to justice."

"The boy got shot because you and I broke protocol. If you want justice, tell your story to the Bahamian Police and the FBI. What you're talking about is a personal vendetta to erase your own guilt and pain."

"What makes you think I'm in pain?"

Carl's eyes grow huge as he laughs out loud. "Looked in a mirror lately? You're tortured. Hell, those bruises are an improvement."

My face heats up, and it's not from the beer. Carl still jabs at me, just like when he was my team leader.

"Sorry to be so harsh, but I talk this way to anyone who wants me to do something dangerous. I did it when I wore a uniform, and now I do it when I wear a suit and go into a corporate office. There's no difference. You're still asking me to pick up a weapon for you."

A trade wind blows across the bay, drawing a line as it crosses the water. It finally comes ashore and hits the balcony and cools the sweat on my forehead, bringing with it the scent of flowers and sea salt. A bell on an ocean buoy rings far away.

"You're right, I won't ask you again. I'll do it myself."

"No, you won't."

"What's that supposed to mean?"

"It means I won't let you. As long as your actress is on Elysian Cay, you're not leaving this island."

CHAPTER 20

JULIA

Day 7: Wednesday Night

I t's 9:00 p.m. A film crew buzzes around me on the veranda, hanging lights, moving fake plants and wetting down the marble until it glistens. Grips raise a square pop up tent and arrange chairs in front of three monitors. This will be the "video village" where the director, cinematographer, producer and others will watch and listen to the live video feed of our performances.

I'm trying to be invisible. It's working; no one seems to be watching me. There's a garden wall ten feet in front of me. I could take four steps, jump over and disappear into the darkness. I could hide for a few days and then flag down a fishing boat. Is this my chance? I've gotten away from Xander once before—

"Miss Travers?"

Toni the makeup girl stands ten yards away. She's a dark-haired girl, around twenty-five, with a cute face and a killer body, which she shows off in black leggings and a Ramones T-shirt.

"Can I finish your makeup?"

I nod, and she skips up to me grinning like we're high school pals gossiping after volleyball practice. She pulls a brush from her makeup belt and dabs my cheeks, looking everywhere on my face except into my eyes.

"It's so humid here, I can't believe how much base I have to put on you. You are so lucky your skin is so light. People with olive skin? Forget it, especially when they're tanned. Too shiny, their foreheads are mirrors, you know?"

"Help me."

"Don't worry, you'll be fine. Your hair looks great. Marjorie and I will be right at the monitors. You are runway ready, girlfriend."

"No really, help me. I've been kidnapped."

"Kidnapped? Are you, like, making me part of how you prepare? Awesome."

My senses tingle. I glance over my left shoulder. Rolando stands just six feet away. He folds his arms and smiles.

The assistant director, a man named Walker, strides up. He is a bear of a man with a booming voice that cuts through any crew noise.

"Is she camera ready?!"

"Camera ready." Toni gives me a final dab and walks away.

"I heard what you said to her," Rolando says. "What do you think she'll do?"

I watch Toni, who skips over to the monitor and joins Marjorie, the set hair dresser. Toni seems to have already forgotten everything I said.

"Nothing."

"Pray she doesn't. Because I'm watching you and I can see everything." He grabs my elbow. I resist, and he pinches my funny bone and pain shoots up my arm. I knock his hand away and try to punch him in the chin with my upright palm, but he catches my hand in midair and squeezes a nerve in my thumb.

"Don't touch me." I yank my hand away.

Two grips carrying extension cords pause. Xander spots us from video village and runs over.

"Getting into character!" he says, so all around can hear him. "Good, I like it."

The grips glance at each other, but neither of them steps closer. A good crew always has blinders on—especially to the ugly stuff—and this crew is professional to a fault. They keep walking.

Xander comes close. "Just work with Rolando, my dear. It makes things so much easier."

"There's no need for him to ever touch me."

"Then behave. If anyone on the crew expresses the slightest concern for your situation, you will be creating a problem for them as well. Don't be selfish."

"This is never going to work. I can't do this."

"Yes, you can, you just don't realize it yet. You will give the best performance of your life, Julia, and you'll get what you so desperately want."

"My freedom?"

"No, to be taken seriously as an actor."

He's taunting me, but he's right about one thing. My acting talent is my only strength in this situation, and I'm already better at it than he could ever understand.

I close my eyes and exhale, pausing for effect. I open my eyes and look at him.

"Teach me, then. You obviously still see things that I can't."

He smiles. He likes the idea that he's my teacher again. "In the first half of the film your character is naive, and so were you five years ago. The second half of the film is where your character is tested, just as I am testing you now. Anything you're feeling is perfect for the film. Just use it. As you start to do good work, you'll embrace your role."

He's spewing actor-speak that he's heard before, but it's partly true. I must embrace *two* roles now: I'm playing ex-cop, Risa Baker, but I must also play Julia Travers, the kidnapped actress who is slowly falling back in love with her captor. That is the role I must play to perfection in order to survive this.

Xander smiles. "Trust me. You can do it."

I stare into his eyes, and force myself not to blink. As my eyes moisten I look away and bite my lip, then look back at him, as if I'm torn with indecision. I nod.

He smiles, buying it. I played him. This could work. But I don't feel grounded yet. I have tools, but don't have a plan.

Walker waves at Rolando. "Hello? I need her over there."

Rolando gestures that we can follow Walker. We pass a long dolly track across the marble veranda and reach the camera crew, which is ready with the first set-up.

Bernard St. Jacques paces in front of the fountain, running his lines to himself as he fans his seersucker suit with his Panama hat. He has crepe paper stuck into the neck of his collar so his makeup won't bleed onto his shirt. He smiles and air-kisses me hello.

"Actors! Places please!" Walker shouts.

I find my starting mark alongside the track, four feet from the camera lens. The camera is on a dolly on the track, like a train ready to roll backwards. The camera operator, Anthony, sits on a suspended seat on the dolly, and his face disappears behind the camera as he peers at me through the viewfinder.

"Focal length?"

The second assistant camera, Sammie, does a tape measure from my eyes to the lens, and then from Bernard's eyes to the lens and adjusts the focus. Anthony looks up from his viewfinder and stares at Rolando, standing behind my left shoulder.

"You know you're not in the movie. Right, dude?"

Rolando stares back at him. Then Paul, the sound guy, motions to Rolando to move so that he can check the microphone cable that runs up the back of my dress and into my bra.

"I'm sweating. The moleskin is coming loose."

"I've got a new one ready." Paul holds up a tiny piece of sticky moleskin.

I lean forward. Paul reaches into my cleavage and tapes down the tiny microphone to the skin of my left boob so that it won't show and then quickly retreats.

I look down. My summer dress, red with white polka dots, now has a crease, of course. I point at my dress and the costumer rushes over with a portable steamer. She jets some hot steam on the crease, pats the dress and then dashes away.

Rolando is still there, but I see something new in his eyes—confusion. This mad activity is chaos to him. He can't follow it. I feel a surge of power, because the madness of a film set is my comfort zone. This is a tool as well.

Josh the boom man steps up beside the track. He carries a long pole with a microphone on the end, which is covered with a fuzzy windsock. He waves at Rolando. "You can't stand there, dude, sorry. That's my spot."

Rolando looks at him, not ready to concede.

Walker strides over. "Yo, we're not doing your portrait, we're doing a movie."

Rolando backs away. A feeling of freedom floods over me. But how much freedom do I have?

"This is a low chest shot?" I ask, into the lens.

Anthony flashes thumbs-up, his eye still on his viewfinder.

I look over at the video village. Nathan the director, David the cinematographer and Xander sit under the pop-up tent, and crowded behind them are two more technicians along with Toni for makeup and Marjorie for hair. They all stare at monitors showing the video feed from the camera. Rolando joins them and stares at the monitors too. He may think he sees everything, but if I'm in a chest shot he can't see my hands.

"Can my first mark be gaffer's tape?" I ask. "I see the reflection better." I walk to my first mark. A production assistant appears with a roll of thick sticky silver tape, kneels in front of me, and rips off a strip with his teeth. I stick out my hand and offer to hold the roll. He hands me the roll and then carefully lays the strip of gaffer's tape down on the patio tile next to my toes.

"My pits are starting to sweat, boys, we better do this!"

I tap the assistant on the shoulder and motion for him to move. As I head back to my starting mark, I toss his roll of gaffer's tape off to the side, near my chair.

"Sorry," the crew all says, and they settle into their places.

A slate appears in front of my face.

"Roll sound…roll camera!" Walker yells.

"Rolling," Paul the sound guy says, from his sound cart.

"Rolling and speed," Anthony says from his camera perch.

"101, take one," Sammie says, and snaps the slate next to my nose.

"Action," Nathan says in a low voice.

I become Risa Baker, former New York cop on her honeymoon. My husband Nicholas takes my hand and we stroll. I hit my silver mark perfectly and the dolly moves back as I walk.

"Do you believe people can change?" Bernard asks, who is now Nicholas.

"No, I don't. Being a cop makes you—"

"Jaded?"

"Realistic."

"But I've changed. And you're the one who's changed me. I'm better with you."

The dolly stops when I do, and the camera lowers with me as I sit on the edge of the fountain. I touch the water with my hand, then look in his eyes, and in synch, Bernard sits and turns his back to the camera as it pans over to favor me. The shot is now a single of me, with the camera looking over my husband's shoulder.

"Then why didn't you tell me you were once in prison?" My voice trembles. A rage builds in me, which I fight to keep it under control.

"I thought I'd lose you. Now I want to tell you everything."

"So do it. Tell me everything."

"It was a long time ago, in Marseilles. I was twenty and a thief. I stole to escape my life."

Bitterness rises up from my gut.

"Usually I can tag a thief straight away," I laugh. "I guess love really is blind."

"You couldn't see it because I'm not that man anymore."

Our eyes lock. "Tell me. Have you ever killed someone?"

"I came close in prison, to survive. But no. I am not a killer."

My tears gush. I fall into his arms, relieved. He kisses me on the lips.

"Cut!" Nathan yells.

Reality returns. Josh, Anthony, Bernard and the dolly grip look at each other and smile. Everyone in video village breaks into applause. Toni is crying.

"Did I tell you we have a good movie?" Xander says, and everyone laughs.

"That's a decent start," Nathan says. "Let's do Bernard's reverse."

"I need to sit down for two minutes," I say.

"She can have three, that was so good," Nathan says, and Walker flashes him a thumbs up.

I walk to my chair. In one smooth motion I take off my shoes and toss them on the marble, then pick up the roll of gaffer's tape. Dangling off one chair arm is my canvas satchel that holds the fashion magazines they allow me to read. As my butt hits the canvas, the gaffer's tape goes into the satchel. I close my eyes and exhale slowly.

I just stole a roll of gaffer's tape with all eyes on me while delaying the shoot three minutes. If I can delay it longer, maybe I can steal more, while figuring a way out of here. Now I have a plan: stay close to the crew, keep away from Rolando, and create delays. This buys me time to gather information and supplies so Trishelle and I can escape.

Most important is performing for Xander without fear or anger. My performance as Risa must be great, and he also must believe his twisted seduction is working, and that I'll want to go back to him. That buys me safety from Rolando, while my escape strategy comes together.

I open my eyes and look over at Xander, who smiles at me.

He mouths the words—I told you so.

I smile back and wait a beat for effect, and then look away.

I may be his puppet, but I can pull some strings too.

CHAPTER 21

Day 8: Thursday Morning

Nicole's kisses wake me up. It's before dawn, with just grey light in the room. I kiss her back and we touch each other under the sheets. Her skin is the color of dark caramel, and my skin is tan. In the weak light, the contrast of my skin against hers is lovely. Our arms and hands brush as we explore each other. More than once she slows down my hands as I caress her.

We smile and kiss. My morning breath must be bad, but she doesn't stop. I probe her mouth with my tongue and she sucks on the tip of mine with her lips. Her breasts are small and perfect, like champagne glasses. I kiss her nipples, which are almost black compared to her skin.

"Is this for me?" she whispers and pulls me on top of her.

She raises her knees and I slide inside of her. Her eyes roll back. This time I don't climax immediately. When it happened last night, she just laughed, waited for me to recover and then let me try again, thank God.

My body rushes again, and she motions for me to slow down.

"Hold still." She arches against me while I hold my body in a plank position. She rises against me, controlling our motion—then the blood rushes to my wounded face and my head starts pounding.

"I have to be on my back." I roll off of her.

She wastes no time and straddles me right away. In seconds, she finds her rhythm. I cup her perfect bum cheeks and support her as she moves against me. She arches back and lifts her knees up and we climax. I try to hold her in place, but she tilts over. We detach and she collapses next to me, laughing and panting and we pass out again.

When my eyes open, Nicole is already showered and dressed with her purse dangling from her shoulder. She smiles and gives me a tiny kiss on the lips.

"Why are you leaving?"

"I've been lying next to you awake for an hour. I've got to go to work."

"You're the first girl I've been with in a long time, you know." I tug her back down on top of me.

"I could tell," she giggles.

The look on my face must betray my crushed ego because she kisses my forehead like I'm a sick child.

"Stop, I loved your enthusiasm. It's like being a teenager again."

"Will I see you again?"

"Is that why you came here? To fall in love with the first island girl you meet?"

"No."

She traces her finger around the bruise on my cheek, which makes me wince and pull back. She gets off the bed.

"Carl told me to be careful with you. He says that you got those bruises because you're not careful enough. You're distracted. You've got too much on your mind."

"Carl is also a perfectionist."

"Cherie has my number." She kisses me and shuts the door behind her.

I get out of bed and take a shower. The three purple spots on my face hurt, but other than that, my body doesn't feel too bad. I'm even relaxed. Awake. Alive. Usually I have to surf all day to feel half this good.

Carl laughs in the kitchen. I pull on my last set of fresh clothes—shorts and a blue long sleeve T-shirt and sneakers.

My pits sweat right away. How do people live in this heat?

I walk into the kitchen and find out: Carl and Cherie are nude. Carl shakes a bottle of hot sauce onto a big plate of scrambled eggs. He looks up and sees me staring.

"What? You don't like spicy eggs? D'Vanya's sauce is the best, man."

"You're naked."

Cherie's round brown butt bends over the counter as she reaches for a coffee cup. She fills it, then turns and shows me her perfect brown breasts. She is all one color, light brown from head to toe, with a splash of freckles across her face.

"Sugar or milk?" She holds out the cup.

"Milk, please." My eyes stay locked on the cup.

Carl laughs. "It's island living, Steven, get used to it."

Cherie takes pity on me and tiptoes away. She tosses Carl a pair of board shorts hanging on an open window sill and then heads upstairs. Carl and I tip our heads sideways to catch a long glimpse of her bum swaying back and forth up the stairs.

Carl pulls up the shorts and slaps his flat six-pack belly. With his cue ball head he looks like a tough Kelly Slater, only fifteen pounds heavier. He also sport a gold earring in his left lobe. "You're wearing an earring. That wasn't there last night."

"Cherie pierced it with a needle and an ice cube mid-party. I was telling people my sailing stories and she said I had to get an earring. It's supposed to protect me."

Carl pours milk into my coffee and then points out the window. Bobbing a hundred yards offshore is a forty-five-foot sailboat with a sleek white fiberglass hull and a teak wood top.

"That's my sailboat, *The Murdina,* named after my grandmother. She's a Hanse 470E, one of the best designed yachts in the world. Cherie says that she's her only rival."

"She's beautiful."

"Let's go sailing."

"But you said I couldn't leave the island."

"You'll be coming back, trust me."

We make bologna sandwiches and put them in a cooler with beer, water and ice. I grab one of my cameras and Carl grabs sun hats and windbreakers. We walk out the front door.

"Tu reviens quand?" Cherie asks, leaning over the upstairs balcony. *You're coming back when?*

"We'll be back late. Lock the house and go to Nicole's place until I call."

"Are you kicking me out? You are a very bad boyfriend."

"I'm a fantastic boyfriend thinking about your safety. Promise me."

"I promise."

We use a Zodiac with a tiny outboard motor to putter out to the sailboat. Her white hull is long and smooth, and she rides high in the water. We tie up to a buoy and climb aboard.

"Been sailing recently?"

"Windsurfing. But I still understand how it works."

"Good, because you have to raise the sails while I boss you around."

Soon Carl stands behind the wheel and barks instructions like Captain Ahab while I pull up the anchor, raise the main and jib sails and run the sheets back down around the winches. We pick up speed and tip sideways as water flows over the heavy keel. I climb on the high side and feel the warm trade wind rushing past my face.

Carl steers the forty-five-foot boat out of the harbor and soon we are racing alongside the island. Carl shouts over the wind and points. To our left is a double rainbow, two arcs of color suspended over the island where a rain cloud has just passed. I snap photos—the best one catches the double rainbow arching from a cloud and seemingly ending at our sailboat's mast. This is nice.

Carl points at me. "You're smiling. That's new."

We clear the southern edge of the island and a full blast of ocean air hits us. Carl turns the boat so the wind falls behind us, then lets the sails out and pulls the boom across. We surf up and down the ocean swells, but it feels quiet and calm since we are moving with the wind and not against it.

"How fast are we moving?"

"Six knots. About seven miles per hour."

We surf up and down the ocean swells, and in twenty minutes we're out of sight of land.

"So are you Quintana yet? Or do you still go by Quinn?"

"I use Quinn for the Hollywood work."

"So when are you going to embrace your beaner side? I thought you were going to use your real family name when you left the Army."

Webb knows my whole life story. I once told him how my dad changed our name from Quintana to Quinn so that his pale half-Mexican kids could pass for Irish growing up in San Francisco. It says something about Webb that he remembers my story.

"I start right now. I'm always Quintana, from this point on."

"Good. So Quintana…let's talk."

"Is that why you took me out here? For a chat?"

"Wind, water and sunshine always stimulate a good conversation. Plus you're a captive audience. I'm not turning the boat around until I get the answers I want."

"What answers are you looking for?"

"Let's start simple—what's your verb?"

"What do you mean, my verb?"

"A nurse *nurses*, teachers *teach* and preachers *preach*. If you could only choose one verb to describe what you do best, what is it?"

"What's yours?"

"I protect. I'm always on guard, watching out for my men, my clients, my friends and my family. I can't help it, it's what I do, and it's what I do best."

"I can't choose one word."

"If you don't choose an action in life, then you are simply reacting to life."

I shrug to avoid answering. I'm not ready to get deep with this baldheaded Yoda, but I also know he's not going to turn the boat around until he gets the answers he wants.

"Start with what you're good at." Carl nods at the camera on my chest.

"My verb is 'to reveal.'"

Carl nods. "I get it. You see people and situations that the rest of us miss, and you somehow get it in your frame. Then we can see what you see. I like it."

"Do I get T-shirts made now?"

"Is that why you joined the Army? To reveal?"

"I joined the Army because ROTC at Berkeley gave me a free ride. But I found my place when my service started. I found my skills. Before the Army I had no clue what I was good at."

"Reveal anything worthwhile out in Hollywood?"

"It depends. I can't tell."

"Well, I can tell you this–you have talent. A gift even. You're the best recon shutterbug I've ever had on my team. We bagged some big ones together."

"I haven't captured anything real since Colombia. If anything, it's been just the opposite."

"What do you mean? The opposite?"

"People are using my photos to tell lies. Like the photo of Julia getting on the yacht. And now people are going to get killed again because of me."

Carl sighs. "Different place, same dilemma."

"Do you think about that night in the village?"

The sails flap on the edges. Carl tightens a sheet and trims them taut.

"Every day."

"But you did everything right that night."

"I was in charge. We should've disappeared, but we were fixated on success. We had done so well that summer we thought we could do anything. We lost our Situational Awareness. That led to improper procedure where I let you to talk to the boy."

"My gut told me that it would work."

"And my gut told me that staying was a mistake, yet I still let it happen. If we had left, we would have escaped uninjured. We would have partied in Cartagena. The village would still be there, and the boy would be alive. But I didn't obey my verb. I didn't protect. That's what I think about."

I got the first ever photo of Caballero—but one of the photos also showed the boy pointing at us. The Colombians mistook that as proof that the villagers were FARC sympathizers, and nothing we said could change their minds. They torched the entire village.

Carl breaks open the ice chest and tosses me a beer and a bologna sandwich. We stare out over the gleaming water. The sailboat coasts along the passing swells as we eat.

I finally break the ice. "Caballero is going to do the same thing to Julia that he did to the boy. But this is our second chance. We can finish what we should've done in Colombia, and stop a new problem from getting worse."

"It's a second chance, all right. It's a second chance for me to say 'no' and to protect you. That's why I'm keeping you here."

"Then Julia Travers will die, and I'll have two deaths haunting me."

"Those are two different issues—the girl's safety and your personal feelings. Which do you want to talk about first?"

I don't want to play this game, but he won't turn around the sailboat until we do. "Julia's safety."

"I suspect her situation isn't as bad as you think, which means other people can handle it. And if her situation is really as bad as you say, then other people should definitely handle it. Professionals with clear heads who aren't plagued by anger and guilt."

"And where do we find these professionals?"

"While you were passed out yesterday, I called officers and agents in three different countries. Research is being done."

"We're running out of time."

"Today's Thursday. You got here Tuesday afternoon."

"Caballero might kill her tomorrow."

"Or she may be dead already. But I doubt it. If he kidnapped her and brought her all the way to that cay, it's for a reason. That's what we have to figure out."

He looks at me, his eyes asking if I know the answer.

"I don't know why he took her. I just know she's not coming back unless someone does something soon."

"That's your fear and guilt talking, which is the second issue. But even if you went and saved her and killed Caballero and died like a hero, that wouldn't bring the boy back. That deed is done. And if you were lucky enough to survive? You'd still be haunted. Probably worse."

"How do you know?"

"Experience," he sighs. "Guilt is a wound. If you pick at it, it never heals. All you can do is bandage it up and wait for it to turn into a scar. The scar never goes away, but at least you can live again."

"So that's it? I come all this way, and you tell me I have to wait?"

"There are worse places to be stuck. You've had fun since you got here."

We stare at each other as the sailboat rises up and down the fronts and backs of the ocean swells we're floating across. It's a Bahamian standoff.

"I appreciate your hospitality. Anything else?"

"Nope, I think we're done."

Carl steers the boat back into the wind for the trip back to the island. The wind that was rolling with us a second ago is now coming across our bow, and we pull in the sails for the first long tack back to the island. There is now too much wind to talk over, but there's nothing left to talk about anyway.

CHAPTER 22

JULIA

Day 8: Thursday Evening

Seven people crowd into Xander's darkened library and gather around a TV monitor to watch two days of work; the scenes we shot Wednesday night and Thursday during the day. There's Nathan the director, David the cinematographer, Paul the sound guy and Eric the editor who has downloaded all the footage into the edit system. The last three are Xander and me, and Rolando, standing by the door.

We each have a blue aluminum canteen emblazoned with the film's title—*Betrayed in Paradise*—with the "t" in Betrayed shaped like a palm tree and the "d" in Paradise shaped like a dagger. It's the line producer Rebecca's way of saving money and being green so we're not all drinking expensive bottled water on set.

The six men watch the screen as they sip water from their blue canisters, their eyes locked on the floating images. I peek back at Rolando. His eyes are on the video too. My plan is working—my performance as Risa Baker is compelling enough that they're watching *her* and forgetting about *me,* giving me time to look around.

This library is almost directly below my bedroom. I might be able to get in here. The windows are locked tight behind thick curtains, but if I break a window maybe the fabric is heavy enough that it might muffle the sound.

What can I use in here? A tool? A weapon? A map? On the bookcase is a conch shell. Useless. On another shelf there's an old spyglass. That could be good, but only if it works. A handmade straw hat. Very good. I'll need sun protection out there. Four painted masks hang on the wall. Colorful, but worthless. The closet door is ajar and inside is a man's jacket and deck shoes. The jacket I could use, but the shoes may be big.

Papers are in piles on his desk—some worthwhile information must be there. My eye catches something on the far side of the room, above a credenza—a nautical map of an island in a wooden frame. Is it this island? It has to be.

Everyone laughs. I glance back at the screen. I just slapped my police detective ex-boyfriend across the face, and he blinks from the sting. The shot is vivid, our skin tones perfect, while the water in the background is aquamarine and framed by pink sand. It looks great. The sound is crisp and the acting is good.

"I feel the tension," Nathan says. "We have something here."

"It's a good first two days," David says. "We got a lot done."

"Let's get some rest then; we have a full day again tomorrow," Xander says.

Eric powers down the edit system, and the screens go dark. Rolando opens the door and the herd rises and leaves, laughing and chatting:

"We're ready for the first stunt shot…"

"The hair held up…"

"We should get a fan going for the next beach shots…"

They are headed to the veranda to join the rest of the crew. They'll watch the sunset, talk, swim in the pool and enjoy the breeze until they grow tired and amble off to bed, sometimes alone, sometimes in pairs. The instant camaraderie is one of the good parts of working on a movie, and I miss it.

Rolando closes the door, leaving Xander and me alone. "Feeling better after what you just saw?"

"It's good. I admit it, okay?" I do my best to sound petulant.

"See? I know what's good for you. And not just in your career. Imagine how far you could go if you trusted me with everything."

I must pick my response carefully. I shake my head slowly. "Xander, you are such a strange and complicated man."

"But maybe a man you could love again?"

I keep my face blank. If my face is empty, he can fill it with whatever emotion he wants to be there.

I fall in back in a chair. "I hate it when you ask me that."

"That's not yes, but that's not no either. I'll take it."

There's a light knock on the door.

"Come in."

Rolando swings the door open and Trishelle comes in. She's dressed for the tropics in blue shorts and a red print shirt. Her hair is pulled back and her reading glasses are in her hair, so she looks relaxed but dressed for business.

"Found the love birds!" She wags her finger. "I think this rekindled romance could be great publicity. We could drop some more hints to the tabloids, keep the story going?"

"Let that fade into the background. Instead, drop a hint that Julia and Trevor Pennington are spending time together. Draw the focus to the project."

"That's good…if you're both okay with it?" Trishelle flashes the "A-OK" sign to me. She knows something is up and is trying to communicate.

"I trust Xander. He's the producer." My face stays blank.

"Am I going to see you two on this shoot? Or is it going to be all work and no play for seven days?"

"I know I haven't spent any time with you, I'm sorry," I say.

"What about now? We're all hanging out on the veranda."

"Not tonight," Xander interrupts. "Write up your blast and we'll send it tomorrow."

Rolando opens the door. Trishelle laughs, but there's hurt on her face.

"Rolando is always escorting me from place to place. I think he has a little crush on me," Trishelle touches his chin. "Don't you, Rolando?"

Xander points at her. "Careful, Trishelle. Rolando has a reputation as a real lady killer."

"He seems harmless to me." She pats his cheek.

Glaring, Rolando grabs her hand and puts it at her side. Everything gets weird and quiet.

"Good night, then," Trishelle says. She raises her eyebrows at me as she leaves.

Rolando stays and shuts the door. I turn in my chair to avoid looking at him, then sigh and pretend to close my eyes. Their reflections line up in the two dark computer screens.

Rolando hands Xander a large manila envelope. Xander pulls out one photograph, then three more. He grits his teeth and jams them back into the envelope.

"You should have waited to show me this."

"You said to give you updates immediately."

"Just handle it." The tension rises in his voice.

I stand up. "I have to use the bathroom."

"It's right there." Xander says and points at the office bathroom six feet away.

"I'm just asking permission."

Xander waves for me to hurry up. I shut the door, but don't lock it. I move the curtain over the toilet and uncover the window, then reach up and unlatch it. I turn the crank and open it two inches, then let the curtain drop back into place. Their conversation is muffled through the door. I swing it open and both men stop talking and look at me.

"I can't go to the bathroom in here."

"What's wrong with it?"

"I need things in my own bathroom upstairs. Can someone just take me?"

Rolando moves to the door, but Xander stops him.

"I'll do it."

Xander glares at Rolando as he tosses the envelope with the photographs onto his office desk. Whatever is in that envelope bothers Xander, which makes me want to see it.

"Come darling, you've had a long day."

"Yes, I have."

We walk upstairs. Diego opens the door to my room. He's a short Venezuelan tough guy who guards my door all night. I go straight into the bathroom and lock it. I yank open and slam shut drawers, rip open a tampon package, flush the toilet, run the water and wash my face. After ten deep breaths I step back into the room.

"You okay? I get worried when you step into bathrooms."

"It's a female thing. Do you really want to know more?"

Xander sits down on my bed. "Let's talk then. That's the best thing we can do."

"Good. You can help me run lines. I have a lot of dialogue to-morrow." I hand my script to him. "Who do you want to read first? Nicholas my murderous husband, or Mike my heroic ex-boy-friend?"

Xander leafs through the script and then hands it back.

"I'm not an actor. Let's watch the sunset instead. We'll watch from your balcony and I'll have some dinner brought up."

"I've embraced the role. I'm doing good work, like you wanted. That's enough."

Xander walks around the room, touching my clothes, my ear-rings, my hairbrush, my makeup. He's choosing his next approach.

"So maybe you admit that what you wrote about me was wrong?"

For him, it all comes back to what I wrote in lipstick on that mirror five years ago. He drugged, kidnapped and tortured me, then kidnapped Trishelle and threatened both of our lives, but that's not his reality. Getting me to admit I was wrong is all that matters.

I look away. "Maybe. About some of it."

When I look back at him, he grins.

"If you won't say 'yes' tonight, then will you at least give me—what do you call it? A rain check?"

I try to look reluctant, yet curious—and perhaps willing.

"A rain check, then. Sunsets in the Bahamas are nice. That I remember."

He smiles. "You're very good at this."

"Good at what?"

"Playing the game. And I do love games." Xander touches my cheek. I don't stop him, but when he leans in to kiss me, my head turns. The look on my face is half-willing, half-confused.

"I can't," I say. "Not yet."

"Yet." He smirks with triumph. "I can wait."

He kisses my cheek and leaves the room.

I collapse on my bed. My acting for the day is finally done. All the artifice and false emotion falls away from me, like weighted bags of sand dropping off my shoulders. My lungs breathe slowly, searching for any remaining strength. The crew laughs on the patio, with glasses clinking and a guitar strumming. My strategy is working. My acting just bought me time and solitude. It's time to use them.

I force myself off the bed and go to my closet. On the top shelf are spare sheets. I grab three and go into the bathroom and turn on the shower, so Diego will hear the water running. In the middle bathroom drawer is my canvas bag. I dump out all the magazines. In the bottom is the stolen roll of gaffer's tape.

I twist the sheets, tie them together, and then tie knots into them, creating one long length. I rip off a dozen long strips of gaffer's tape and stick the ends to the bathroom counter. I wind tape around each spaced knot on each sheet, making as big a tape wad as I can. I then open the cabinet under the sink and tie one end around the bathroom pipe beneath the sink, then open the bathroom window and look outside.

The sun hasn't set yet, but it's getting dark. There's a glow from the patio lights around the edge of the building, but nothing else. The dark grey trunk of a young banyan tree blocks my view, but also anyone's view of me.

I go back into my room and pull on jeans and a T-shirt, then dart back into the bathroom and lock the door. I grab the canvas bag and slide it over my shoulder.

I toss the rope sheet out the window and pull myself up into the tiny opening. My legs go through first as my body squeezes through the window. The thin aluminum rail digs into my legs, then thighs, and then stomach as I slide out. It's a good thing I'm wearing jeans.

I just hope there are no red marks on the back of my thighs when this is done.

I ease down the sheet, using the knobs of gaffer's tape like rungs on a ladder. My butt bumps into the wall on the way down and my arm scrapes against the rough stucco. That will leave a mark.

The library's bathroom window is now right in front of me, and it's already open two inches. My hand fits inside, finds the knob and cranks it the rest of the way open. My heart is pounding.

I swing my heels onto the window ledge, get my legs inside, then shimmy through until my butt plops down on the closed toilet seat. The bathroom door is open a crack. No one is in the library. I dash in, lock the door and get busy. The spyglass and the straw hat go inside my canvas bag. I open the closet and throw in the man's dress coat and the pair of deck shoes.

Next is the map on the wall. Nothing says Elysian Cay, but the shape of the island is the same as what I see looking north from my balcony. The island arcs like a finger, ending at a jagged tip that has an electronic beacon and the ruins of an old lighthouse. An inset in the corner of the map displays a larger geographic area—Elysian Cay is the second cay in the Ragged Island Chain, which has twelve small islands. Cuba is fifty miles to the south and the nearest large Bahamian island is one hundred miles to the north.

This isn't Eleuthera, which has four thousand people, four towns and a major shipping lane off shore. Elysian Cay is in the middle of a vast stretch of water, surrounded by uninhabited islands.

Tiny numbers dot the map in the water offshore—the depth. It's shallow on one side of the island, fifteen to forty feet deep for a long way out. On the east side, the depth drops to a thousand feet fast. A deep underwater canyon called *The Tongue of the Ocean* cuts through the middle of the Bahamas, and the Ragged Islands start at its southern tip.

There's noise in the hallway. Time is running out. I scan Xander's desk next. There are monthly statements of stock holdings in Europe, REIT accounts, bond purchases and pink copies of the Financial Times of London—

—and the manila envelope that enraged Xander.

I open it and pull out four 8x10 color photos. The first two show a man in a harbor talking to a boat captain. He's in his late twenties or early thirties, in good shape, with dark hair, light brown skin, not handsome but with an interesting face. He's wearing a long-sleeved red T-shirt and blue jeans.

The next two pictures aren't as crisp. They show the same guy fighting off six men in a narrow street next to a taxi. Then in the next photo there is a new man swinging a long metal stick, hitting the attackers. This new man is tall, also in good shape, bald, masculine and quite handsome.

My eyes are drawn to the first man's face, as he fights off his attackers. He grits his teeth and his eyes are wide with fear as he blocks the punches. He looks familiar…

He's my paparazzo stalker. My curry and rice dinner churns in my stomach.

Someone tries the door.

"We're good. It's already locked," a voice says.

"We still need to get a key and check it," a second voice says.

It's a race now. The photographs go back in the envelope and onto his desk. The canvas bag goes over my shoulder. I dart into the bathroom, step on the toilet and almost dive out the window. Once both legs are wrapped around my bed sheet ladder, I reach back inside and crank the window closed, then start climbing. The thick globes of tape are perfect grip points for my hands and feet. I reach my bathroom window. Bringing my canvas bag filled with loot back into my room is too risky, so I hang it on a branch stump of the banyan tree.

I swing my feet back in the window, heave my body through and land in the tub. The shower is still running, and my shirt and jeans get soaked. I have to move fast now. I pull in my sheet ladder, stick it under the sink, then pull off all my clothes and step back under the running water.

I turn up the heat and rub out the scrapes on my legs, arms and belly from the windowsills and the coarse stucco wall. I then shut off the water and rub in oily cream. My skin must look red, smooth and shiny, not bruised or scraped.

I wrap myself in a towel and open the bathroom door. Diego waits in my room.

"You were in there a long time."

"Why do you care? Is there a water shortage?"

"Puta," he mutters and closes the door.

My fingers go to my temples and my breathing slows. I scan the room for a place to hide the sheet ladder. Lamp, bed, bureau, desk, rug, curtains…

The curtains. The ceiling is high, and the metal curtain rod that stretches across the sliding windows is ten feet off the ground. I have to close the curtains though, which people will see. I can't raise suspicions.

I put on a nightgown and comb my hair, then step out the open glass doors onto my balcony. Showtime again. My fingers curl on the ledge and I tilt my chin so the light hits my face. It's a fifty-foot drop down to the marble patio below. People are gathered at tables and around the pool.

I feel their eyes on me. It's an animal instinct, like the feeling you get when you are driving and you glance over and catch someone watching you in the next car. We all have it, but I just use it more, like a muscle you exercise. With one micro-glance, I can spot people watching me, but still keep my own eyes looking where I want.

I let them watch me, and then glance down. Xander and Rolando are still arguing, until Xander glances up, and we make eye contact. The chatter drops. Everyone is looking up at me now. There's even a sound track for my scene, low romantic Cuban music from someone's MP3 player, pumped through a speaker. Trishelle is in a chair in front.

I wave. Everyone waves back. It's a harmless gesture from the lead actor. I then flash a thumbs-up, aimed right at Trishelle. At first she doesn't move, and then she flashes thumbs-up back at me.

Behind her, I see that Rolando is not looking at me anymore— he now watches Trishelle.

I toss my hair and then head back to my room, but not before looking over my shoulder at Xander one more time. The music is still playing. Our eyes meet, he nods, but I dip my eyes and go back inside my room. I draw my curtains shut. Scene over.

I push the chest of drawers close to the windows, then run to the bathroom and pull out my taped sheets. I lay my sheet ladder across the top of the curtain rod, folding it carefully so that it's flush against the wall and hidden from view. The roll of duct tape fits on the finial that juts out from the end of the curtain rod. I jump down and look. It all blends in. I push the chest of drawers back into place, and then collapse into bed.

I made progress today.

CHAPTER 23

STEVEN

Day 8: Thursday Evening

It takes us three hours to crisscross against the wind back to Long Island, and only when we are within a half mile of shore does the island shelter us enough to finally have smooth sailing. It's just before sunset as we come close to Deadman's Cay and the windows of the town are lit up like they're made of gold, reflecting the setting sun behind us. In less than thirty minutes it will be dark and the town's few streetlights will come on.

Carl stares hard at the island. Something is bothering him because his thick worry lines are popping on his bald head again.

"What is it?"

"I have a feeling Cherie didn't go to Nicole's like I asked."

"We're close enough now. Just call her on the cell phone."

He turns the sailboat into the wind and lets the sails luff. He keeps staring as we drift.

"Carl, what is it?"

His eyes narrow and he points at The Screw Pump, the decrepit bar leaning out over the harbor. A nautical flagpole juts out of its roof and marine flags fly on the cables that run diagonally down to the base of the pole.

"When a stranger comes to town, Tyler at the bar flies the yellow flag. If they're looking for me, he also flies the green flag. If they mean to do me harm, he flies the red flag. Right now a yellow, a green and four red flags are flying," Carl says. "And that means four bad guys are looking for me."

"What do we do?"

"We don't call Cherie. We'll anchor in a cove a mile south and Tyler will pick us up."

Carl turns the boat downwind. We head back around the southern point, out of sight, and into the next bay. He peeks over his shoulder as if waiting for a speedboat to come tearing after us, but we're alone.

"When do we call Tyler?"

"He's already there. Like I said, I plan things out."

We get to the cove and pull alongside two anchor buoys bobbing in the water. As the sun sets, I walk up on the foredeck and attach the bowline to the front buoy and Carl ties up to the one in the back. A black Zodiac speeds toward us—it's Tyler. We grab our stuff, lock up the boat and step over the rail and down into the raft. Tyler hits the gas, throwing us back against the rubber walls as we race away.

"Relax, Tyler. I'm in no hurry to get there," Carl says.

Tyler eases up on the throttle until we just chug along. The sun is now gone and his hands are shaking in the dusky light.

"So what are we looking at?"

"Four guys. Young, but trained. I can't tell where they're from. They came to the bar and one guy stood outside while the others ordered beers that they didn't drink. One guy got up to pee and spent a lot of time looking around and then they all left. They didn't ask questions…they didn't say anything."

"What happened next?"

"I got on the roof and watched them head down your street. A car dropped them off and they were carrying bags. They've been there ever since."

"Anything else?"

"Simon was in the bar, so I gave him a postman's hat and satchel with some letters and sent him down there about an hour ago, but he didn't come back. That's when I raised the flags."

"Is Cherie still there?"

"I don't know. I called her cell phone, but there was no answer."

Tyler beaches the Zodiac and we hop out and pull it up high onto dry sand. We scramble up a bushy path to the road above. Although it's now night, the limestone gravel still shines white in the darkness.

Tyler's car is parked in a rutted driveway lined with sea grape trees that hide us from the main road. Tyler opens the trunk and a small light illuminates Carl's weapons stash—a single barrel shotgun, a Colt M16 rifle and inside a metal box, two Beretta handguns.

Tyler glances around while Carl puts on a shoulder holster and secures the pistol in place under his left arm, then puts two more clips in the deep pocket of his cargo pants.

He glances at me and nods for me to grab something.

"I haven't touched a weapon in five years."

"Take the shotgun then. You're less likely to miss."

Carl also makes me grab a leather harness with a long pocket so that I can carry the shotgun snug against my back, then hands me a belt bag full of shotgun shells.

"Loop that through your belt. You'll know when it's time to load up."

I obey, and he hands me a small knife in a belt sheath next.

"And put that on too." I loop that through my belt as well.

Finally he opens a plastic storage bin and pulls out surgical tubing in three-foot pieces, and flat exercise bands that are used for stretching.

"Are we doing surgery or working out?"

"Neither. Tubes are for tying, bands for gagging and blindfolds, and they fit in your pockets. Take a bunch and be ready, because I know you'd rather tie people up than shoot them."

He knows me well, and I stick a handful into the pockets of my windbreaker.

Carl shuts the trunk and turns to Tyler. "You need me to drive?"

"I can handle it." Tyler's back stiffens. He stops shaking.

"Drop us past town, at the pothole farm."

Carl gets into the front passenger seat, Tyler jumps into the driver's seat and I slip into the back. Tyler kicks up dust as we barrel back onto the island's main road.

We climb and pass the town of Deadman's Cay. Carl's street comes into view in the distance. It is lit up by the one street lamp, on the far end of town. We rise more, and farmland appears again on either side of the road. Tyler pulls over onto the sandy shoulder where Carl and I jump out.

"You want me to wait?"

"No. Stick to the plan. Go to Clarence Town, tell the constable what's going on and bring him back. Whatever is going to happen will have happened by then."

Tyler drives back onto the road and disappears going north. Carl heads into the scrubby farmland, walking fast and I have to jog to keep up.

"Maybe they just want to scare us."

"Or kill us."

"Why?"

"Because you told people you wanted to go to Elysian Cay, and someone got pissed."

Carl moves fast through the sparse fields. The limestone rock is pockmarked with erosion holes that the farmers have filled with soil and planted fruit trees and vegetables. Carl darts between the plants with me right on his heels.

We reach the rocky ledge that overlooks his street below and hunch down. A dog barks in the distance. A light wind blows in from offshore. There's nothing else.

"Strap on that weapon and get secure."

I pull the harness over my shoulder and pull the straps tight. Carl slides the shotgun into its slot so it's tight against my back. It feels odd to be carrying a weapon again.

"From here on, things get real. Ready?"

I breathe deeply. "Ready," His confidence feels mine.

Carl kneels down, pulls up a wooden stopper and uncovers a limestone hole. Inside is a knotted rope, which he tosses over the edge of the cliff. Like he said, he's always prepared. He hands me a carabiner, then clips his own onto his belt and slides the rope into place. He steadies his feet against the wall and drops over the edge.

When I feel the rope go slack, I tie in and back my feet over the edge. The physical stuff is easy for me and doesn't feel rusty even in the dark. I belay down the cliff, staying silent, and land next to Carl inside a wooden fence, surrounded by propane tanks and barrels of diesel fuel. Carl peeks out. Still nothing.

Carl draws his weapon and gets it ready. He looks at me, which is the signal for me to do the same. I draw out my shotgun, slide a cartridge into the open barrel and close it as quietly as I can. We creep out from behind the fence and ease up to the side of the first empty house. We see our first "red flag"—a dark-skinned man stands in the shadows next to Carl's house, holding a rifle. He looks south, waiting to ambush whoever comes up the road into the light of the street lamp.

We wait. The man in the darkness rubs his eyes. He puts down his rifle, lights a cigarette, takes one drag, then puts it out and picks up his rifle again. He's not a total slacker—he took just enough nicotine to keep him alert.

The guard then sighs and stares at the empty street, waiting again for Carl to appear.

Carl re-holsters his pistol and taps the pockets of my windbreaker and nods. He wants me to be ready with the tubing, and I nod that I will be.

He stays low and darts across the grassy space with his hands in front of him. He slides his right forearm around the man's neck from behind, and just as he lifts him off the ground he uses his left hand to grab the man's rifle from in front of him—all in one fluid motion. Keeping the flow going, Carl leans over so that the man's back lies flat against his own huge broad back and continues to choke him—while also gently lowering the man's rifle onto the grass with his left hand. I've seen him do this before; while his opponent struggles like a trapped overturned beetle, Carl looks like he's doing Tai Chi.

The man twists sideways and even tries to flip his legs over, but Carl keeps adjusting his feet and the angle of his back to counter any move the man attempts. There is no noise.

It doesn't take long. After two minutes without air, the man loses consciousness. Carl turns around and wraps his legs around the man's waist and thighs and rolls them both back gently onto the grass.

I run up and place my shotgun down next to the rifle. I tie the man's feet tight with one strip of tubing, then tie a flat exercise band tight around the man's mouth, leaving him just enough room to breathe. Carl lets him go and rolls him onto his stomach. I hand him another piece of tubing and Carl ties his wrists behind his back. Fast and easy, just like the old days.

I grab the walkie-talkie off the man's belt and we lay him down next to a bougainvillea bush.

The walkie-talkie crackles in my hands. "Tommy, position three?"

I click the walkie-talkie once—an easy binary answer—and wait. They click back once as well.

Carl motions for me to stay and that he is going around, then disappears leaving me in the shadows next to his house—a house that twenty-four hours ago was pulsing with people and music. Now it's dark and shuttered as if it's closed for the winter, though three more guys are in there somewhere, along with Cherie and maybe Simon, the fake postman.

"Taxi!" Carl shouts. "Where's my taxi?"

Carl staggers up the street, wearing a hat low on his face and acting drunk. He shouts up at the houses.

"Where is everybody? Don't you Bahamians know how to party?"

The front door opens. A young white guy with close-cropped hair wearing army fatigues exits the house carrying a rifle. My face is right next to his feet on the steps, so I sink down on my haunches to stay hidden. He walks down the stairs but stays in the shadows.

I turn down the walkie-talkie in my hand just in time.

"Tommy, where are you? Move to the front," he whispers into his headset.

Carl spots him and waves.

"Hey! I'm wasted! Can you drive me to my hotel in Santa Maria? I'll pay you."

I lift the shotgun off the grass and dash up behind the man hoping he won't turn. The man clicks his walkie again. "Tommy, get to position three, I have—"

Carl draws his pistol. The man swings his rifle up to shoot Carl—just as I hit him hard in the back of the head with the butt end of my shotgun. Too hard, because as he crumples my body keeps moving and I collapse on top of him—just as gunfire from the balcony tears up the street around me. Carl returns fire at the balcony and runs up to the next building. I scamper behind him, cowering.

"Boy, did I blow that." My body won't stop shaking.

"You did fine."

Carl pulls out a key from a chain around his neck and motions for me to follow him. We reach the back door of the neighboring house. He sticks in a key and unlocks it. "Go to the front of my house and try to draw them out on the balcony."

He eases inside. I hear him going up the stairs. The two men inside his house have the advantage of height over us, but they won't for much longer. I dart around the side of the building and look up at Carl's home.

The lights are off, but the windows are open. Two men with guns are up there in the dark, waiting. I take the walkie-talkie, turn the volume up high and throw it hard at the open window. It goes in and smashes against something, which gives me time to run across the empty space between the two houses while they shoot random bullets out the window.

"Tommy, move around!" The voice blares from inside the house before they realize it's the echo from Tommy's open walkie. All goes quiet. The only noise from inside is a woman crying.

I sneak around to the front of the house, pull Tommy out of the bougainvillea, cut the tubing around his ankles and yank him to his feet. I stick the shotgun up the front of his shirt so the barrel rests against his chin, then pull him into the street.

"Hey! Out here!"

Dark figures move on the balcony but don't step forward.

I keep Tommy in front of me while staying close to the sea wall so I can jump over. The second man is still unconscious in the middle of the street. I must not glance at the house next door.

"You have Cherie? I'll trade her for Tommy!"

"Where's Webb?"

"Down against the house."

"I want to see him too."

"You shot him. He can't move."

"Say something, Webb! I need to know where you're at!"

"He can't answer! It's me you want anyway! Just let Cherie go."

There is a pause. The men move out onto the wide patio balcony, the same outdoor patio where Carl and I talked just last night. One of the silhouettes holds Cherie from behind, just like I'm holding Tommy.

Tommy tries to pull away, and I pull down hard on the tubing on his wrists and jam the shotgun up hard against his chin.

"Fair trade, right. Tommy for Cherie?"

"Sure," the voice says. "Fair trade."

Nothing happens. I extract the shotgun from under Tommy's shirt, then push him face down in the street. My arms are open and my head is up—an easy target. The one man lets go of Cherie as they both step to the edge of the balcony and raise their weapons.

I dive for the street as a gun pops twice, like a car backfiring. Two heavy thuds hit the wood floor of the balcony. Cherie screams.

I look up. Carl lies flat on his back on the sloped roof of the next house, his handgun aimed between his thighs, with a straight shot down onto his own balcony.

CHAPTER 24

JULIA

Day 9: Friday Morning

I wake up at 5:30, two hours before my call. Looking west, the light on the water out my window is slate gray and the thin clouds reflect streaks of orange. The sun must be peeking over the horizon somewhere to the east.

I need to memorize my lines and nail my performance today. I also must delay shooting. It's strange to want to perform well in a movie while also trying to subtly sabotage it, but I can't be stuck here when shooting ends. On the day this movie wraps, Xander will expect me to return to him—and if I don't, both Trishelle and I may become playthings for Rolando. Right now I'm in a safety zone; as long as shooting continues, I have time to strategize. Therefore, I must do a fantastic job, while also making sure my job lasts as long as possible.

It's day three of a seven-day shoot, and today we will do all the outdoor scenes with my mysterious murdering husband, Nicholas, played by Bernard St. Jacques. By tonight we'll only have four more days left. That's not enough time.

A maid brings me fruit, yogurt and coffee at 6:00 a.m., and Diego knocks on my door an hour later and escorts me down to the set. I don't have to worry about wardrobe; I'm in a black bikini and a pareo all day, with a white robe to wear between takes.

People dart back and forth on the veranda and say "hello" as I walk past. Most of them have been awake for hours. They're paid good money to do their jobs fast and well, which leaves little time to sleep.

This morning we're shooting all the outdoor honeymoon lovey-dovey stuff before the complete truth about my husband's murderous past comes out. It's all montage action that's not strenuous on my brain, which hopefully will give me time to look around.

Diego leads me across the veranda straight to Rolando, who gestures for me to sit in my canvas chair. Rolando pulls up a chair of his own and joins me as Diego walks away. The hand-off is complete, and no one even notices.

Rolando doesn't smile, nod or grimace. He just stares straight ahead.

"Hi, I'm Richard. Can I get you ready?"

Richard wears Bermuda shorts, a blue T-shirt and a makeup tool belt around his waist. He holds an open dish of base in one hand and a makeup brush in the other.

"Sure. But where's Toni?"

Richard does nothing until Rolando gestures that he has permission to approach. Richard moves directly in front of me. I tilt my face up and he dabs at my skin.

Rolando whispers in my ear as Richard's makeup brush skims across my face.

"Things didn't work out with Toni. She was terminated."

My skin turns cold as the blood drains from my face. I must put my hand on Richard's shoulder to keep from fainting, and he grabs my arm to hold me up.

"Whoa, steady." Richard leans me back in my chair. "Want some water?"

"Sorry, I didn't get much sleep last night." Rolando gets up, moves behind Richard's shoulder and stares down at me.

"Oops. Am I replacing someone?"

"Toni talked too much," Rolando answers, staring at me.

"Ouch. Cardinal sin for makeup artists," Richard says.

The brush hairs skim my face, but I can't feel them. My hands clutch the wooden arms of the director's chair to keep from shaking, but it doesn't work.

Rolando grins. His eyes, usually dead, are now wide and alive. He wanted to see my reaction and moved to get the best view of my horror.

"I know how hard it is to switch makeup artists midstream. But you're so beautiful you barely need anything. It'll be easy to match her look, I promise."

"That's enough talking," Rolando says. "Just work."

Richard rolls his eyes and winks at me. A minute later he smiles at Rolando, makes a zipping motion over his lips and walks away.

Rolando sits down next to me again, making my skin crawl. It makes me feel more vulnerable than when he faces me. He gestures at the bustling crew around us.

"It's wonderful when you can pursue your passion and make money at it," he says. "That's what we all dream for, isn't it?"

"I'm not making money on this film, and this is not my dream."

"I'm not talking about you. I'm talking about me. I make movies too."

He holds up his smartphone and touches the screen. A small video comes on. It's Rolando, lit by a single flashlight. He's on the black speedboat, bobbing somewhere out on the water at night. Someone is crying. He heaves something over the edge of the boat and then holds it in the water. He says something in Spanish and whoever is holding the smartphone comes closer and shoots down into the water. The other person with the flashlight follows and lights up the scene.

Rolando is holding Toni, and her hands are tied in front of her. She is straight up and down in the water and Rolando's arm muscles are taut as he holds her up.

"Please! Why are you doing this? What did I do? Please, please…"

Toni begs Rolando and then looks up at whoever is holding the smartphone. Rolando lets go and Toni's eyes widen. She tries to scream, but her mouth is already under the water as she sinks below the choppy waves. The clip ends and Rolando pockets his phone, then looks at me. I fight to control my reaction because I know that's what he wants to see.

"You're a monster."

"And you're disobedient. She's gone because you misspoke. Think of that before you speak out of turn to anyone here again."

My eyes close and Toni's terrified face stays in my mind. Her face morphs into Trishelle's.

Rolando leans close and whispers with excitement. "But I also like it when you misbehave. I get to make my own movies. If you misbehave enough, maybe I'll get to make one with you."

"Remember who you're talking to. Xander won't tolerate you speaking to me this way. I'm his lead actor."

"Only until shooting ends," he says and pats my hand.

"Xander's in charge and if he is happy with me, you'll do nothing. And be careful. I may even have something to say about what happens to *you* by then."

"We're ready, Julia," Walker says, striding up.

I follow Walker without even looking back at that skunk for permission. Toni's pleading face is stuck in my brain. She's dead because of me. I hold my breath to keep from crying, then grab Walker's belt to stop him.

"Whoa, Trooper. You want to sit down?"

We grab forearms. "Sorry, I got up too fast."

He waits, holding me steady. I glance back and Rolando's eyes lock into mine with his dead shark stare.

My mind flashes back to Trishelle. Rolando saw us trade the "thumbs-up" signal last night. Now I doubt my entire strategy. If I get caught, Trishelle dies. The safest choice is to submit and sleep with Xander. Then she'd survive and Rolando would disappear…or not. No, surrendering guarantees nothing.

"The blood is back in your face."

"That's because I'm angry."

"We all are, sister. But not at you."

I step into the set. "Let's get 'er done!"

"Julia Travers says 'let's get her done!'" Walker shouts, and a collective "whoop" rises up from the crew.

Their affection fills my with warmth. This is my comfort zone, where I'm safe from Rolando. He can watch me all he wants, I'm sticking with my plan.

We start with a scene by the pool. Bernard walks up and lies down on the lounge chair next to mine. "Good morning, my wife," Bernard coos.

"Good morning, husband."

Bernard wears blue shorts made of raw silk, and an open white shirt. He is lean and just a little muscular. It's believable that Risa Baker, my character, would fall for him despite our age difference.

I open my robe and turn towards him, showing off my bikini body. "Why do you get to wear clothes and I have to be in a swimsuit?"

"Because you're why people buy movie tickets."

Sammie, Anthony, Paul and the rest of the crew circle around us, tweaking the lights and getting the final measurements. The red tally light flashes on the camera. Over at video village Rolando joins Nathan and David who are already watching Bernard and me on the monitors.

I laugh and put my hand on his leg, and he puts his hand on top of mine.

"Are you flirting with me?"

"It's not flirting if we're married and in love. And we get to be in love all day."

He smiles at me and puts his hand on my hip.

"I'm fat. I had to gain weight for this shoot."

"You look fine to me." He adds a light stroke to my leg.

"Oops, look at your hand." His hand comes up with a streak of yellow.

"I should have told you that part of my tan was sprayed on," I offer him the sleeve of my terry cloth robe.

He wipes his hand, and it leaves a stain on my white robe. We both wince and look at video village. Richard hurries over with his makeup kit just as the costumer arrives with a new robe.

"No touchy touchy," Richard says.

"Sorry, we'll be good." I stand up so he can fix my fake tan while I change my robe.

It takes five glorious minutes for Richard to get my skin tone set again.

"Let's just get the wide shot with no hands!" Nathan shouts.

I cover my microphone with my hand as I snuggle close. "We're supposed to touch, don't worry."

Bernard doesn't need much encouragement to touch my leg or tummy or face, which creates continuity, wardrobe and make-up problems. I milk six takes out of a shot that should have been done in one. Rolando comes over after twenty minutes.

"No more fooling around."

"People have to believe we're in love. If they don't, they won't care when they find out I'm in love with a killer."

"Then love each other without touching."

"Why must I explain this? If you have a problem, tell Xander, he's the producer. Where is he, anyway?"

Rolando turns around and walks away.

"I like how you handled him," Bernard says.

"We're the ones on camera, not him."

My gut tells me that Xander is away from the set because of those photos with the paparazzo. Adding drama here may draw him back and misdirect his time and attention even more.

The pool scene goes well. Our characters share childhood stories as we lie on our sides, staring at each other and touching. Then, between takes, Bernard shares his own real childhood stories about growing up outside Montreal.

He whispers, his face inches away from mine. He grew up poor with an obsessive mother and a father who drank. He holds my hand while he shares, all the while staring at my boobs. I nod with sympathy and stroke his thumb with mine. He moves his hand to my hip. Rolando whispers into his walkie-talkie, probably updating Xander on the torrid touching going on out by the pool.

We move to the beach for the next scene—strolling on the sand after snorkeling. We start in hip deep water with masks, snorkels and swim fins, then wade onto the pink beach holding hands. We stop and kiss on the beach, and then keep walking while he puts his arm around my waist.

It's a simple shot, but it's easy to make it complicated. There's a camera dolly with rubber tires on the beach that rolls back with us as we walk. The palm fronds we have to cross under make it hard to get the pacing just right. I make sure to drop my snorkel gear twice.

Then there's the makeup. Richard must create the perfect combination of oil and salt water on my skin, and slick my wet blonde hair back perfectly. I mess it up just enough that Richard must fix it after each take. Richard has an even worse time with Bernard, whose fake six-pack lines keep dissolving away, and as co-producer I insist that my husband look sexy and cut.

It's one gigantic hassle, but Bernard loves it. Ten times we stroll into the water and ten times we stroll out. Ten times he kisses me, tells me he loves me, then puts his hand on my waist and walks me down the beach. By the fifth time, he gives my ass a squeeze before sliding his arm around my waist. I giggle, but don't object. By the tenth time, he doesn't even bother with my waist and just cups my ass.

Most of all, we need the swim fins I'm holding. The map in Xander's office comes back to me, and the distance between the islands isn't that far. If I can escape with these fins and get to the next island, we might have a chance. I never put them down, or even make a motion with them. These fins must become such a part of me that no one sees what I do with them. Everyone can watch Bernard grab my ass instead.

Rolando's calls finally get through. Xander arrives and says hello to no one. He taps David, the cinematographer, on the shoulder, gestures for him to move, and then takes his place next to Nathan. They whisper.

Walker and Sammie, the second AC, stand ten feet to my right, in the water, holding their walkie-talkies over their heads to keep them dry. Walker hears a request crackle through his earbud.

"Copy." turns to Bernard. "No more ass grabbing. Got that?"

"Completely." Bernard hides a smile. "I apologize, Julia."

"Let's slate it!" Walker shouts, and Sammie sticks the clapper in my face.

"Scene 16, Take 11." Sammie snaps the slate shut.

After eleven takes, everyone is happy.

"May I have your snorkel gear back please?" a woman asks.

She's tall with red hair and I've only seen her once before. She's the prop master, and not the type of person I can just wave away like I did with the production assistant when I stole the gaffer's tape. We hand over our fins and masks.

I put on my sunglasses and a sun hat and pretend to listen to Bernard gossip about his second wife, but my eyes follow the prop master to see where she puts the snorkel gear. She plunges the gear into a bucket of fresh water and tosses it all into a blue rubber bin.

Xander appears and kisses me on the cheek. Rolando is five feet behind him.

"Hello, Mr. Constantinou," Bernard says. Xander waves his hand at him and Bernard slinks away.

I shoot him a pouty look. "You were gone all morning."

"I've had some challenges to attend to."

"You're not upset with me, are you?"

Xander smiles. "So now you care if I'm upset with you? When did that happen?"

"Stop it. I did some good work this morning, and you weren't around. That's all."

"I heard all about it." He looks over his shoulder at Bernard.

"I didn't cast him, you did. I'm just doing my job."

173

"You're playing games."

"And you're not?" I raise my eyebrows at him.

Xander's face softens. Walker tries to walk over, but Rolando stops him. Walker, who towers over him, just raises his voice.

"Just tell them their lunch is ready at their table," he says and walks away.

"I want us to eat alone. I don't want that pig Rolando anywhere near us."

"You know how to make Rolando disappear. Just accept my offer."

The table with our food is in the shade, close to the stone stairs leading up to the villa. As we sit, Xander gestures to Rolando that he can stand a little farther away from us. That's a relief. It allows me to gauge Xander's emotions with a little more privacy.

I also have a clear view of the blue bin just over Xander's shoulder. I don't dare look at the fish and rice on my plate, otherwise the prop master may move the bin while I'm sliding food on my fork. Finally she lifts the bin onto a red wagon with all her other props and tugs it away.

My attention turns to Xander instead. "Something is bothering you. You're sure that you're not upset with me?"

"I already told you, no, I'm not."

"You can't expect me to change overnight. You're asking a lot of me."

"Stop it. I told you, that's not it."

"This is how girlfriends talk to their boyfriends. Are you sure you want that?"

Xander lifts his finger and motions for silence. I obey, but also smile, which makes him smirk. This weird sassy obedience is what he wants from me. Easy enough, if I can make it work for me.

Rolando answers his phone. Xander looks at him. I keep eating, but watch the signals that pass between the two men. Rolando issues some curt answers into his phone, hangs up and shakes his head at Xander.

Xander leaves the table without a word and he and Rolando walk ten yards to the side. My eyes stay looking forward, but with sideways micro-glances I see Xander poke Rolando hard in the chest and ask him a question. Rolando doesn't answer.

This is all about the photos in his office, but how?

CHAPTER 25

Day 9: Friday Morning

News spreads fast when there's gunfire. Soon everyone knows that down at The Screw Pump there are two bad guys handcuffed on the floor and two bodies in the freezer. Gawkers stroll by the outside of the bar and peek into the darkened interior. Every five minutes a kid darts in to look around and Tyler chases him out.

Me, I'm in the freezer, shivering, looking at two dead men lying on the cold floor. My stomach churns from lack of sleep and my head and body ache from my bruises and cuts. None of it registers in the front of my brain, though; not with Death right in front of me.

Last night, Cherie and Simon were in the house, alive but terrified. Cherie had welts on her wrists from where they had tied her but otherwise she wasn't physically harmed. Mentally, she wasn't so good though. She kept crying and wouldn't answer when Carl spoke to her. Simon was in worse shape. They had broken his hand with the butt end of a rifle and locked him in a closet.

Right away Carl phoned and got Dr. Hassan out of bed to attend to their injuries. Then he called Nicole to come and help comfort

Cherie and take her to her place. They both got to the house within ten minutes to treat and soothe the patients.

The inside of the house was trashed. The four guys upended every shelf and dumped out every drawer. It was hard to see the kitchen floor between all the utensils and broken dishes strewn everywhere. In the bedrooms, they'd ripped down the curtains and sliced up the mattresses. My bag was ripped up and cut to shreds. All I have are the clothes I'm wearing, my wallet, and my one camera that I took on the sailboat.

We had four problems: two dead guys on the balcony and two angry living ones tied up in the street. We dragged the two corpses down the stairs and lifted them into the back of Carl's pickup truck. Their two friends fought so hard that we duct taped their ankles and wrists and then heaved them into the truck bed as well. We drove to The Screw Pump and laid the dead bodies in the freezer and let the living guys sit on the floor. Carl forced me to drink a glass of water and eat a mango, which I did while standing in the freezer. Now it's Friday morning, and I'm still standing here waiting for the police to arrive, staring at two dead men on the freezer floor.

It's surreal yet familiar.

I whisper a prayer from my catechism lessons back at St. Cecilia's in San Francisco, growing up:

"Eternal rest grant unto them, O Lord, and let perpetual light shine upon them. May they rest in peace."

I walk out of the freezer and Carl latches the door behind me.

The two bad guys sit on the floor tied up and blindfolded. I tip their heads back and give them water just like I did with prisoners of war back in Afghanistan. It's what you do while you wait.

The police arrive; four Bahamian constables in two police cars from Clarence Town. Three of them are young cops in their twenties, wearing blue pants and white short-sleeved shirts with gold badges, which makes them look more like school crossing guards than cops. They stare wide-eyed at the bad guys on the floor. The chief constable is in his fifties, with white flecks in his curly black hair. He seems more irritated than shocked.

"It's a fine mess, Mr. Webb. Real muddy trouble."

"Sorry, Chief Andrew." Carl says.

"Any of you seen any of these guys before?"

"No, but I bet somebody in the boat harbor has," his first constable says.

"Don't go down there. Whoever sent them already knows what happened," Chief Andrew says. He walks over to the two men sitting on the floor. "Either of you want to tell me your story?"

Neither of them reacts.

A car drives up and Carl peeks outside. It's Nicole driving Cherie. Carl starts to step out and the chief constable motions for one of his men to go out with him.

"Can I have a moment alone with her?" Carl asks.

"You're in custody, Mr. Webb. You're lucky I even let you outside," Chief Andrew says.

I look out the window. A dozen people stand in the narrow street and watch as Carl and the constable walk over to the car.

Cherie gets out and weeps. Carl whispers to her and moves close. When he tries to put his arms around her, she pushes him away and hits him in the chest. Carl jerks back in surprise. She hisses something, then gets back in the car and Nicole drives away. Carl watches until the car rounds the corner and then he and the first constable come back inside.

"Can we do this then?"

The police chief nods at his three constables. Two of them lift the bad guys off the floor, un-tape their ankles and take off their blindfolds and steer them outside and into the first squad car. One constable gets behind the wheel and locks the doors, while the other constable comes back inside.

The crowd steps closer to the squad car and stares at the men inside.

Carl puts his wrists behind his back and Chief Andrew puts handcuffs on him too.

"What are you looking at? Turn around, you're going in, too," Carl snarls at me.

The last young constable turns me around and takes my wrists. The cool metal clicks tight against my bones. Chief Andrew and his constables escort us outside for our walk of shame through the crowd, and help us tilt our heads down as we slide into the backseat of the second squad car.

The doors close. The people press closer, peering in at me. I make eye contact with two faces from Tuesday, the day I arrived— Marcus, the fishing boat captain, and the taxi driver.

Chief Andrew tells two constables to stay behind. "You guard the bar, don't let anyone in," he says to the youngest cop, then turns to the other officer. "You go back down to Mr. Webb's house and do the same. I'll call you both later."

Chief Andrew slides into the driver's seat and honks at the squad car in front. The cars inch through the crowd and then head up the street and out of town. We turn left on the island's one main road—The Queen's Highway—and head north toward the main police station in Clarence Town.

Carl stares out the window at the blue water of the Bahama Bank. He shifts, probably trying to get blood to flow to his hands behind his back. He must know I'm looking at him, but he won't turn my way.

I look out the window on my side. Green scrub brush flies past, and in the distance is the blue Atlantic Ocean. This narrow island is a strip of green growing out of bright white rock, under a blue sky with white clouds, surrounded by turquoise water that changes to deep azure on the distant horizon. It's paradise, but it's on the other side of the glass, in a parallel universe that's now impossible to reach.

The bright sun makes me blink. My clothes are filthy and my skin is covered with a layer of white dust. I close my eyes and lean back against the warm headrest. A shower and a nap will be nice. There'll be plenty of time for that in jail.

The car stops and jerks my eyes open. We aren't in Clarence Town. We are alone in a white semicircle of dusty rock off the main road. It looks like a private driveway, sheltered by mango trees and a circle of short palms. There's no house though…it's a building site for a house that was never started.

Chief Andrew opens the back door and helps Carl out, then takes off his handcuffs. Carl rubs his wrists and puts on his sunglasses, and they whisper in front of the car for a good five minutes. Finally Chief Andrew gestures with his palms up, as if asking Carl something. Carl glances back at me...then nods.

Chief Andrew walks over, opens the door, helps me out and takes my cuffs off.

"You have two days. Then I come looking." Chief Andrew slides into the car and drives away.

"What's going on?"

"Follow me." Carl walks into the trees.

The path weaves through thick brush and then bursts into the open sunshine. We're on the edge of high cliffs that encircle a sheltered cove. In the middle of the cove is a fishing boat anchored to two mooring buoys.

"Ready?"

"Ready for what?"

"To go to Elysian Cay." He jumps off the cliff.

I watch him fall two seconds and plunge into the blue water and send up a jet of white spray. He surfaces, and swims toward the fishing boat.

"Come on! We're in a hurry!"

I jump. I feel the air rush past my chest and then I hit the warm cleansing water.

CHAPTER 26

JULIA

The crew is not happy. For three shoot days they've been on schedule, on budget and doing excellent work, yet they just got news that they must pick up the pace. It happened right after Rolando got that phone call and Xander poked him in the chest.

Xander told the line producer to redo the schedule and Walker is handing out the updated call sheets to the crew. People are crumpling their papers and tossing them on the veranda in a group display of passive aggression. This is bad, especially me.

"We make the impossible look easy," one grip says. "That's our problem."

That phone call and the photos in the manila envelope are causing this, I'm sure of it. The crew, however, suspects that Xander is just trying to save a dime. They've experienced this before on other shoots. The producer sees the scenes are going smoothly, so he pushes the production to go faster. If they shave a day off the schedule, it's a big savings, even if the producer must pay overtime.

The crew hates it. They don't need the overtime pay that badly. They're already killing themselves, and this was one of the few afternoons where the schedule was going to finish early so people could go swimming and snorkeling, which is half the reason some of them came. Now they get a two-hour break before starting the scenes slated for day four. They'll end up doing two days of work in one eighteen hour day.

Walker approaches with my new schedule, which Rolando intercepts and takes from him. Walker just rolls his eyes and walks away. Rolando examines it and hands it to me.

"Thank you," I say, trying to soften him.

Rolando stares. He's not buying my act for a second. He squints his shark eyes at me, which makes my skin feel like insects are crawling all over it.

My schedule doesn't change that much. I have two more scenes with Trevor and Bernard, which means I work until 6:00 p.m. tonight. Then both my day three and my day four will be done. My co-stars have to work until midnight, however, to get their new work schedule completed.

I must get out of my wet swimsuit, clean off the oil, salt and sand, get my hair and makeup done again and then put on a dress, all in an hour.

"No more delays. You must move fast."

Rolando and Diego escort me upstairs where I shower and put on a fresh robe. I then rush down and get back in the chair for Richard, who must do my make-up and give my hair a blowout. Yet he's in no hurry. Everyone else seems to work in slow motion, too.

Waiters set up tables of food for the crew. It's a working meal of sandwiches, fruit and junk food that they can grab while setting lights and gear. Their next real meal won't be for hours.

It's a kind gesture from Rebecca, the line producer; she knows food might soften this blow. The crew is already rebelling however. Empty soda cans, blue *Betrayed in Paradise* water canisters and half-eaten sandwiches on paper plates are strewn everywhere. When the wind blows away the napkins, no one chases them down.

A film crew is not like a disciplined army platoon. It's more like a pirate ship that will mutiny if they feel they're being cheated. They suspect greed, and they are muttering.

"I turned down a union gig for this…"

"That's why we have unions, brother. I can get this abuse at home…"

"So much for a day off. I haven't even dipped my toe in the water…"

"I thought I would snorkel at least once. The only time I even walked on the beach was lugging gear…"

"Betrayed in paradise is fucking right. I don't even get to keep the cheap ass metal water bottle…"

Their discontent may work to my advantage. I get lucky—Rolando's cell phone vibrates. He answers quickly, mutters a response, hangs up and yells for Diego. Diego rushes up, Rolando whispers to him, points at me, and then leaves.

Diego glares at me. He wants to show me that he means business, but I feel only lightness. I can look around and perhaps even speak to someone for longer than ten seconds without worrying about the Skunk reading my thoughts.

They light and prep my big confrontation scene. My "husband" and I will sit at a cafe table on the veranda, and my ex-boyfriend Mike Nomad will appear and throw down a police dossier that proves my husband is a killer. I will look through the dossier with bemusement, but as I turn the pages, my face must fill with horror as I learn the truth about who my husband really is.

Nicholas my husband will demand the dossier, and when Mike refuses, Nicholas will pull out a gun. Mike will fight him and knock the gun from his hand. I must grab the loose gun and aim it at my husband, but I won't be able to shoot him. Nicholas will then grab the dossier and flee, but not before stabbing Mike Nomad in the back with his stiletto knife.

My character, Risa Baker, will then be betrayed in paradise.

It's a complicated action scene, with a book, a gun, a knife, a fight scene and stage blood. On a big movie, this usually takes a day to pull off. We must do it in two hours.

While the grumbling grows, I stay in my chair and pretend to go over my lines. It's a perfect chance to study the set, the people and the environment.

Bernard and Trevor arrive, ready for our big action scene.

"Look how calm our star is, as beautiful as ever," Bernard coos. He flirts, while Trevor, who plays my ex-boyfriend Mike, poses like the hunk he is.

"You're terrible. Flirting got you into trouble earlier today."

"I love taking chances." Bernard nudges Trevor. "You'd take that chance, wouldn't you?"

"With Mr. Constantinou watching? No thanks."

Diego stares at us with the angry disgust of a high school outsider. All he sees are two actors flirting with me.

"Why don't you boys pursue someone you can actually catch? There are other pretty girls here, you know."

"Like who?" Bernard asks.

"Like my friend Trishelle."

"Trishelle? Who is she?"

Trevor perks up. "The tall curvy brunette? I think she's the publicist. She was taking photos of our scenes yesterday."

"She was taking photos yesterday? I never even saw her."

"I have spoken to everyone here and I remember no Trishelle."

I lean close. "Just go find her. She's worth it."

Bernard wags his finger at me. "Now I understand. Since you can't have fun with me, you like playing matchmaker."

"And I know she'll adore you. Just tell her that I sent you with a big 'thumbs-up' and she'll know it's from me."

He strokes my arm. "Of course. Thank you."

I wag my finger back at him. "But you must be a gentleman. No breaking hearts on my movie. Understand?"

Bernard grins, thrilled with his on-set reputation. Trevor can't help rolling his eyes.

The tall prop master walks up, pulling her red wagon full of gear. Diego stops her just as he has seen Rolando do, then escorts her the last ten feet to us.

I offer my hand. "What's your name? I haven't met you."

"Renee. And I have your props for you." She pulls out a fake police dossier. Inside are just random photos and newspaper articles and blank pages—no pictures of Bernard as my evil husband Nicholas.

"Sorry, that's the best I could do with the pushed schedule."

"It's okay. I can pretend that terrible things are written here."

She reaches into her wagon and pulls out the prop pistol, the prop stiletto knife, and the bag of prop blood to be taped to Trevor's back and puts them on the table.

Trevor pick up the bag of blood. "You are good."

"Where do you keep all your wonderful toys?"

"There's a gardener's shed at the edge of the veranda. That's my little workshop."

And that's where she keeps the two sets of swim fins—one for me and one for Trishelle.

Xander and Rolando return, followed by Nathan and David. Xander scowls like an angry dad, while Rolando has a snarl on his face that makes me suspect Xander just yelled at him again. Nathan and David trail behind them with wide eyes, like confused children unsure of what's really going on.

Xander stays close, and waves at Nathan to do his job. He straightens his back and becomes a director again. "Risa and Nicholas, you can both sit down." He guides Bernard and me into two chairs at the table. He then guides Trevor to a spot behind my chair, over my left shoulder.

"Mike, your first mark will be here. In the wide shot you come up and slide the dossier into her hands. Move close to her shoulder so we don't have to pull focus."

I look up at him. "Thank you, Nathan."

"You're welcome."

He shoots stink eye at Xander, then walks over to video village, leaving his crew to make their final adjustments. Anthony tweaks the camera while Sammie runs his measuring tape to my eyes.

Rolando pulls Diego aside out of the shot, which gives me space to operate. I smile at Xander and he steps closer.

"I heard you've been a trooper, darling," he says.

"Trying to be. I need to impress you, right?" I wink at him.

"Everyone settle, let's do a take!" Walker yells.

Xander leaves us to join Nathan and David in video village. Rolando follows Xander and isn't looking at me, so I make my move. I cover my microphone and whisper to Bernard.

"Find Trishelle and come to my balcony tonight."

"But it will be the middle of the night."

"And oh so illicit. So be careful. Be there at two a.m."

Bernard grins, he is thrilled to join my conspiracy.

"Let's get 'er done!" I shout, with my best country accent.

"Done and done!" Sammie repeats. A laugh runs through the crowd.

The crew still likes me, and they will work hard for me as long as I stay a trooper. When I glance over at Xander in video village, his face shows that he appreciates it.

CHAPTER 27

STEVEN

Day 9: Friday Afternoon

I'm seasick. We've been motoring through rolling swells for two hours and I've been working with my head down, moving ice chests with food, unrolling sleeping bags, setting up fishing rods and putting sardine bait on ice. It's all for show; if we get stopped we have to appear like we're on a fishing trip. The smell of diesel and rotting fish is a bad mix, and when you add in the rolling deck under my feet, it throws my stomach off-kilter. Being nervous doesn't help.

It's time to move to the real work, which I haven't done in years—assembling and prepping two M4 assault rifles. Can I still do it? Then my muscle memory kicks in and my hands move quickly.

My old rifle was such a constant companion that she had a name: Tina. Carl called his weapon Mary. Tina is in my life again, which churns my stomach more. Chances are good that I'll have to use her.

There's a set of dark camouflage outfits for each of us, along with helmets, two Beretta handguns, flak jackets, night goggles, food and water, an emergency medical roll and a change of socks. It all has to fit in two "three-day" packs.

It takes me an hour. When I stand up, my hamstrings cramp, my stomach heaves and my body falls forward and I retch over the side. My body screams from exhaustion. I haven't slept since my night with Nicole.

Carl hears my primitive yakking and pulls back on the throttle. The drone of the engine drops away and the sound of the ocean returns, and with clean air, thank God. Carl comes out on the back deck and hands me a peeled banana, which I wolf down, then a bottle of water, which I sip lightly. You can't add too much liquid to your belly when you're seasick. He motions for me to come inside the front cabin.

It's an all wood fishing boat with a powerful engine. The inside is sparse and simple; a wheelhouse with a radio and GPS, padded benches, a small kitchen with a table, and a sleeping area in front. The boat is motoring forward via GPS navigation.

"What's the story with the boat?"

"It's a Gollywobbler 38."

"A Golly what?"

"A Gollywobbler, thirty-eight feet long. It's a hand built wooden fishing boat from the Northwest, they use it a lot in Puget Sound. There's a sail we can raise above the engine house and it holds a ton of fuel, so we can be out to sea for a while in this thing."

"What's it doing in the Bahamas?"

"Chief Andrew, who arrested us, is a fishing buddy of mine. We bought it together in Seattle, then motored it down from Washington and brought it through the Panama Canal."

"When we climbed aboard it was already stocked with food and water, extra fuel, and supplies and gear. Like he knew we were taking the trip before he even arrested us."

"He was about to take his monthly fishing trip, but we interrupted it."

"Lucky coincidence." I don't ask how the rifles got on board. Knowing Carl, he planned for this trip, in case he had to take it.

"How's the gear?"

"Ready for you to check."

"Good. Do you still have that weird skill?"

"Which skill is that?"

"Seeing something once and remembering every detail."

"I'm a little rusty, but I think so."

Carl spreads out a large map of the Bahamas on the table. He stabs at tiny islands at the bottom. "This is the Ragged Island Chain. His is Elysian Cay, which is the second island from the top."

He opens a cabinet and throws more maps and books on the table.

I leaf through them: *Boating in the Southern Bahamas*, *The Island Survival Guide*, *Flora and Fauna of the Caribbean and Bahamas* and *Game Fish of the Gulf Stream*.

"You have to memorize the map and go through these books. I've been in the Bahamas four years. You have four hours to know as much about them as I do. Then I want you to sleep for eight hours. By then we'll be at Elysian Cay."

He stares at me, waiting for me to ask the question. "You changed your mind. Why?"

"The night in Colombia, Caballero saw my face in that flashlight beam."

"I remember."

"Five years later, that taxi driver sends him photos of a tourist asking too many questions about Elysian Cay, then sees photos of me saving your ass in a street fight...and it's my face he sees and remembers."

"I'm sorry I brought you my problems."

"Well, they're mine now too. Maybe they always have been/" He brushes my apology away with a wave of his hand. Then he leans closer. "The bigger question now is, do you think he'll stop? What do you remember after he shot the boy?"

"You shot off a burst and we rolled under the fence. We ran zigzag down an incredibly steep hill dodging trees. I got shot. It was like a sledgehammer slamming into my right shoulder and I pitched forward and rolled downhill for a while. I landed on my back with my shoulder on fire. The front of my shirt was bloody, and torn. One bullet had gone clean through."

"But you got up and kept moving. Do you remember that?"

"Sort of. Everything was in slow motion. My head collided with a tree but my face didn't hurt that much, it just felt sticky. I'm pretty sure that's how I got this scar in my eyebrow." I touch the small red line on my forehead.

"The rebels were chasing us and spraying gunfire. We couldn't outrun them with you hurt, so I pulled you down so that you were lying flat down next to me."

"I was losing it by then." What I don't say is that I was hallucinating. My clothes felt cold and wet, so my mind morphed it into something that made sense. I was back with my brother Anthony camping at Kirby Cove campground across the Golden Gate Bridge from San Francisco. I was wet and cold in my sleeping bag from the thick ocean fog that was rolling in. I even heard the foghorn under the bridge and tried to sit up hoping to see the lights of the city, but the fog has already blanketed it. Anthony then pushed my forehead back down, and when I looked over, he morphed back into Carl again.

"You pushed my forehead down. To men came close. One even stepped on my hand as he passed us. You sat up and there were two pops as your Beretta went off. People higher up on the hill started shouting. You pulled me to my feet and lifted me into a fireman's carry. A lot of blood came squishing out of my shirt, and then I passed out."

Carl nods, then sighs. "What you don't know is that Caballero and the others kept pursuing us for three hours, even when they knew the Colombian army was coming to extract us and to chase them down. After I clipped us into the rope and the helicopter started to rise, they popped off a shot and got me in the ass." He slaps his right butt cheek.

"We got lucky."

Carl leans on the map with both hands and looks at me with his blue lasers. "We did that time. So let me ask it again. Knowing him, do you think he'll stop chasing us?"

"He won't stop."

"Then neither can I. If someone else handles this, he'll escape and come after me again. We do this now, while we can get the jump on him."

Carl's face hardens until his forehead lines pop out. He grips the table and the muscles in his arms and chest stiffen. I've seen this transformation before.

"What's our time frame?"

"Two days. Everybody thinks we're in jail in Clarence Town. That gives us a day to surprise them. Caballero and Constantinou know we are on to them though, so they'll be expecting something. Whatever happens, Chief Andrew is alerting the Bahamian Coast Guard, which is coming to look for us in forty-eight hours."

"Game on."

"Time for a plan, Stan. Let's get busy."

A rush of adrenaline hits me and I enter a zone of heightened awareness. My vision, hearing and thinking—even my sense of smell—have a new acuity, and the world seems vivid and alive. This shift happened before every mission, and it would stay with me for days, long after the job was done. It's been years, and I miss it.

A mental checklist appears in my brain. The first thing on it is to eat and drink, and I grab another banana and water. Carl sees the change in me and grins, the air between us crackling again.

"Let's start from the beginning. What do we know?" I ask, my mouth full of banana.

"I may know more than you. The research came in."

"When?"

"My people called back yesterday morning while you were passed out with Nicole."

"So yesterday on the sailboat you had intel you weren't sharing?"

"Yesterday was different."

"What did you find out?"

"Caballero was part of FARC until that night. Then he disappeared. He popped up in several places over the years, including working for Gaddafi in Libya. That's because Fuzzhead helped fund FARC for years, and then hired them as assassins to kill his own people during the uprising against him. When his government fell, Caballero disappeared again and popped up in Greece. That's when Xander Constantinou hired him as his head of security."

"Security. That's rich. No one is safe with that guy around."

"And Constantinou isn't Greek, he's Egyptian. He comes from a wealthy family with deep ties to the Egyptian military, and they made a fortune selling weapons. But times are tough since the regime change. The new government froze most of his assets. He was previously worth 250 million, and now he's worth 30 million, if he's lucky."

"Having 30 million doesn't seem like much of a problem."

"Not to you and me, but to someone like him, losing that much tweaks you. And his lifestyle is way above 30 million. Just maintaining his island is probably a million bucks a year, and that's just one property. He's probably leveraged and bleeding money to creditors. If that's the case, he can burn through 30 million easy, unless he has a plan."

We stare at the maps and books on the table, as if they had the answer. "It doesn't make sense. If you're desperate to turn 30 million back into 250 million, you buy companies, you invest, or sell more weapons. Or smuggle drugs or blood diamonds or nuclear fuel. Instead, he kidnaps his ex-girlfriend?"

Carl doesn't answer. I point at his little island on the map for emphasis. "I think his motive is revenge, not money. It's about her."

"But there are a few new wrinkles since your arrival in the Bahamas. On Tuesday he flew twenty people to the island. A film crew and actors."

"What for?"

"To shoot a movie. Just like the tabloid article says."

"It's got to be bullshit."

"Twenty people and their gear left Miami by seaplane. It all checks out."

I shake my head. "But that first article is a perfect cover. Caballero can kill her and they can stage it like a boating accident or a drowning. Then he has his revenge. But a film crew? That doesn't make sense."

"Which brings us back to my favorite motive. It's about money, not revenge. And movies make money, right?"

"Most don't. Gambling in Vegas is safer. And if he's forcing her? Once that hits the Internet it'll be bigger gossip than anyone can control."

"Unless she wants to do it. Is there any chance of that?"

"She doesn't. The photo doesn't lie," I answer.

Carl nods. "You may be right. A friend with the RCMP in Canada contacted Julia Travers's parents. They admit that she's changed since she's moved to Los Angeles, but her decision to go to this island without telling anyone is out of character. They also insist that she ended the first affair with Constantinou and that she fears him, which makes them even more suspicious of what's going on. But they have no way to reach her."

"The RCMP should tell the FBI and the Bahamians."

"I'm sure they have, but they won't do anything. It's only been four days, and there's no evidence of a crime. So far, your photos have worked—everyone thinks they're in love and finishing a movie," Carl says. "Except for her parents and us."

"What about last night? Caballero sent four guys to kill us."

"We can't prove it was Caballero. If we had died, they'd assume it was a drug smuggling deal gone bad, or one of my cases came back to bite me."

"They can't be making a movie? It doesn't add up, there's no way he can make that kind of money."

"He's got some kind of plan, and he's willing to kill us to keep it going. We just haven't figured out what it is yet."

Carl gets up from the table and walks back to the wheel. He checks the GPS, then pushes the throttle. His boat slices through water that's as flat as a bathtub. He keeps his eyes on the horizon through the window. "Memorize that map. Know where we're going, in case you have to find your way back."

The Bahamas are spread out on the table in front of me— several groups of small islands between the massive peninsula of Florida and the huge island of Cuba. The deep ocean is to the east, and the shallow Bahama Bank and the Gulf of Mexico is to the west.

Long Island is at the bottom of one curve of islands, and now we're following the next big curve south—the Jumento Cays, Torzon, Flamingo Cay, Man of War, Jamaica Cay—and then there is open water until the Ragged Island Chain pops up last. Carl leaves the helm and points to a spot of open water on the map.

"We're about here right now. We'll stay far west, and then when we're past Elysian Cay I'll turn and head in from the southwest. I want to arrive just before dawn."

"I like that. Safer for us, more surprise for them."

"It won't be Club Med. There will be well trained bad guys. We have the jump on him, but we did last time too, and we know how that turned out. He may even be thrilled when we show up."

My eyes scan the Ragged Island Chain and suck in the details. The depths, the reefs, the beacon lights, which islands have landing strips, anchorages and blue holes which hold fresh water.

"I'm going to check the packs you prepped." Carl goes on the back deck.

I open the books and read quickly. Elysian Cay has coconut palm trees, part of a plantation that failed years ago. It is less than a quarter mile south of Nurse Cay, which has low scrub trees and no water. Elysian Cay has a small blue hole on its north end, which is an eroded limestone cave filled with water that's linked to the sea, but may have fresh rain water on top. My fingers fly through the pages as my eyes scan the words and pictures. I learn about limestone caves, land crabs, ocean fish, edible scrub trees and curly tailed lizards.

Carl touches my shoulder, making me jump. "You've been at it three hours."

"I'm almost done."

"Eat something and sleep. I'll wake you up at two in the morning. Then you can take the helm."

I grab a power bar and a banana, wolf them down, then crawl into a sleeping cabin under the foredeck.

Carl pushes the throttle to top speed.

It seems impossible to relax over the drone of the engines, but my team leader told me to sleep, so my training kicks in and I fall unconscious as commanded.

CHAPTER 28

JULIA

Day 10: Saturday, Before Dawn

It's one in the morning; all is quiet and I'm awake. My call time is 6:00 a.m., five more hours of rest, and then day five begins. Three more days of shooting, including today.

Then what? What happens to me? Xander feels I'm gradually moving back to him. Once the movie is done, there's no more gradual. He'll have kept his "promise" to me, and he'll expect me to close the gap between us.

My heart pounds, making my chest hurt. I have to get out of this room, out of this building, and off this island. But how? I jump out of bed and pace to keep from hyperventilating, but too much air still rushes to my head, making me dizzy.

I flash back to when I was a teenager with so many learning disabilities that I thought I'd never finish school or amount to anything. Life was an intense pressure cooker that got worse every day, with no escape...like now. I had a trick that helped me when my despair became too much for me to bear. Maybe the same trick can help me now.

I grab a towel, sit on the floor, stick it against my mouth with both fists, and scream. The sound echoes in my brain, but the towel muffles my cry, so there's no noise in the room. Growing up I screamed this way at night and no one heard me, and no one can hear me now. I scream silent howls until I can scream no more.

After the screams come the tears. My body lets loose with deep sobs of hopeless desperation. I can't fight or flee—all I can do is weep this hopeless fear out of me.

After an hour of screaming and crying into my towel, something magical happens. I become calm. There is no emotion left. Just emptiness. It's 2:00 a.m.

I open my curtains and step out on the balcony. There is no moon and the Milky Way is splashed across the sky above me with so many stars I can't even pick out the constellations. A star moves across the sky—it's either a distant plane or a satellite. Another streaks past, a true shooting star.

The sea breeze draws my eyes back to the horizon. With no moon I can't see the water, just the beacon light on the distant point that flashes every four seconds. The warm breeze rustles the leaves and palm fronds, but otherwise there's no noise. The veranda below is dark, with the grey shapes of film carts and tents. My eyes strain to see. A minute passes. Nothing.

"Julia?" It's Trishelle. Relief and excitement hit me at the same time—and then fear.

"Are you okay?"

"Thumbs-up."

Good girl. She knows something's up. "Is Bernard there?"

"I am right next to her, darling," Bernard whispers up to me. "It was very hard to sneak her past all the men in dark clothes wandering around."

"How are you two getting along?"

"She's wonderful. But I have a problem."

"What's that?"

"I'm falling in love with both of you." Trishelle giggles.

"You're not in love. It's just the excitement of being on a movie set," I say.

"You are so jaded, Julia. I have feelings for you, yet you toy with me."

"You love it. Trishelle, where is your room?"

"Same floor as yours, but in the main building. Above the kitchen, overlooking the pool."

"Don't you want to know where my room is?" Bernard asks.

"You'll get your fun with us, soon enough," I tease.

"Come down now, we can all walk on the beach together," Bernard whispers.

"You two have fun. But tomorrow night I want to do something special."

"What?" Trishelle asks.

"I want to go skinny dipping under the stars."

Bernard sighs. "That will be wonderful."

"Bernard, I want you to go get the swim fins out of the gardener's shed now, and leave them in the bushes right there. Then I'll meet you both on the beach tomorrow."

"When?"

"Same time tomorrow. Can you sneak away?"

"But of course. It's what I am good at."

"Be careful tonight. I want us to have fun tomorrow."

"We'll explore and find a perfect spot for the three of us," Trishelle whispers.

"For that I will find a way past a hundred men in dark suits," Bernard whispers.

The bushes rustle and then there is no more noise. They're headed down to the beach. Trishelle saw my hand signals so she knows everything is not right with me. If she can't get answers from me, she will get them from Bernard. She will hold his hand, hear his story, let him kiss her and more, and pull all the knowledge she can from him. I am thankful for her expertise in sexual politics.

I walk back inside and fall on my bed.

The water will be warm but not if we're in it for a long time. We'll need to bring some clothes. I need some plastic garbage bags to keep them dry. Maybe I can get them from Wardrobe somehow. Our canisters can hold fresh water, but we'll need food. I need to steal candy bars and peanut butter from the set today.

Gathering food, water, clothes and supplies takes time. But the more days we stay on Elysian Cay, the bigger the risk of getting trapped forever.

The time to run is coming soon.

CHAPTER 29

STEVEN

Day 10: Saturday, Before Dawn

I've been at the helm for five hours, staring at endless dark water in front of me, beneath a billion stars. The GPS tells me we're on course, but the boat is doing all the work. All I know is that Cuba is straight ahead of me over the horizon, and somewhere to the left is the tiny island of Elysian Cay.

We've used a third of our fuel already, which worries me, but the boat has a small mast and sail if we need to catch the wind, and there's an extra drum of diesel fuel on the back deck.

I finish the last book Carl gave me between glances out the front window. There are no blips anywhere near us on the radar screen. We are alone in the inky blackness...except for a trail of glowing green water streaming behind the boat.

I step on the back deck. it's bioluminescence—the water is full of tiny animals that light up as our engines churn past them. There's one cloud far to the east, backlit by a distant sun that won't rise here for two hours.

I almost enjoy the view, but can't—just like I can't quite enjoy the sunrise while surfing in Tivoli Cove back in Malibu. My shoulder aches, reminding me again of my injury, the boy, my anger and regret, and Caballero.

I move back into the wheelhouse and stare out at the horizon, alone with my thoughts.

My eyes spot a line in the water, barely visible in the weak light. It's a strange kind of sloshing, like water moving everywhere in a bathtub. The line is a slightly different color and a good hundred yards away, but it's definitely there.

I pull back on the throttle into neutral, but we're still coasting forward at about four knots. I step outside and onto the foredeck. Glancing over the edge, the water is so clear you can see straight down to the sandy bottom. It's less than twenty feet deep. No— fifteen.

I run back into the wheelhouse and slam the engines into reverse. "Carl!"

He's already on deck. He grabs the wheel from me and spins it hard to the left.

I rush to the stern. The boat is in less than six feet of water now and not turning fast enough. Carl kills the engines. I grab the railing and wait for impact. We hit the sandbar on the front starboard side, and the boat lurches to a stop. Everything not bolted down keeps going forward, flying everywhere in the cabin, including Carl. He spins the wheel the opposite way and slams the motor in reverse, but we're stuck.

"Jump over and push!"

I run to the bow and jump. I land in only a foot of water, and my knees buckle. I dig my wet shoes into the sand and push against the high wooden bow. I feel the engines struggle and see sand whirling around me. The boat rises up off the sandbar and drifts back.

Carl eases the boat back until he's thirty yards away in deeper water. I walk higher on the sandbar. At its shallowest point it's only six inches deep, but nowhere does the sandbar break the surface. This underwater mountain of sand stretches hundreds of yards in front of me, and the only clue that it's even here is the slight ripple in the water at its summit.

"We need to find a way through! The cay is still to the southeast!"

I walk along the ridge for five minutes, parallel to the Gollywobbler motoring to my left in deeper water. It's strange to be wading like this, with nothing but water around me in all directions. It's a bathtub at the end of the world, with only dark clouds lighting up pink in front of me to give me a sense of direction.

My brain clicks with facts from the books Carl tossed at me. *"Sandbars often hug the Bahamian Islands on the Bahama Bank, pushed by the wind and currents. There are famous sandbars in the Bahamas, like Mackenzie Sandbar and the Corman Sandbar, which are closer to the larger islands."*

A black triangle cuts the surface of the water two hundred yards to my right, clearing my mind instantly. It disappears, but a moment later reappears as a thick black shape in the darkness only ten yards to my right. It's a bull shark, about six feet long. It's the third most dangerous shark in the world—another fun fact from my reading. There was nothing written about how to stop them with your bare hands. The shark swims parallel to me, unable to come any closer.

"There's one behind you too!" Carl shouts. Behind me, another black shape comes close. Two six-foot bull sharks are keeping pace with me.

Lucky for me, there's a shallow hill of sand separating them from me and the Gollywobbler on the other side. They could probably scrape their bellies across this ridge and bite me if they wanted to taste human flesh.

After ten minutes of walking, Carl waves for me to come back. I wade deeper out on the safe side and swim to the boat like an Olympian. I switch to backstroke to look behind me, and no black shapes crossed the sandbar. Carl helps pull me aboard.

"They showed up fast," I say.

"Fishermen toss over their fish guts and bait. When they hear a boat motor they'll show up and follow it for miles."

The morning wind makes me shiver, so I grab a towel to dry off. The clouds to the east glow pink on their lower edges, reflecting sunlight that still has not peeked over the horizon. We still have more than an hour until true sunrise, but there's enough light for us to see how long and dangerous this sandbar really is.

"Good eyes, Quintana. You're more water wise than I thought."

"I see that surfing, but close to shore."

"It's not on the map either. It may disappear in six months when the squalls come."

"What would have happened if we'd really hit it?"

"It could've busted this hull wide open. And it's the Sahara desert out here. People sometimes abandon their wrecked boats, thinking they can follow the sand to an island. But the sands are always shifting and have different finger paths, and once you lose sight of your boat, you're screwed. And then the bull sharks come."

We motor alongside the sandbar for five minutes before we spot a rivulet in the sand deep enough for the Gollywobbler to pass through. I hang over the port bow and point which way Carl should turn the wheel until we ease through the tiny passage. Our bull shark friends are there to meet us on the other side.

Carl pulls back on the engine so the boat idles south. We move inside and he notes our location on the GPS, and then moves to the map. "Elysian Cay is ten miles away, just over the horizon. What's the name of the cay just north of it?"

"Nurse Cay. About a mile long and half a mile wide, not much vegetation, but a good anchorage on the north side."

"That's where we're headed. The delay set us back, so we don't have time to head south and come from below. We'll come above Nurse Cay so they can't see us, anchor, and head ashore with one raft. Then we cross Nurse Cay on foot and swim to Elysian Cay."

My brain makes the mental calculation. It's about three hundred yards between the two islands. We'll both have backpacks and rifles strapped to our backs, but we'll also be kicking with swim fins. We should make it across in five minutes, ten if there's a current.

"It has to be daytime?"

"We lose any time advantage if we wait until nightfall. By tonight people on Long Island will know the jail is empty, or someone will notice the Gollywobbler is gone. People may follow us. But if we move now, we'll be on Nurse Cay in less than an hour and on Elysian Cay by 6:00 a.m. The estate is on the south side of the island and they can't be looking everywhere. And they'll be looking for a boat, not two guys swimming."

"Sounds like a plan."

"What can you tell me about Elysian Cay?"

"Elysian Cay is three miles long and half a mile wide, with thicker trees, including coconut palms planted in the 1930s by former owners hoping to start a plantation. There's a blue hole on the north end, which may be their fresh water supply, or it may be too brackish."

Carl listens while going through the packs yet again. He examines each flashlight, water bottle, first aid kit and power bar. He picks up the rifles last.

"How many men are we facing?"

My mind flashes back to the photos of Constantinou and Julia Travers boarding his yacht. My mind's eyes sees the camera frame and the photo shutter clicking:

There's a skinny unshaven white guy with a cigarette…

There's a tall muscle-bound blond guy…

There are two Latin types, with darker skin…

There's a black guy, but he's not American. He's either Bahamian or Jamaican…

There's another tall guy, American-looking, with dark brown hair. He's maybe Italian…

Finally, there's Caballero, tall with the dark hair and the streak of white.

"There are six I know about, plus Caballero."

He then hands me what looks like a tiny cell phone with a flip top—but it's not a phone—it's a WorldTracker GPS location device. He holds up his own.

"Our devices are linked, so your screen displays both your location and mine. But no maps are loaded, so your screen shows only a bird's-eye view of our direction and distance from each other, nothing else. If there's a mountain or a coral reef between us, it won't show up."

"What about communication?"

"It's also a two-way radio," Carl points to the side of the device. "Your headset plugs in here. The battery will last eighteen hours. If we have to separate, we check in every hour. Two short clicks means everything's good. One click means things are bad. Got it?"

"Got it."

"We go in, find her and get out. No full sentences until we're back on this boat."

I clip my WorldTracker to my belt. "Do you have standard walkie-talkies?"

"Why would you want standard walkies?"

"If they're really making a movie, a crew uses 13-channel walkies and they're chatting the entire time. If we have one, we can listen in and even ask a thing or two."

Carl goes to the bulkhead on the starboard side, moves the cushions and lifts the lid to a storage box and rummages around inside. He pulls out an old black walkie-talkie with an old wire plug-in headset with microphone. "It's so dead the battery is rusted on."

"I'll take it. All I need now is some canvas work gloves, a baseball cap, a roll of duct tape and a foot-long piece of rope."

Carl smiles, digs deeper in the bin and comes up with a roll of duct tape, a sweat stained baseball cap that says "Gone Fishin" and a small roll of rope. He hands it all to me. He goes to another bin, lifts the lid, rummages some more and hands me a pair of oil stained work gloves.

"Anything else?"

"Got any gum?"

He goes to the steering wheel, opens a drawer and tosses me a half pack of spearmint.

"Now I'm ready." I force them into my pack.

"Let's get to Nurse Cay then." Carl steps back behind the wheel and pushes the engine throttle. We leave the bull sharks behind and head east toward the pink-edged clouds. We're moving fast now.

Carl looks at me and we trade grins.

CHAPTER 30

JULIA

Just before dawn I twist the doorknob to my suite, but it's still locked. Diego opens the door and sticks his face in the crack. "You need something?"

I push the door closed. He curses me on the other side. It's 5:00 a.m. I have one hour before my call time, and my day is supposed to run fifteen hours.

I leaf through the script. What scenes are left to shoot? Where can I stall for time? How can I snatch supplies?

Scene 25: *Risa finds a local doctor to bandage Mike's stab wound. Mike then leaves to pursue the murderous Nicholas despite the doctor's warnings.*

We shoot this on the patio first thing today. It could be an opportunity to steal bandages.

Scene 26: *While Mike pursues Nicholas, Risa searches her husband's computer and discover he is an assassin, and he always returns to this island after a killing.*

That scene is just my character Risa alone in a room, staring at a screen. We shoot that today too, but we'll be in a small room with too many people to steal much. Creating a delay is possible, however.

Scene 27: *Mike chases Nicholas and catches up to him in the harbor, trying to board a seaplane. Mike and Nicholas fight on the pontoon of the plane, and Mike pulls Nicholas into the water before he can escape.*

They're supposed to shoot this scene tomorrow. There will be a dozen camera setups for this, and I'm only in two of them. My character Risa runs down the dock and watches the fight happening out on the water. They will need my wide shot and close up. There will be opportunities to gather food, garbage bags and sunscreen amid the commotion, but that means waiting a day and not leaving tonight. That may be too risky.

After that stunt, there are only four more scenes in the movie:

Scene 28: *Mike handcuffs Nicholas in his room, then comes to Risa's room and asks her to return to New York to testify against Nicholas. Risa says that she'll give him an answer in the morning, along with Nicholas's computer.*

Scene 29: *Alone again, Risa digs into the computer files. She discovers the whole island is on Nicholas's payroll. He comes here after every paid murder, and the island helps him hide and get away. Risa recognizes names, including the doctor. They all profit from his murders.*

We also shoot both these scenes today, with duvateen to black out the windows so we can play day for night. It'll be tight quarters, with all eyes on me, so again there's little chance for me to lift anything.

Scene 30: *Risa rushes to Mike's room and discover that the loyal islanders have helped Nicholas escape his handcuffs. He's about to kill Mike, but Risa bursts in and shoot Nicholas first.*

Scene 31: *Risa is on a plane (a mock-up) and bringing both men back to New York, in bandages and on stretchers.*

This is the end of the film, which we shoot the day after tomorrow after the seaplane scene. We must be gone by then, or Trishelle and I may die.

My choices are clear. I must gather water, food, and garbage bags today. If I get enough, we can leave tonight. If I don't, I must wait to do my collecting during tomorrow's seaplane shoot, when my chances may be better. Then we have to leave tomorrow night, no matter what.

I close the script. It's a decent story with a good twist at the end, but Xander is deluded. This is no blockbuster hit. It's a typical cop thriller, which can earn $50 million at the box office if there's a star attached, but I'm not famous enough to draw that many people to the movie theater. If it's a flop it could slowly make its money back from DVD, Internet and TV sales over the next five years, but that can only happen if he has a studio and distributor backing him. That's the worst case scenario, but even that can't happen.

He says he's back on top and can turn a profit, but how? Or is he just trying to prove that what I wrote on the mirror is wrong, and his version of reality is right? Or is all of this revenge for me daring to leave him?

There's a knock on the door and Xander steps in. He's wearing designer jeans and a loose blue silk shirt, and he's drenched with cologne. My God, he's trying to look attractive for me, at this hour of the morning. We smile at each other. My smile is from relief though—relief that he's not Rolando.

"Good morning, my love. Going over your lines?"

"These are the big scenes, I want them to be good."

"I came to tell you tomorrow is the last day of shooting. We're going to press through and get almost everything done today. Tomorrow we will shoot the climax when you rush into the other room and shoot your own husband and save Mike. Then we will be done."

"What about the fight on the seaplane?"

"A second unit shot that scene in Nassau earlier this month, using stunt doubles. David and Nathan looked at the footage and all we need are your close reaction shots. We can shoot those today on the patio as inserts, with a wind machine."

I act impressed. "Good idea. But what about the last shot of me on the airplane, bringing both wounded men back to New York?"

"Don't need it. The movie ends once you shoot your husband. The look on your face will say it all."

"That saves time."

"In fact, we only need a skeleton crew for the climactic final scenes in the bedroom tomorrow, so most of the crew will wrap up today and leave on *The Petrokolus* tomorrow morning," he says. "I think they'll be glad to be going, considering their attitude."

"Will Trishelle be leaving with them?"

"That's for you to decide. That choice is still yours, Julia. It always has been."

"I've already decided. I want to have dinner with you tomorrow after the shoot wraps. I want to celebrate—and more," I whisper, and put my hands on his chest and kiss his lips.

"No. We celebrate tonight."

"Tomorrow is my biggest day, I need to prepare."

"We celebrate tonight. That will help you prepare."

"Of course, darling. Tonight then." I fake a smile for him.

"And tomorrow we'll use this room for the climax scene where you shoot your murdering husband. But I want the crew to set the lights now. That way, tomorrow we just have to put the camera on the tripod and shoot the final scene with the skeleton crew."

"You want them to light the final scene now? But I have to take my shower and get dressed."

"So? Grab some clothes and close the bathroom door. It'll take you five seconds to get dressed. They're on their way up the stairs."

"Can I have a minute?"

"Why?"

My hand touches his arm. "Tonight is special, I want to find the right lacy things to wear without six gaffers and grips staring at me."

He smiles back. He likes that idea. "For that I'll give you two minutes." He leaves the room.

I'm smart enough not to lock it. I push a chair to the sliding glass door and step up, then jump and knock the roll of gaffer's tape off the end of the curtain rod. I catch it on the way down and throw it on the bed. I jump again and catch the end of the long taped-up sheets and pull them down, almost yanking the entire curtain mechanism down with them. I land on my knees, then gather the sheets and stumble into the bathroom. I throw them into the tub and yank the curtain shut.

With forty seconds left, I run back into my room and yank open my drawers, which are full of the clothes he bought for me. I pull out a black push up bra, pink panties and some white stockings and lay them on the bed.

The roll of gaffer's tape is still on the bed. I toss it through the open bathroom door just as Xander walks in. The tape sails over the curtain rod and lands in the tub, where the sheets absorb its landing.

Xander looks down at the lingerie on the bed.

"You like?"

He smiles. "I like very much."

"Until tonight then." I pull the duvet cover over them.

Xander steps forward, kisses me softly on the lips, and puts his hands on my shoulders and presses down. He smiles, keeps pressing, and nods.

He won't wait. He wants it now. This was part of our relationship—he needs to dominate. I rebelled against it then, but that won't work now. My knees buckle and hit the floor. I unzip him and reach into his pants.

He stops me. Why? Then I remember that he needs his blue pill to rise to the occasion.

"Come on in guys, she's ready!"

Six guys plow into the room while Xander zips himself up and I rush to get off my knees. One man snickers. The other five are embarrassed, and they hide their discomfort by starting to work. One rips open the curtains and the pre-morning light flows into the room.

"I'm taking my shower." I walk into the bathroom and lock the door.

Xander laughs on the other side of the door, and the one gross guy in the bunch joins in. I grab a towel and scream into it.

My plan is ruined. How can I escape with Trishelle if Xander is going to be in my room tonight? I hyperventilate.

Then a voice tells me—*stop.*

He just humiliated me in front of other people. Why? He confused and upset me, which is the opposite of how he should want his lead to feel on a stressful shoot day.

Then it hits me. He's not thinking clearly, because he's stressed as well. The photos in the office and the rushed phone calls prove it. His plan is being threatened somehow, which is why he's pushing the schedule.

He's frustrated and he's lashing out at me, which is revealing. Since I woke up on his yacht I've been unclear on his true motivation, but he just exposed it.

He doesn't care about my performance, or about making a good movie, or getting a return on his investment. He's not doing it out of love, whatever love means to him. What he wants most is to make me suffer, and he wants other people to see him do it.

But why go through all this madness? Of a kidnapping? A movie?

I don't know yet, but if I end up with Xander tonight, he'll hurt me. That means we must leave tonight. But if I want Trishelle to be safe, that means I should stay and be with Xander tonight, so she can be on that yacht tomorrow. What do I do?

The voice in my head returns—do one thing at a time, and start by taking a shower. Get water running on your face and think.

I hide the sheets and the gaffer's tape under the sink cabinet and then turn the water on. I look at my watch. It's 5:30 in the morning and the sun is just rising. I have a little more than twelve hours to make my choice.

CHAPTER 31

STEVEN

W e're five hundred yards away from Nurse Cay when Carl waves me inside and points at the radar. There are three blips heading our way.

"I'm not sure who they are, but they're tracking us."

The VHF marine radio chirps to life. Carl looks at me and turns up the volume.

"Boat out at Nurse Cay, any fishing there? Or are you pleasure cruising, over?"

Carl turns the channel from 7 to 10 and we hear the same message repeat, with a different voice, then he changes it to 11, and then to channel 18, and we hear the same message.

"He really wants to talk to us. He's hailing us on every channel there is," Carl says.

"They know we're coming."

"So we're changing the plan. I'm going to motor past the top of Nurse Cay, slow down enough for you to roll into a Zodiac raft and head to shore, then head out past the cay and into the deep water of the Tongue of the Ocean."

"I'm doing this alone?"

"This ship is the only way back to Long Island and we can't risk anchoring it. If I can get into deeper water I can avoid them, join some other fishing boats for cover, and then circle back and get you."

We're getting close to shore. A half mile away there's a small break in the shoreline that marks the separation of Nurse Cay from Elysian Cay.

"You better get ready."

I take off my clothes and pull on the camo pants and boots Carl brought for me, then strap my pistol and GPS to my belt. I then slide the Kevlar vest over my head, tighten the straps, and pull the dark camo T-shirt over it. I roll up my shorts and blue T-shirt that I just took off and stuff them into a zippered pocket in my pack.

The sun is rising directly in front of the Gollywobbler, a yellow ball on the horizon that turns the grey water around us instantly blue. Silver fish dart back and forth in the shadow of the boat. The sandy bottom rises fast and we are soon next to the cay on the starboard side.

Carl cuts the engine and lets the boat coast. He comes back and we each pull a cord and the Zodiac dinghy falls off the stern and into the water. I climb over the railing into the raft and he hands me my pack, my M4 rifle in its nylon scabbard, and two oars. The boat has a tiny outboard motor, but it's too risky to start it. Anyone listening will hear its high-pitched whine a mile away.

"I'll pick you and Julia up right here at 0300 hours," he says and then holds up his GPS. "No matter what happens, you wear yours, and I wear mine. Got it?"

"Got it," I only have to row a hundred yards to get to shore, but I'm afraid to start. Instead I just stare at Carl, wondering what the hell I'm doing.

"You'll be fine, Quintana. No one is better at disappearing and staying alive than you. And don't hesitate with Tina's trigger, because they sure won't," he says. "Antennae up and head down, right?"

"Antennae up and head down." I repeat his mantra back at him, and then start rowing.

Carl waves at me like I'm some hitchhiker he just dropped off, then heads back inside the wheelhouse and pushes the throttle. The Gollywobbler zooms off and passes the cay in less than a minute. Out in the distance the water turns from light blue to deep blue, where the depth drops from fifteen feet to over a thousand.

I row hard. There's no current, just a warm wind rippling the water. The Zodiac hits the sandy bottom and I hop out with my gear. I attach my rifle scabbard to the side of my backpack with clasps that attach to the molle webbing. I can tell Carl had this designed special for him. I pull the pack on my back and everything feels snug and flush, but if I reach over my right shoulder I can pinch one clasp and pull out Tina. It's muscle memory, and it's strange how after five years my body still knows it.

I grab the bowline of the Zodiac and drag it up on the sand and hide it in the mulberry bushes. I then run south, parallel to the beach, weaving through the high grass. I spot edible stuff here too, like horseradish trees and sea grapes. It's good that Carl made me read the books.

I reach the end of the island in ten minutes, kneel down and look at my watch. It's 5:50 a.m. I look out across from Nurse Cay to Elysian Cay, which is three hundred yards away.

Five minutes pass and I see nothing, just a bigger island with more palm trees. I take off my pack, pull out binoculars and watch for another five minutes until my gut says it's safe. I pull my swim fins and mask out of my pack, take off my boots and socks, put them in the waterproof bag, attach it to my pack and slip it on my shoulders again.

I dart out of the trees and down to the shore and ease into the water on my hands and knees. I tug on my flippers and slide the mask on my face. I ease into deeper water and pull my rifle out and hold it against my chest—then push off the sandy bottom and start kicking on my back. I want my rifle already in my hands when I get ashore, in case someone spots me. When I reach deeper water, the current hits one side of my body. It's moving fast, and I must kick hard to stay pointed at the island.

I look over my shoulder and pick a landing spot. Only another thirty yards.

Then I spot them—two men with rifles, looking north toward Nurse Cay. They're standing in the exact spot where I was aiming to go ashore if this current hadn't pushed me. The rising sun is behind me and throws glare on the water, but they will still see me when they look my way.

Underwater there's a rocky bottom only eight feet down. I have to get there. I suck in a breath, drop below the surface and kick. My lungs are in good shape from surfing, but swimming with a heavy pack and rifle is not easy and my legs use a lot of oxygen. My free hand grabs a rock, but the current tugs me off. I kick back to the rock and grab it with my free hand again, and the current pulls me off a second time. My lungs ache, but I can't risk going up or losing my grip again—so I let go of Tina and grab the limestone rock with two hands. It takes just a moment to get a decent grip, and I reach for my rifle—and she's gone. Over my shoulder I watch her slowly descending in a current pulling her into deeper water.

After ninety seconds underwater, my mouth breaks the surface and I grab just enough air to go under for another minute. My lungs hurt, but I've been held under for longer in heavy surf. I break the surface and raise my head. The men are gone.

I crawl out of the water, pull off my fins and scramble into the trees, kneel down and listen. Voices are talking a hundred yards away from me. One of them laughs, which is a good sign.

I open my pack and dry myself off with a synthetic chamois towel. I squeeze water from everything, put on my boots, put away my fins, and eat a candy bar. The whole time I'm thinking one thing – I'm an idiot for losing my rifle.

There's no point worrying about it now. As long as I can see them but they can't see me, which is what I'm good at anyway. If things get rough, I still have a weapon on my hip.

I scan the horizon and spot a white dot heading north. That's the Gollywobbler. I click twice on the two-way GPS Worldtracker. He clicks back twice.

"I'll see you in eighteen hours, Sergeant Webb." I move into the trees.

CHAPTER 32

JULIA

I'm back on the patio in the same outfit from yesterday, a spotted sundress covered with the fake blood splatter from when Nicholas stabbed Mike in the back and then fled. We shot that scene yesterday, but it feels like a week ago.

The crew bustles around me, eating their Bahamian breakfast burritos while simultaneously raising lights and pulling cables. An HMI light shines through the silk material and then through a window into the "honeymoon suite." This is where we will shoot almost all of today's scenes, day into night.

I grab four candy bars from the craft service table and put them in my magazine bag and sit down. Did anyone notice?

My eyes scan the set. No, I'm alone. Rolando isn't hovering right next to me. Either Xander told him to back off, or Xander and he are arguing about whatever crisis is pushing them.

Maybe I'll get lucky. Maybe tonight will work. Maybe I can dodge Xander—

"You need anything, Julia?"

It's tall and lanky Walker. He's wearing cargo shorts and a vintage Star Wars T-shirt, and he's sporting a three-day beard. He's a good assistant director; loud and assertive, but kind. He's the on-set traffic cop who makes sure everything flows the way it should.

"No thanks, Walker. I'm just thinking."

The crew works hard around me. They're all smiling again; it's close enough to the martini shot that they can now imagine happier days ahead.

"You sure you're okay?" Walker still stands next to my chair. He peers into my eyes, like a doctor trying to see diagnose me.

"It's been a tough shoot is all."

"You're our trooper. You need anything, you just let me know."

I'm about to take him up on his offer when Rolando sits down next to me. Even though Walker is three inches taller and thirty pounds heavier than Rolando, he doesn't dare speak to him. He turns on his heel and leaves.

"You can relax, Rolando. Xander and I understand each other again."

Rolando narrows his eyes. "Too bad. I so badly wanted to work with you. I'm an artist too, you know. Art is about expressing the feelings inside you, don't you think? When I was a child I was ashamed of my gifts. But now, I pursue my passion without shame."

"Your passion makes me sick."

Xander arrives, thank God. I pop out of my chair and kiss him on the cheek, which he loves. He's got a razor cut on his neck, so I kiss my finger and touch it. "Did you cut yourself shaving for me?"

Xander smiles as I stroke his smooth face. I want him and the crew to think that we're back together. Then he'll relax enough to loosen my leash. Three crew people swivel their heads, then keep going. The word will spread fast, especially after the bedroom tableau he created in my suite this morning.

"You'll be with me all day, won't you?"

"Right next to Nathan and David at the monitors."

"Then tell Rolando that he doesn't need to hover like I'm a flight risk."

"He's doing his job. It's all over at the end of the day tomorrow."

"After tomorrow I never want to see him again."

"You won't, darling, I promise. But until then, he stays close." Xander then pats me on the ass and goes over to video village.

Rolando grins at me. I don't think I'll be snatching any more Snicker Bars today.

I make my decision. Trishelle comes first. The chances of us getting away are nil. I have to make sure she gets on that yacht with the rest of the crew tomorrow and gets away. That means I must finish today's shoot, and spend the night with Xander. It scares and disgusts me, but it's my only option. Once she's safe, I'll look for my chance to get away.

The only thing left to do is to get a message to Trishelle. I can't risk her showing up with Bernard under my balcony tonight, when I'm with Xander.

Trevor paces on the patio, going over his lines. Renee the prop girl follows after him, trying to get the right amount of blood dribbling from his back wound. His work ethic impresses me. Trevor is a good actor preparing like he should.

Risa Baker is the answer. When I'm a great Risa, they're watching the monitors, not me. That's where I'll get my wiggle room to get my message out.

"You're Julia Travers."

The voice belongs to a short bald man wearing a stethoscope and carrying a black bag. He smiles. Rolando is a foot away watching us.

"He said it was okay for me to speak with you," he says, nodding at Rolando. "You were great in *Junk Conspiracy*. You acted circles around Clooney."

"In our two scenes together? You're sweet. And you're playing the local doctor who sews up Trevor's wound."

"Fred Cisneros." He offers his hand and we shake. "I just got here by seaplane. I'm doing this scene, and then one insert shot during the climax where I give first aid to your husband after you shoot him. One day of work, and then I go back with everyone tomorrow on a yacht. Crazy business we're in, huh?"

"Crazy is the word for it."

Rolando stands behind him, sneering.

"Can I ask you something then? Pro to pro?"

"Ask away. Pro to pro."

"Why am I sewing him up out here on the patio? Don't they have a doctor's office, or at least a hotel room we should do this in? It doesn't make sense. They can't find a table and a chart and some bottles of alcohol? Know what I mean?"

I wave Walker over.

"What's up?"

"Fred thinks we should shoot his scene inside, and I see his point."

"It's the last big day of shooting, we just have to finish."

"Why are we rushing this anyway? We don't want this to suck just because we have wrap fever. We're doing decent work here."

Walker holds up his hands. "It's not my call. Let me get Nathan, David and Mr. Constantinou over here."

"And can you get Trevor? He's in this scene too."

I grab Fred's hand and pull him toward Rolando. "Fred, this is Rolando, one of the producers. Tell him what you think we need."

God bless Fred, because he does. He launches into his design concept for the doctor's office. Rolando's lips curl with disgust, but Fred keeps plowing on.

Renee, Trevor, Nathan, David and Xander surround Fred and Rolando, which gives me a ten second window. I touch Walker's hand.

"I need something from you."

"Say it."

"Find Bernard and Trishelle and tell them tonight is off. And tell Trishelle that everything's A-OK now and she should go home with the crew tomorrow."

"Done." Walker leaves.

"What's the problem?" Xander asks, suddenly there.

"Walker is just getting me a towel."

Rolando still stares at Fred the chatterbox as Walker walks away.

I hope Walker gives Trishelle the message.

CHAPTER 33

STEVEN

Elysian Cay is shaped like a long backwards capital C, with beaches on the Bahama Bank side, and rough rock on the Atlantic side. The ruins of an old lighthouse grace the northern tip. Now there's a metal tower with an automatic pulse of two quick flashes followed by one long one to tell passing ships where they are, and to steer clear of the shallow water and rocks between its northern tip and Nurse Cay. The north end of the island has a large blue hole. That's where I head first; if something goes wrong and I must hide in the bush for days, I'll need fresh water or a rainstorm.

I move fast for two hundred yards, then stop and listen for five minutes, then run another two hundred yards and pause again. Even with those pauses I end up covering a lot of ground, and meet no one. Everything and everyone are on the south end of the island. That's where the estate is, the dock, the diesel generators, the desalination machine, the waste evaporator and all the other luxuries of Western Civilization that Constantinou has built for himself. That's good, because it means no one is looking for me anymore.

I find the blue hole. It's a white rocky hole in the ground, thirty yards across. I leave the cover of the trees and creep up to the side and peer down into it. The blue water starts ten feet down and goes so deep I can't see the bottom.

A blue hole is a sunken limestone cave filled with fresh rainwater. Deeper down the water may be salty and rise and fall with the tide if it has a cave passageway that leads to the sea. This one is deep enough that there's definitely salt water down there or worse, a smelly toxic goo of bacterial waste from dead animals and people who ended up at the bottom. This island has had people, pirates and plantation workers come and go since the sixteenth century, so there's crud down there. Maybe enough to poison the clean water on top, if it gets stirred up.

I take out an empty canteen from my pack, tie it to my wrist, then crawl over the ledge and rock climb down to the water. I dip in the canteen and watch the water slide in. It's clear, with no smell except for a hint of salt. I think I can drink it—

Something flies past my face. My heart races and I almost lose my grip. It's a bird, circling above me. It dive bombs my head again, then flies deeper into the hole, vanishing somehow into the rock wall.

The wall curves under at the water's surface, hiding a ledge where a bird can fly under and disappear into a small cave. It's probably a Caribbean cave swallow building a nest. There's an air pocket there—big enough for a bird, maybe bigger.

I climb back to the top and slip back into the trees. I pull out my BCB water purifying straw, which yanks out any bacteria or poisons, and sip the water from the canteen. It doesn't taste terrible. I have two days of water built into my survival pack on my back, but if that runs out, it's good to know there's more here.

I zigzag through the trees and come out on the beach south of the lighthouse ruins. I'm halfway down the island now, and through my binoculars I see a dock with the white yacht from Palm Beach alongside, a black cigarette boat, but no villa.

There are big holes in the sand—blue Bahamian land crabs live in there. Cracking one open will give me protein, if it comes to that.

I keep moving then stop after two hundred yards. The only noise comes from birds singing in the trees, and small waves hitting the beach, and a distant shout from the villa. Two trees in front of me look as straight as telephone poles. They *are* telephone poles, or sections of them. They're part of a small shack that's so overgrown with vines that it blends right into the brush.

It's a fisherman's shack, made from four cut pieces of a telephone pole buried in the sand, with faded wooden boat planks hammered in for the walls and a rusted tin roof bolted to the top. The hut looks decades old, but it's still standing. It wasn't built to be pretty, it was built to last any hurricane. Whoever built it could come back months later and know that it would still be standing and get a little shelter from the wind and rain.

The door is flimsy plywood. Its hinges are dozens of aluminum cans that have been ripped open and hammered into the edge of the door edge and the frame to create a flexible seam. I push it open with my foot and peer inside. The shack is ten feet square with one window that has no glass, and it lets in less light than the dozens of gaps in the wood planks. As the wind blows the trees, it sends patterns of flickering light dancing on the wood walls. There are two old canvas army cots, some shelving, a counter and a table. There are rusted fish hooks and spinners on the shelf. It could have been here since World War II, and repaired every ten years.

This is no place to hide. It's a square trap where people can surround you. I step out slowly, making sure not to bend one grass blade.

I keep moving, and in fifteen minutes the villa appears. It sprawls for five acres, and looks like a cross between a luxury hotel and a Spanish plantation from old Jamaica. It has stone walls and balconies and colored wood balustrades with roof made of tile and wood.

A six-foot wall surrounds the estate, with two terraced walkways below the main patio level. That's why they're not out looking for intruders—it's easier to defend their raised fortress than to comb the bush looking for me, even if they suspect I'm coming.

I get close, staying hidden in the trees. The first guard leans against the cement balcony railing at the top of the first wall. He's thin, has a stubble beard, wears dark sunglasses and he's smoking a cigarette. He stares down at the trees and bushes, walks twenty yards, and then scans the trees again. He was in the photos—the skinny unshaven white guy. He finishes one cigarette and lights another. His cigarette pack is blue—Gauloise. He'll be French Smoker.

I move through the trees back toward the beach. The estate looks inviting from this angle, lit up by the morning sun. There's a wooden dock, two boats on the water, tables and umbrellas in the sand, and two staircases leading up to a villa with balconies. This is a damn nice vacation spot.

Another two guards are at the top of the stairs to the main patio. They were on the dock in Palm Beach too. One looks like a tall German body builder type, with white blond hair. He's Arnold the Austrian. The other is the dark-skinned black guy, with Rasta hair cut close to his head. He'll be the Jamaican.

There are four more tough guys somewhere—one American with brown hair, two Latin types with skin like mine, and Caballero. They may be the ones who were roaming the beach when I dove underwater and lost my rifle.

Someone is hanging a light from the ceiling in the highest room of the villa, the one with a balcony. He's wearing cargo shorts, and his hairy belly pops out the bottom of his yellow T-shirt and spills over the top of his pants. He also has a walkie-talkie on his belt, along with a pouch for his tools and a ring of rope with six different colored rolls of gaffer's tape. He takes off his leather gloves, yanks off his baseball cap and wipes sweat off his brow. He's a crew guy, straight out of New York or L.A. There really is a movie going on.

I move back into the brush and find a thick Mulberry tree. I unzip my pack and find my civilian clothes and change back into them. I strap the dead walkie to my belt with the GPS device Carl gave me, and then put on the sweat stained baseball cap and the headset. I tie the duct tape to my belt with the loop of white cord, and put on sunglasses and work gloves. I hide my pack, my clothes and my weapon in the mulberry tree, then move back toward the beach.

A wad of gum goes in my mouth and helps me channel my best "whatever" attitude. *Just doing my job, dude.* I walk out on the sand.

Aware that both Arnold the Austrian and the Jamaican are now looking at me, I trudge with deliberate disdain across the thick sand, making sure not to look up. I walk over to a beach table with the umbrella and drag it across the sand twenty yards and look up past the guards and toward the high balcony room where my crew buddy was hanging lights earlier.

"Is this good?" I say out loud to no one, as if I were talking into my headset. "Copy that," I say, and drag the table another five feet and stop.

The two guards come down the staircase and onto the sand, but I still don't look at them. I drag another table ten feet, pause and look up, then drag it another two feet. By then my two new friends are right beside me.

"Where'd you come from?" the blond guy asks.

I hold up my hand to show that they're interrupting me, then drag the table another four feet. "Copy that, look now." I look my new friend in the eye and motion that he's allowed to speak.

"I said—where the fuck did you come from?"

"Whoa, Arnold. You didn't say 'fuck' last time, because I would have heard you. Just chill, we're all going through enough shit on this production without you going aggro on me."

He glares at me. He takes a step closer and so does the Jamaican.

"Nah, I can handle Team Mission Impossible," I say into my headset, looking up. They follow my eyes. Three crew guys are hanging lights in the balcony room now.

"I came from the beach. I've spent the last hour cleaning every palm frond and rock bigger than my fist off the sand, for a thousand yards up that way. When they shoot from the balcony room, they want to see perfect sand in the background." I look around and sigh. "And believe it or not, now I need a rake. Okay?"

Both guys blink, still looking up at the balcony. I shake my head and trudge up the stairs past them to the patio. I expect one of them to tap me on the shoulder, but it doesn't happen.

On the patio there's a real movie set, with a generator and HMI lights blasting into one of the rooms, with power cables stretching across the tile and twenty people with clipboards, makeup kits and soda cans crossing back and forth chatting with one another. Some scene has just ended and a new one is being set up, so there's a chaotic energy into which I quickly disappear.

There's a pile of cables in a corner, so I grab one off the top and start walking. Put something in your hand, walk with purpose and people will ignore you. It's time to learn the layout of this place, and if I'm lucky I'll steal a working walkie from someone and listen to the chatter.

There's a main hall with a wing on each side, so the villa looks like a rectangle missing a side. It's got thirty rooms at least and is set up like a hotel retreat. I head inside and wander through the halls, pass the kitchen where cooks are preparing food for the crew, then the laundry room, and then out the back door to the guts of the place. There are garbage bins, the compost, a cargo container which holds a desalination machine and big septic tanks for the waste. There are also two diesel generators and solar panels that provide electricity to Constantinou's fortress. I walk back into the main hall and see people on the second floor, so I head up the main staircase. A short stocky guy stops me at the top of the stairs. He looks Mexican—one of the two Latin guys—and he pokes me in the chest.

"No one comes this way."

"Not even once?"

He answers by pushing me back down the step. I don't fight and show him the power cable instead.

"Go up the back staircase like everyone else."

His name will be the Hot Angry Poker. "Hey, I'm just trying to get to Julia Travers's room."

He grabs the staircase handrail and aims a kick at my head, which I dodge.

"I just told you, if you want to get to her room, go up the back staircase like everyone else!"

I dart down the stairs. Her room must be the one they are lighting.

I get back on the patio, pull my hat down and follow a line of people past the craft service table, grab a handful of BBQ potato chips, stuff them in my mouth and keep going until I find the back staircase. Another guard appears—the tall American guy with brown hair is scanning the crowd. There's something about him I don't like. He's too attentive, and he'll spot me as a new guy in a second.

He touches his earbud and looks around. I bend down behind a table to tie my shoe. The Austrian and the Jamaican must have radioed that I haven't returned with a rake, and the Angry Poker has just confirmed that he saw someone who looked like me on the staircase, and now this guy—his name will be the Watcher—is looking for me in the crowd. There's not much time left. These guys have figured me out.

I wish I could hear what they were saying.

A tall crew guy wearing a Star Wars shirt pushes through the crowd, waving his hands. "I'm not feeling the love, people! I need you all to find your places, everyone, and hold still!"

This man must be the AD, because everyone obeys him and freezes. That also means I can't move yet, which may be a good thing, because no one else who is looking for me can move either. I crouch next to a hedge and pull down my cap.

A crew guy flips a switch on a big floor fan and a breeze kicks up across the patio. A camera on a dolly wheels into place, and two guys prep the shot. To my right is the little tent where all the bigwigs hang out watching the monitor.

Then, out of the ground floor suite, she emerges—Julia Travers—the woman who filled my bank account, the actress who tried to run me over and who kicked me in the teeth at the Egyptian Theatre less than two weeks ago. She looks different; she's somehow more beautiful, more poised and more confident than I've ever seen her, and it radiates off her like heat. She's watchable and seems larger than life. She really is a movie star.

All eyes are compelled to be on her as she walks past, flanked by two escorts.

"Let's just start, Julia. We'll ease into it," a voice says from the tent.

The AD shouts. "Okay then! Roll sound...roll camera...and slate it."

A slate snaps in front of Julia's face and she tosses her hair in the artificial wind. She stares out in the distance and begins to react to events that are not even there. The camera rises up and down as she emotes, then passes back and forth in front of her.

"Can you look left to right with your eyes, Julia?" the voice from the tent asks. "We'll cut to the seaplane which will be moving left to right across the screen."

I look closer at the bigwigs at the monitors who are running the show. Under the little pop-up tent is the guy talking to Julia, who must be the director. He looks a few years younger than me, under thirty, and is dressed in black jeans with Converse Chuck Taylors, and an Atari T-shirt on top. Next to him is a heavyset guy with a trim black beard, wearing jeans and a blue shirt with stains under the pits. That's Constantinou, and he looks the same as he did in Palm Beach. He points at the monitor and whispers something, and the director immediately agrees.

"Slower...stare hard like you can't quite see them fighting," the director says. Julia moves her head slower, her face tortured by an imaginary scene in her mind.

She's flanked by two escorts, who must be standing just outside the shot. They haven't left her since she came out of her room. Closer to me is the last bodyguard from the Palm Beach dock, the other Latin looking guy. He's tall and thin, while Angry Poker is stocky and short. This guy will be Thin Poker.

The Thin Poker, the Watcher, Angry Poker, the Jamaican, Arnold the Austrian, and the French Smoker. All six. There is only one missing. Her other escort turns and scans the crew from behind his dark glasses—it's Caballero. He's tall, powerfully built, with that dark hair sweeping off his forehead with the lock of white. He stares at Julia with a detached desire that is so easy to read—he wants to walk five feet, grab her by the throat and strangle her.

He looks right at me. I look down. He felt that he was being watched. They're expecting visitors, so they're looking for something out of the ordinary.

Their antennae are up, and so are mine.

I pretend to do something with the power cable while dipping my head behind the coffee dispenser. Caballero is looking at me, and if we make eye contact it will all be over.

"Cut," Constantinou says.

"Cut," the director says louder.

"Cut!" the AD yells and the crew is suddenly moving, voices rising, crossing back and forth. The AD keeps yelling. "That's the last exterior, so strike the outside! Next is interior night Scene 28 with Risa Baker and Mike Nomad!"

A guy wearing a L'Oreal T-shirt, a pink baseball hat with a brush behind his ear moves through the mix with a tall folding director's chair under one arm and a long mirror under the other. I glide alongside and help take the mirror from him.

"Where to?"

"Back inside. I can touch up her makeup in her bathroom. I haven't seen you. Did you just get here too?"

"Kind of."

I use the mirror to hide myself and follow him back inside the main entrance to the villa.

"Hey! You in the blue shirt!" the Angry Poker shouts from the top of the main stairs.

I walk under the staircase and lean the mirror against the wall. I walk down the hall, turn into the kitchen, go past the cooks and out the back door, then weave through the garbage bins and reach the villa wall on the south side. It's a six-foot drop down to the lime-stone rock below. I vault over the wall and land softly, then run into the trees. I take off my T-shirt and jam it into my shorts so they see no flashes of blue between the branches. I weave back and forth, staying low.

There are voices behind me.

I'm running full speed now, but I'm not scared. This is what I do best. I'm disappearing, and in twenty minutes I'll be back in my dark camos and completely invisible.

CHAPTER 34

JULIA

Day 10: Saturday Evening

We are working on the last shot of the day and I'm exhausted. I worked fifteen hours today after getting only three hours of sleep, with fifteen hours of work yesterday.

A film set gets ugly sometimes, especially after endless hours of shooting. A couple of the crew guys have been farting the conch fritters they had for lunch and my body odor is worse than a hockey player after a playoff game.

"We're still rolling, everyone," Walker says.

"Lean forward again, Julia?" Nathan asks.

I am in a tight sexy tank top that pushes out my boobs. It's hard to make this scene dramatic—all I'm doing is typing and staring at the screen, trying to look confused, afraid and then outraged. But if I'm wearing something tight and my bare skin is glistening as my bosom dangles over the keyboard, they find the shots a lot more interesting.

"And…cut. We got it," Nathan says.

"That was the last shot for the day everyone, and a wrap for most of you!" Walker shouts, and a cheer goes up from the crowd.

"There's a party on the patio, but then it's an early night. *The Petrokolus* leaves for Miami at 6:30 a.m., and we want everyone on board."

"Julia, you coming to the party?" Sammie, the second assistant camera guy asks. He's been next to me for the entire shoot, measuring the distance from my nose to the lens for every shot.

Rolando falls into place beside me. Xander stands in the doorway, filling the entire frame. He nods and smiles and taps at his watch. It's time to prep for my next performance.

"I can't. Tomorrow's my biggest day," I say, and a moan goes through the crowd. "But I'll see you all on the next one."

"Can we clap out our trooper?" Walker asks. The crew claps in unison for me for a good twenty seconds, and then we're done. People smile at me as they break down gear and walk away. They already have their minds set on going home. A crew can get close fast on a film set, but when it's over they drift apart just as fast. It's been great but it's time to go, so it's too late to get personal.

Walker shouts over the low hum of voices. "Everyone! Turn in your aluminum water bottles to Rebecca outside, who will make you sign when she gets them back—otherwise you can't get on the boat tomorrow! She's serious!"

Everyone snickers, but complies. Every shoot has its weird eccentricities, and this is one of them. Walker comes over to me and hands me my water bottle, which I don't remember losing.

"Don't forget yours. I want you to get off this island too."

"Thank you, Walker."

Did he give my message to Trishelle? She's somewhere deep inside the villa, and he either reached her or he didn't, but with Rolando standing right there, all he can do is smile. Then he gives me an ever so slight nod of the head.

"Like I always say, I'll miss you," he says.

"And I'll miss you too."

He turns to Rolando. "You, however, I will not miss," he says, then walks away.

Rolando points for me to go to the door. "Time to go upstairs."

We cross the patio, and the crew falls silent as their eyes follow me. We turn left into the villa's main entrance and head up the staircase. Their low chatter doesn't start until I get to my room. If they're talking about me, it will only last a few minutes. Soon the wine will flow and all will be forgotten.

Diego is at my door sporting his usual frown. I'm too exhausted to care and walk past him into the room, which has been rearranged for tomorrow's final shoot. The bed is pushed to the side, the credenza is gone, and the gear is all in place. The second camera is already on the fluid head dolly with fresh digital cards and batteries. All they have to do is turn on the lights, power up the camera, focus and shoot.

Diego and Rolando enter behind me and look around.

"Can I have a little privacy please?"

"Mr. Constantinou said to be ready in an hour," Rolando says and leaves.

"And don't touch anything," Diego says, tossing in his own comment before closing the door behind him.

I yank back the duvet cover. The lingerie I left this morning is still there.

CHAPTER 35

STEVEN

Day 11: Sunday

It's midnight and the island is quiet. Whatever party was going on ended an hour ago and people have drifted back to their rooms. Most of the lights are off. The tough guys searched for me for only an hour after I escaped the film set. It was easy to lose them, and now five of them wander around the exterior, staring into the blackness of the trees.

They wave flashlights as they scan the trees for me, which just makes it easier for me to spot them. The French Smoker and the Watcher monitor the patio, while the Austrian and the Jamaican pace back and forth on the beach. The Angry Poker is probably indoors. I move to the back of the villa, which is where the Thin Poker is patrolling. He's like a metronome—twenty paces one way, twenty paces back. He's so predictable that he's the best way in.

I wait in the trees below the road that runs behind the villa. When he reaches the far end, I climb up the six foot wall, dart across the road, grab the posts to the cargo container that holds the desalination unit, and climb fast. I get on top without a noise and lie flat. Thin Poker turns around right at twenty paces and heads back, but he looks out at the trees and not up at me. He walks his twenty paces, looks around, then turns and heads out again.

On the wall in front of me is the metal tube that exits the villa's main electrical box and flows up to the second floor. That pipe holds fragile electrical wiring, but the outside is sturdy enough to climb. When Thin Poker is ten paces away, I channel my inner Spiderman, run across the top of the container and jump out into empty space. My hands grab for the tube while my toes land on either side, I climb fast up to a window, get my feet on the ledge and push myself up. I reach a patio balcony to one of the back rooms. Four wooden posts rise up from the balcony and support a pergola with beams criss crossed with flowers. I grab a post, climb, swing my legs up, then walk across a beam and scamper onto the roof.

It took me less than a minute to climb up and my lungs are hurting, but after a minute of deep breaths everything is back to normal. I lie flat on the roof and wait, half expecting a gun click next to my ear, but hear nothing. These are my skills—climbing, running, hiding and photographing. I'm like a professional squirrel. Rifles? Those I lose.

I click my GPS twice. Carl should respond, telling me that he's heading back my way, but there haven't been any clicks back from him in three hours. If he's circling he may be coming in and out of range. If he doesn't respond soon there's no point in going on, since there's no way off the island.

Then it comes—two clicks back. He's good. He must have dodged the bad guys. Good for you, Carl. In three hours he'll be exactly where he dropped me off, at 3:00 a.m.

That gives me an hour to rest before I drop down onto Julia Traver's balcony and make my move. I stare up into the Milky Way.

It was strange watching Julia working on the film set today. She was like a magnet, drawing all eyes to her. No one could look away, which is why no one on the crew noticed me.

Caballero noticed me, though. Why didn't he just cross the patio and grab me from behind the coffee dispenser? The work on the movie was more important than catching me—at least at that moment. Why?

I close my eyes, but I don't think I'll sleep.

CHAPTER 36

JULIA

Day 11: Sunday

I shower, put on the lingerie and lie on the bed and wait, staring at the camera and lights less than five feet away. Having my bedroom transformed into a set is bizarre and sets me on edge, but my body is exhausted and I fall asleep.

Xander walks in well after midnight. The noise of him coming through the door shoots adrenaline into my bloodstream, and I bolt awake and jump off the bed. Hiding my fear, I rush to him like a little girl greeting her long lost daddy.

"Why did you make me wait so long?"

"We've had some unexpected challenges to our little production, but they've just been handled." He holds my face in his hands. He stares into my eyes as if he's looking for an apology. When I smile, he holds my head tighter and I don't know if he wants to crush my skull like a melon or kiss me.

"We have a good movie, don't we?" I ask.

"Yes, I think we do."

"I'm sorry I didn't trust you sooner."

"You have all night to make it up to me." He sits on the bed and pats the mattress, gesturing for me to come sit next to him.

I sit at his side and await his instructions. He strokes my hair. I stroke his arm with a light touch.

"I want you to put clothes on over this lingerie. Blue jeans and a white shirt."

"Why?" I ask.

"That was what you were wearing the last time we made love…or almost made love, and then you left."

I don't dare ask why. I pull jeans out of the bottom drawer, and take a white shirt off a hanger. He pops a blue pill and sips water. That will work its magic in about ten minutes. Not much time left. I pull the jeans over my hips, then button up the white shirt.

I sit down again. He leans in and kisses me, and we fall back on the bed. We stare at each other as he strokes my breasts through my bra, and his likes and dislikes come flooding back to me. He likes to play peek-a-boo with my flesh, stroking me through my clothes and then having my breasts and nipples slowly emerge. He pinches me until it hurts.

He strokes me between my legs. He is purposely rough and the denim hurts. I don't dare recoil, so instead I lean into him and arch against his body. My hand reaches down and touches him between his legs. I try to imagine myself in another place but it's not working.

He sits up, perhaps sensing my discomfort. "I want you to dance for me." He motions for me to stand.

I toss back my hair and smile. "I need music."

"You're an actress. Imagine the music."

I close my eyes and dance, touching my breasts and sliding my hands between my legs.

"This is what we should have done that last night together," he says.

I sway my hips back and forth and run my hands through my hair, then throw my head back to show him that I'm getting excited.

"Strip for me. That's what you were supposed to do next."

I get it now. He wants to erase the memory of me leaving him that afternoon and create this new one. The better I am at erasing the old and creating the new, the less he may hurt me.

I take off the white shirt and toss it to the side, then unzip my jeans and pull them half way down my hips. I turn and undulate my backside for him as I step out of each leg. With just my bra and panties on now, I pull one bra strap down, moan a bit, and then pull down the other. I lean forward and hold my breasts with the bra cups.

"We're together again. You were wrong to leave me."

"I know that now." I drop the bra completely, showing him my breasts. I stroke my nipples while looking into his eyes.

"I want you to touch me like this," I lie.

I can't feel my legs under me and my stomach churns. Depression and nausea hit me in waves, like it must for the millions of women every day who must pretend passion for men in order to survive.

Xander stands up straight, takes a vial out of his pocket, snaps off the lid and pops another blue pill. "I want to recreate this moment a million times tonight."

"So do I." That's a million moments of pain he's been imagining.

"First, I want you to blow me while I sit on the edge of the bed."

"Perfect."

He comes around the bed, grabs me by the nipples and pulls me close. I put my arms around his neck and kiss him hard on the lips, forcing them open with my tongue. I feel him harden between my legs—and I stop.

"I need to get some lubricant."

His face darkens. "Why?"

"I'm too dry. It's from the work and the weather. I'm dehydrated. I want to put my lubricant in now." I pull away, then stop at the bathroom door. "You have your blue friend, I have my pink friend."

"You're coming out, aren't you?"

"I'm on the second floor with just lingerie on! Yes, I'm coming out, you silly."

I close the bathroom door, grab a towel and throw up into it. I wipe my mouth and look at myself in the mirror.

My blue aluminum water bottle is on the bathroom counter in front of me, left over from the shoot. I pick it up and it's still full, so I twist off the lid to drink—and something hard and smooth slides into my mouth. I gag and spit it out in the sink. It's two lipstick tops taped together with gaffer's tape.

"Are you okay?" Xander asks through the door.

"I'm just putting on lipstick for you and I dropped it. I'll be right out."

I peel off the tape and pull apart the two tops, and inside is a long rolled up piece of paper, which I unfurl on the bathroom countertop. It's a note from Trishelle.

I told you once you were a fool not to sleep with him. Now you are a fool if you do. If you're doing it for me, I'll never forgive you. By the time you read this, I will already be outside. We can make it.

She knows me. I'd rather die trying to get away than submit to him, and if she's up for it, then so am I.

I yank off my panties, grab my black bikini off the towel rack and put it on fast, then pull on my bathrobe and cinch it tight. I grab my sheet ladder from under the sink, tie one end to the pipe, step into the tub, open the window, and toss the other end out. I grab the shower head with two hands, lift my legs up and get my butt on the ledge, and then grab at the window sill. The metal window edge digs into my thighs, but I grab the rope and I'm out.

The banyan tree is right in front of me. I grab my canvas satchel off the tree branch where it's been hanging for the last week. Inside are the few stolen supplies—a man's jacket, some shoes, a hat, the gaffer's tape, some candy bars and water. It's not enough for what we need to accomplish, but it will have to do.

I slide it on my shoulder and climb the rest of the way down the sheet. I pass the bathroom window, reach the ground, push through the foliage and find the blue plastic bin exactly where I told Bernard to put it. Inside is the snorkel gear.

"Good boy."

"Julia?"

I grab the masks and fins and step out on the patio as Trishelle emerges from the darkness.

"Are you ready?"

Three more silhouettes step into the light. Bernard, Remi and Rolando. Trishelle cries as my heart sinks. "I'm sorry, I thought it would work."

I look at Bernard. "You told him."

He shrugs. "Sorry, Julia. I can't act forever, and I need some kind of retirement."

I look down. Remi points a gun at me.

"Okay, I won't fight anymore. It's over."

"It's not over, Julia. We have a movie to finish. And the ending will be a real surprise," Rolando says.

CHAPTER 37

STEVEN

Day 11: Sunday

At 1:00 a.m. my eyes open after exactly one hour of sleep. It's a residual talent from my Ranger days. Time to move. I creep down the tile roof, get to the edge and look at the patio balcony under me. That's her room. After nightfall, I watched with binoculars and saw her on this patio balcony staring at the crew party on the terrace.

There is no way to prepare. I just have to leap in and be ready for whatever happens, having the slight advantage of surprise on my side. I exhale, dangle my feet, grab the edge of the roof with both hands and swing down. I land softly. The curtains and sliding glass windows are open to her suite.

Lights and a movie camera fill one side of the room. I step inside. Julia is not there. Instead, Constantinou stands naked in the middle of the room, fists on his hips and admiring his physique in a full-length mirror. He's sporting a pink hard-on that pokes past his paunch like a flesh colored bird perch.

He senses me and turns, and when he spots me he grabs his crotch and falls to his knees next to the bed. We stare at each other for five seconds, frozen in confusion.

I draw my firearm and aim it at him. "Where is she?"

He points at the bathroom.

I open the door to the bathroom. Twisted sheets start under the sink and go out an open window. She's gone. I run past Constantinou out onto the patio balcony and look down.

On the terrace twenty feet below, Julia Travers is in a white robe, surrounded by three men; Caballero, who is twisting the arm of a brunette woman, an actor type guy I don't recognize, and the French Smoker, who aims a gun at Julia.

Constantinou yells. "Diego! Get in here!"

The Angry Poker bursts into the suite with his gun out. Everyone on the patio looks up at me. It's time to make a choice. I vault over the edge of the balcony and aim my body like a flying squirrel right at the French Smoker.

My legs hit him square on the shoulders, as my body goes into a tumble like an infantry parachuter. The Smoker's gun goes off, then it skitters across the tile, the metal dancing on the ceramic while I keep rolling like a curled up armadillo.

After two full rotations, I bounce to my feet. The French Smoker is down and out, the actor guy is gone, and Caballero stares at me in shock.

"Run, Julia!" someone shouts.

Julia bolts across the patio with her white robe flapping, swim fins in one hand and a canvas bag in the other. She slows to pick up the French Smoker's gun and then leaps over the first wall.

A bullet whizzes past my cheek, followed by the sound of a gunshot. I jump over the wall as more shots ring out. People shout as I disappear into the trees.

The shouting continues and then stops, but there are enough branches cracking and electronic chirps to know that four men are behind me. I notice a flash of white and head for it, and find her robe stuck in a tree. Smart girl. I toss it in the high grass so they can't find it.

I wait for the sound of a small thud or crack in front of me, and then head until her trail appears again.

The fisherman's hut appears in the darkness. The bent grass blades tell me she went inside. Not such a smart girl after all.

Creeping around the side, I find the closed door.

"Julia," I whisper.

I push the door open. It's pitch black. I pull a glow stick out of a pocket in my camo pants and crack it, letting the light leak through my knuckles, then step inside.

Crouching in the corner next to the open window, she's wearing a bikini, a man's suit jacket and deck shoes that are too big, and her legs are scratched from running through the woods. She has her canvas bag in one hand and the French Smoker's gun in the other.

She's breathing hard. Our eyes lock and she freezes. Emotions flash across her face: fear... recognition... confusion...then she really remembers who I am...and her face fills with anger.

It's the same anger from ten days ago when we were last eye-to-eye, and she knocked out my tooth with her foot. She raises the gun and aims it right at my heart.

"I hate you, you asshole."

"Wait!"

The door next to me bursts open just as she pulls the trigger.

CHAPTER 38

JULIA

S omeone else is in the doorway. I pull the trigger and the gun explodes, knocking me back against the wall. The paparazzo drops his little glow stick. The bullet hit Levi, the Jamaican guy, and he's writhing on the floor. Did I just do that?

The paparazzo kneels in front of me. He's dressed up like some Army surplus military soldier with the full-on camouflage getup, including backpack.

He grabs the gun from my hand, steps back, and aims it out the window. He shoots six times in different directions, drops the gun, and then dives headfirst through the open window and vanishes with no noise. His face comes back in the opening and he offers his hand.

"Come on." He gestures that he'll help me out.

I don't move.

"I'm good at two things. One is taking photos and the other is hiding. Come on."

"What's your name?"

"Steven."

I push my canvas bag up on my shoulder and jump up into the open window. He grabs me under the arms and lifts me out, then pulls me down onto the ground with him. He crawls away and I follow. Rocks, stones, twigs and branches scratch against my stomach and legs. All I'm wearing is a bikini, a man's jacket and some bad deck shoes. We crawl two hundred yards, his boots and ass inches from my face.

Behind us, men kick in the door to the fisherman's hut. Levi shouts out in pain and voices yell for him to be quiet. I'm glad I didn't kill him.

Men walk nearby, close enough for me to hear their whispers. I wonder if one of them is Rolando, which makes my heart beat even harder in my chest. Steven motions for me to lie flat. I'm glad we're in high grass. He rolls onto his back, takes his gun out of its holster and holds it next to his chest, and stares straight up. He stays frozen for a minute, then five minutes. I'm aching—I want to move so badly, but I must stay as still as he is.

The voices fade away, but Steven remains motionless. Finally he rolls on his side, goes up on his elbow and listens. There's gunfire in the distance, then it stops.

He gets to his feet and motions for me to follow him. We sneak over behind a thick tree trunk and he gestures for my canvas satchel on my shoulder and I hand it over. He pulls out the swim fins and mask and snorkel and nods. He pulls out my roll of gaffer's tape and candy bars and nods again. He finds the straw hat and the spy glass and tosses them. He examines the oversized men's shoes I'm wearing. He sniffs a little, but nods. He takes off his pack and jams my satchel of stolen goods inside a hidden compartment at the bottom of his bag.

Then he touches some small cell phone thing on his hip and clicks it two times, and waits. Nothing happens, so he clicks it again.

He doesn't look happy. He looks at his watch and then whispers close to my ear, "We're going to move fast. Stay right behind me."

I nod and we're off, running fast through the grass, with me close to his heels. Somehow he ducks every branch, dodges every rock and skirts every ditch, all at full speed. As long as I copy him, I'm fine.

We run that way for fifteen minutes. My lungs are gasping for air. I hope to God there's a boat out there somewhere and that Steven is leading us to it. Then we can get the police and come back for Trishelle.

He stops and clicks the device on his hip again and touches his ear, as if hoping to hear something through his earbud. He shakes his head, and then keeps running.

The sound of small waves comes from our left and now in front of us. We are close to the beach. The light of the flashing beacon cuts through the trees. The island is shaped like a crescent moon, and the beacon is at the tip, so we must be at the top of the island.

A yellow glow also comes through the trees. Steven sees it too, and when we reach the beach, he steps out onto the open sand to see it better.

A quarter mile to the north, alongside the next cay, flames rise high out of the water, like someone lit a match. A boat is on fire, lighting up the sky like a Hollywood premiere. The boat is so far gone that only a vague shape within the flames tells you what it once was.

Steven gets his wits back and pulls us back into the trees. If he's worried about the boat, he's not letting on.

He sips water from a tube coming out of his pack, and then motions for me to sip too. He doesn't let me drink too much. He then pulls out a small plastic package, tears off the top and motions for me to eat it.

My tongue recognizes it immediately; it's a high-energy food substitute goop. I diet with it to lose weight for shoots, and it tastes like chocolate toothpaste. I slurp it down. He also eats one, then digs a hole in the sand and buries both plastic containers.

He pulls the device off his hip and examines it. It glows like the front of a smartphone, but it's something else. He looks at his watch, looks at the sky and then points to his right—inland, away from the beach and back into the trees.

He nods at me, and we're running again but even faster. He's not giving me any breaks, but I don't dare complain. This is serious—our escape boat is burnt and gone. He moves through the trees and grass, with me right on his heels.

Steven slows down and stops. We're below the beacon again. He listens. The scent of salt water is in the air. In front of us is the beach I could see in the distance from my balcony, and the waters of the Bahama Bank. Cuba is out there somewhere, and even farther is Mexico.

He turns back into the trees and clicks his device again. One click comes back through his earbud. He looks down at his device, creeps forward, looks down again, creeps forward and then stops. He snaps the device back on his belt and pushes the grass aside, then moves another five yards and pushes the grass again. He reveals a shape—a human shape.

Steven pulls out a weak flashlight with a yellow filter on the front that barely lets light escape and aims it down. It's a man, dressed in the same army outfit Steven has on, with a backpack, and a pistol resting on his chest just like Steven was doing a few minutes ago. The man is wet with seawater and there's a rifle lying next to him. Steven's light reveals that he's bleeding from a wound in his left thigh.

His face is grey and I can't tell if he's alive or dead—until he opens his eyes.

"What the fuck took you so long?"

CHAPTER 39

STEVEN

Day 11: Sunday

"You have to start taking better care of yourself," I whisper at Carl, and he smiles. I put Carl's hat on Julia's head and motion for her to tuck in her hair. Her blonde strands are like a reflective beacon out here in the darkness.

I take Carl's loaded Beretta off his hip and hand it to Julia. "Shoot at anyone you see."

Her eyes widen, but she nods and puts both hands on the weapon and looks out at the darkness.

I take off my backpack, pull out my first aid kit and unroll it. It's a good think that I checked it six times on the boat, because even in the dark my hands can find everything. Carl raises his head to look at his leg, but I gently push his forehead down. It's the first time I've ever seen him nervous, and I send calm confidence through the palm of my hand.

"You'll be fine. I can handle it."

"I hope so. It's a lot worse than getting shot in the ass."

I tug my night vision goggles on my forehead. They provide just enough clarity to work. I pull on sterile gloves, pull out scissors and snip off the top of his pant leg and expose the wound. There's a small burn cavity where the bullet went in, and it pulses up a tiny gurgle of blood every time Carl's heart beats. It's already weak and rapid. He's losing blood pressure.

The bullet didn't hit the femoral artery, thank God, but it ripped up his muscle and he's been bleeding awhile. I soak up the excess blood with a wad of sterile gauze and find no exit hole. I need to clean this wound and then wrap it and give him some antibiotics. The bullet was so searing hot when it went in that it's sterile and deep in his leg. The problem is, the bullet dragged dirt and clothing into the wound along with it. That's the stuff I have to clean out, otherwise he'll get an infection and a fever that will cloud his brain so he can't function. If he goes into shock, it will be impossible to move him.

I grab a bottle of sterile fluid, squirt it on his leg to wash away the blood and grime, then wipe around the wound with alcohol. I find the pre-filled syringes of Lidocaine and inject him with two shots on either side of the opening.

I stick a piece of plastic in his mouth and he bites down hard. I stick my index finger into the wound and his eyes roll back as more blood gurgles out.

Julia then surprises me by putting the pistol down and holding his face in her hands to comfort him. Smart girl, but more than comfort right now, he needs to stop bleeding. I motion for her to put her hands on the pressure point at the top of his leg, right next to his groin. "Push right here, and push hard. It helps slow the bleeding."

She allows me to place her fingers in just the right spot where his leg meets his groin and she pushes. I stick my finger back in the wound and already there's less blood flowing.

If one of Constantinou's men found us right now it would be over for all of us, but there's no turning back now. My finger feels two sharp bone fragments and I scoop out two femur chips, shaped like tooth picks. My finger goes back in and I pull out what I really want—a quarter-size burnt piece of dirty denim from his pants that the bullet pushed inside. I pour alcohol into the hole to really clean it.

"You can't pass out yet."

He nods back through gritted teeth.

I stick gauze into the wound, and watch the white material turn red. He needs surgery to sew up blood vessels and suture the muscle back together, but if we don't stop the bleeding he'll never get to surgery. I apply direct pressure on the clean would.

"Put on some gloves," I whisper to Julia. She rips open a bag and puts on a set of sterile gloves and looks at me.

"In that first pouch, pull out two bags that say 'Quik Clot.' Open both and be ready to hand them to me. They're going in the hole in his leg."

Julia finds the packages and rips them open. Inside are two small white bean bags full of amazing little beads that will swell up and stop his bleeding. I take my hand away and pull out the gauze and gobs of coagulated blood. His wound is open and gaping, but it's not gushing. I take the bean bags and place them in the open wound and then apply pressure again.

Minutes pass. Julia looks around. The wind rustles in the trees and the sound of waves reach us from the Atlantic side. Carl's breathing is rapid and shallow. He's lost a lot of blood. I want to run an IV to get his fluid volume back up, but there may not be time.

Voices. They are coming.

Julia picks up the Carl's gun again and looks around. My eyes stay on Carl. After three minutes of direct pressure I pull my hand away. The bags have expanded in the wound and the bleeding has stopped. Small victory number one. I have to tape him up next, with just one small roll of medical tape. If he has to move, that amount of tape won't hold.

Instead, I pull out the best tool ever invented by man—the duct tape that Julia stole. I pull a long piece from the roll, which makes a loud enough noise that all three of us wince.

"Lift his leg." When she does he moans and bites down hard, but it gives me enough space to wrap the tape around his thigh, snug enough so that the pressure stops the bleeding, but not so tight that it's an artery-killing tourniquet that will cost him his leg. Without me asking, she takes the scissors and cuts the tape from the roll.

"You're good at this," I whisper.

"I played a nurse once on TV."

Carl laughs. I'm liking this girl more every minute.

It's time to hide him. I open Carl's pack and pull out his survival bag. It's really just a fireproof plastic bag with camouflage coloring which you crawl inside to keep from freezing or burning to death. I lay it out next to him, unzip it, and motion to Julia to come alongside.

"When I push him on his side, slide this under him."

I push on Carl's hip and roll him on his side, and she slides the bag under him. We tug on the edges and zip him in. He's still not hidden well enough. We can't drag him, because that will leave a trail of crushed grass.

The voices stopped, but they're still coming. That duct tape noise was loud enough to get people heading our way to investigate. There's a slight breeze coming from behind us and my ears burn, expecting trouble.

I take off my night vision goggles and hand them to her. "Put these on, find the morphine syringes, put them in his left hand, then roll up the first aid kit. Pull his backpack close and give him water and some goop, but not a lot. Then clean up so it looks like we weren't here."

I get up to leave and she grabs my arm. "Where are you going?"

"I need to hide him better." I sneak away.

Fifty yards to the north I find three dry palm fronds that will work. With Carl zipped in his bag and with the palm fronds on top of him, someone will have to step right on him to know he's there.

A voice whispers and a branch cracks close by. I carry the palm fronds back. Julia did everything I asked, and now she's holding the hydration tube from the water pack so that Carl can sip water. Carl strokes her hand as she touches his forehead. Carl mutters something and she giggles.

Even shot and bleeding, Carl still has life in him to flirt, thank God. Maybe he'll make it, but he has to beat infection and shock and a lot of blood loss.

I want to put fluid in his veins, but the voices are too close. I kneel down and whisper in his ear.

"People are coming. We have to go. Water and food are on your right, but don't take much. We'll be back in a few hours and I'll do more for you then. You have four morphine syringes in your hand. You want one now?"

He nods.

I put the night vision goggles back on and take one of the syringes, uncap it and hold it in my mouth while I straighten his arm and feel for his vein. I find it with my thumb and press until it bulges and feel the pulse throbbing. It's thready and weak, which isn't good. I angle the needle and push it into what I hope is his vein. I push the plunger, and his eyes roll back in his head. He's still awake, but his pain is fading.

I put on my pack, then take Mary off the grass and slide her into the nylon scabbard attached to Carl's pack. I leave Carl's weapon next to his right hand, so he can find it if he needs it. The only weapon I want is the gun on my hip. As we creep back, I brush at the bent grass with the palm fronds, like a hairdresser flicking up some flattened hair, and then gently cover him with them.

Voices are less than fifty yards away. We squat down.

"He's got a bullet in him, he can't have gone this far. He's closer to the Atlantic side."

"No, he's here somewhere."

"Then let's come back in the morning after he's bled to death. My skin is burning."

"That's from the poison wood trees. I said not to touch them."

"I can't stand it, I'm going back," the first voice says, and he trudges past us through the underbrush, swearing. The other voice mutters and kicks at the grass.

I unholster my weapon and we creep away, moving backwards. After fifty yards I stand tall and run. The gun is in one hand, aimed down and in front, and I clear leaves from my face with the other.

After another fifty yards I push hard on a branch, cracking it, to draw them away from Carl. Once they chase me, losing them is easy.

Julia stays behind me. All she's got is an Army hat on her head, a jacket over a black bikini and oversize men's boat shoes, but she's keeping up. Fear is a great motivator, but she's got more than fear driving her. She wants to make it out of here and she's depending on me.

We need our own hiding spot—but where?

We come to a clearing. The half-moon is high enough to reflect off the white coral rock in front of me. It looks familiar. We creep forward and almost walk off a ledge. It's the blue hole, and we pull back just before falling in. My toe hits a rock and it splashes in the water below.

I grab Julia's hand and we sprint around the rim to the other side. Then, from across the blue hole, a man breaks through the trees and aims his pistol. It's the tall Latin guy from the patio scene this morning, the attentive one I called the Thin Poker.

"Stop!" he shouts, then starts talking into his headset. "Encontre la puta," he mutters, and steps forward, one step, two steps—until he reaches the edge of the hole and glances down, just like I did.

When his eyes are off me, my movement is automatic from deep in my muscle memory. My gun goes up and my finger pulls the trigger. I feel the kick and hear the blast as the bullet goes right through his chest and knocks him off his feet. He lands on his ass right on the lip of the coral rock and tries to sit up. His eyes widen in shock as he realizes something is wrong—he grabs his chest, then falls forward and splashes in the water face first.

He floats. Julia stifles a little cry. He's the first man I've killed since Afghanistan, and the first man whose face I saw when I pulled the trigger.

Voices come at us from three different directions. I holster my weapon, then get down and grab the edge of the limestone rock and climb down into the hole. Julia still stands there, stunned.

"I know what I'm doing. Come on, this rock is like a ladder."

She gets to the edge and climbs down into the blue hole alongside me. The hole is almost a perfect fifty-foot circle of white rock that goes down twelve feet before blue water starts, which is still sloshing from the dead man's splash. I ease into the lukewarm water and feel it soak my clothes. Julia comes beside me and we breaststroke slowly along the edge, staring at the rock until I find it—the lip where I saw the cave swallows hiding their nests. I duck my head under the water and come up under the rock lip, and emerge inside a small cave. I reach up with my hand and I feel that there's some space with a ledge above me. I'm about to go back underwater again to get Julia, but she pops up right next to me and wastes no time grabbing at the rock and climbing onto the cave ledge. The toes of my boots dig into the rock and find a purchase point, and I push myself up out of the water.

Julia helps me by pulling at the top of my heavy wet pack and I plop onto the ledge beside her. I pull my feet up and scoot my butt back. The cave is almost pitch-black. Birds are flapping around us.

Voices arrive. Light flashes on the surface in front of us, bouncing through the water and up against the rock walls. Fear forces our bodies together and we push farther back into the tiny cave until our shoulders are wedged against the rock wall. Julia shivers as we hold our breath waiting for the men to finish staring at the dead body floating outside.

Minutes pass.

Their voices die down as they finally walk away.

CHAPTER 40

JULIA

Day 11: Sunday

Steven stays as still as a rock for five minutes just listening, until my shivering is so bad that he has to do something. He pulls off his backpack and cracks open another chemical light stick like the ones the kids use at Halloween, which casts a weak green light inside the tiny cave. The cave is as big as the backseat of a small sedan, with a low ceiling and barely enough room for the two of us to fit sitting down. The cave shrinks down and keeps going into the rock behind us, but you'd have to be the size of a gnome and crazy to want to crawl back there. Water must have carved all this a long time ago, and I'm sure there are creepy crawlies looking at us right now.

Worst of all is the dead man floating in the water just outside. That was horrible to watch.

Steven pulls out food rations, opens the plastic pouches and hands them to me. Each one is a slurry: meat, peas, rice, pudding and chocolate. It's just fuel, but it's amazing how much it restores me. He must see that I'm bolting the food because he pulls the last ration from me and motions for me to drink water from his water pack.

He wraps up the remains in a Ziploc bag and stuffs it away in his pack. Dinner is over. He then signals for me to take off the wet men's jacket I have on, and he pulls out a dry T-shirt from yet another compartment. This guy is like Mary Poppins with that bag of his.

The last thing he pulls out is his own little camouflage bag just like the one in which we hid his injured friend, and he motions for me to crawl inside with him. I hesitate, which makes him sigh.

"I once hugged a guy from my squad for three nights in the snow, and our body warmth is what kept us alive. We both need to stop shivering, and to sleep."

We crawl in and lie down. We both barely fit on the tiny ledge. I wonder how we can do this without rolling into the water, but then he adjusts my arms and legs so we are entwined with each other in a pattern that holds us in one spot yet somehow doesn't pinch any nerves in my limbs.

"We both stink, but you get over that quick." He hugs me tight. It certainly isn't romantic; it feels more like we're two sweating wrestlers grappling.

"What's your friend's name again?"

"Carl."

"So you both came to help me?"

"Yes."

"Is he going to die?"

"He knows how to stay alive. We'll check on him in a few hours."

"What about Trishelle?"

"What about her?"

"They have Trishelle—my girlfriend with the dark hair."

He exhales, then pauses a long time before answering. "They want you, and as long as you're out here, they won't do anything to her."

I want to believe him, but the tone of his voice says he might not believe it himself.

"Now sleep," he says, and within moments he is out as if someone flicked a switch.

I feel the rhythm of his chest rising and falling next to mine. The food and water in my stomach warms me and feeds energy to my empty legs, which feel like cold wood attached to my aching hip sockets.

I'm wet, scared, sore, cut and bruised. The faces of the men we hurt, shot and killed tonight flash in front of me—but I also feel safer now than I have since the night of the movie premiere when this all began. Sleep comes.

My body wakes with a start. How long have I been sleeping? His arms and legs are still tangled around me, with his face an inch away from mine. He's asleep. Everything is damp and smells like seaweed and old gym socks. Except for one piece of rock digging into my hip, the ground is soft.

The sun has risen high enough for light to hit the water and send rippling beams into this grotto. It's amazing how sunlight can get through any crack, even into a cave hidden underwater.

The lip of rock that hides the cave is also higher out of the water like it moved up a half foot somehow, but that's impossible. No, the water must have sunk. It's got something to do with the tides— this blue pond must somehow attach to the sea.

A bird with a little red head and tiny black beak flits above my head, disappearing out into the sunshine, then returns. That bird has no clue or care about what happened to me yesterday. While people are shooting and running and dying, life on this island keeps going on without a thought about us.

The bird disappears into a little hole in the cave wall. Is that her nest? That hole in which she disappeared is surrounded by dark mud. I then notice a dozen mud nests above me. The gooey soft feeling under me is probably a hundred years of bird crap acting as a mattress. Nice. Even worse, it makes me want to pee.

Something hard juts against my thigh. Is that his morning boner? It is, but he's also fast asleep. It's gross, but I know enough about male anatomy that it has more to do with a full bladder than him trying to nail me.

A wave of sadness hits me. I haven't felt a man's morning boner since…I can't remember. You need a boyfriend who stays the night and wants to be pressed up against you in bed in the morning with the sun pouring in the window and both of you wrapped up in sheets. It leads to morning sex, cuddling, talking, showering together and going out for an anonymous breakfast with all the other couples in the world.

It's been years since any of that has happened.

His eyelids flutter. He's having a dream, and it's not a good one. He moans with his mouth closed, like he's trying to shout in his dream but he can't be heard.

His eyes open and we stare at each other. The guilty look on his face tells me he knows exactly what's going on. He extricates himself from the survival bag faster than a man who wakes up next to the coyote-ugly bar pickup that he can't remember from the night before.

He burrows around in his Sergeant Mary Poppins backpack pretending to look for something. I sit up but keep my legs in the bag so I don't have to sit in a cushion of bird poop like he's doing right now. The ceiling is an inch above our heads, and we're side-by-side. A slight breeze comes from the narrow black tunnel behind us, which means it leads to the surface somewhere, but the breeze smells like rotten seawater.

"Hello, I'm Julia Travers." I stick out my hand.

"I'm Steven Quintana." He takes my hand and we shake. "Nice to finally meet you."

"How's your tooth?" I point to where I kicked his face in.

"You got me good. But I guess I deserved it." He laughs to himself and then hands me an energy bar. I take a bite and chew. He bites into his own.

"I'm guessing you weren't always a paparazzo."

"Carl and I were Army Rangers five years ago. We were part of a reconnaissance team that would go into war zones and locate and photograph bad guys. We then fed the information to the authorities so they could take action. Carl led the missions and I took the pictures."

"And I thought you were just a Hollywood scumbag."

"I was, but I'm trying to make up for it."

I want to thank him, but don't, although he did an impressive job last night.

"You know what? In five years of working in Hollywood, no one saw me taking their picture except you. And you saw me more than once. You even recognized me," he says.

"I'm observant. I was that way as a kid, but now it's part of my job. My acting coach calls it being 'attuned.' Sort of like a receiver."

He laughs and shakes his head, which makes me curious and pisses me off.

"What's so funny?"

"Carl and I use different words for the same thing. We call it S.A., or Situational Awareness. We say 'antennae up' instead of 'attuned.'"

281

"Does that mean I have what it takes to be an Army Ranger?"

"Sure. You kick hard and run pretty fast. I could never be an actor, though. I know that for sure."

"Why not?" I ask, expecting some insulting answer.

"I'm not brave enough."

His answer surprises me. Who is this guy?

He grimaces and rolls his right shoulder like he's doing some kind of yoga move.

"Sleep on it wrong?"

"An old injury. It bugs me in the mornings." He stares at me. I can tell he's assessing me now. "How about you? Are you okay?"

"I'm worried about Trishelle. And Carl."

"We're leaving here soon to do something about them."

"Do you have a plan?"

"Kind of. But something else is bugging you. What is it?"

He's good at reading my angry suspicion despite me doing my best to hide it. "Why did you come? Did you work for Xander?"

"Xander? You mean Constantinou?"

"Yeah, him. The Slimeball."

"No. I took the photos for the magazine spread about you 'running away' with him when you boarded his yacht in Florida. Later I realized it was a con to cover up you being kidnapped."

"And that bugged you enough to want to come and get me?"

He finishes his energy bar and wipes his hands. "Sometimes when I took my photos, innocent people got hurt or killed. When I left the Army, I swore no photo of mine would ever get someone killed again."

Steven doesn't look me in the eye when he says any of this; he just stares down at the water in front of him.

"So now you just humiliate them."

I look at him, waiting for a response.

He finally faces me, but he examines my face, my ears, my hair, my nose, as if he's still assessing me—and then he finally looks me in the eyes. "If you want to knock out another tooth I'd understand. I was caught up in the past and I wasn't paying attention to what I was doing to people." He points at me. "What I was doing to you. But I'm aware again—"

"You're attuned," I interrupt.

"Exactly. And I can't fix every mistake I've made, but I'm fixing this one. Or I'll die trying."

"Die? But you don't even know me."

"But if I don't try, then you die. And if that happens again, I can't live with myself. And that's worse than dying."

"What is it about your Miami photos that made you think I'd be killed?"

"Caballero. The guy with the white streak in his hair."

My heart rate picks up and my toes and fingers tingle just hearing his name. "Rolando. You've seen him before?"

"In Colombia five years ago. Have you ever heard of FARC?"

"It's an acronym for something bad, is all I remember."

"FARC stands for Fuerzas Armadas Revolucionarias de Colombia. They call themselves communists, but they're terrorists who controlled a quarter of Colombia up until five years ago. They kidnapped and killed businessmen and politicians every week. Then the new Colombian president got tough. He asked for American help, so they sent Rangers to do clandestine reconnaissance, but both countries deny that. Ever hear of Ingrid Bettencourt?"

"The name sounds familiar. She was kidnapped and then rescued?" I ask.

"In July 2008, our four-man team scouted and secretly photographed FARC hostages, including the former presidential candidate Ingrid Bettencourt. They were all then freed by the Colombian army."

"Okay, so you're not a total scumbag."

"There was pressure to finish off all the FARC factions, so Webb and I had the idea to divide our four-man team into two-man teams so our Ranger RRD squads could cover more of the country. Webb and I got the Caribbean region."

He's acting like he's giving me an official field report, but he's talking so fast that it sounds more like a confession he must get off his chest. He then pauses and blinks like he can't remember something—or doesn't want to say.

"Is that when you went after Rolando?"

"Yes. He was infamous for kidnapping and torturing people. The victims he released told stories of how he enjoyed their pain and took pride in his expertise, even calling it an art form. That's how he earned his nickname—El Sádico. The Sadist."

"He killed Toni, the makeup girl. He recorded it on his cell phone." I can't help crying again. I bite my hand to keep quiet—until Sergeant Mary Poppins hands me a little towel to bite on. He touches my back and pats me like a baby, which is both awkward and soothing.

"I saw him shoot a boy through the heart and smile. And then he tried to kill both Carl and me."

He's doing that blinking thing again. He must be on the verge of tears himself, but that's as far as he gets.

"But you got away."

"A boy died, and they probably torched a village because of the photos I took."

"But you got away."

"Yes, I got away."

"So now we just have to get away again."

His hazel eyes are piercing. His dark brown hair is full of mud and grease, and his face is smudged with dirt that hides light acne scars on his olive skin. He's almost handsome, which actually makes him more attractive in a way, and his confidence makes me feel a little less scared of Rolando.

"What's next?" I ask.

"Take off the T-shirt and shoes. I'll put them in the pack so they won't get sopping wet again and you can swim out of here easier."

I pull off his T-shirt and hand it to him followed by my damp men's deck shoes, then slip out of his camouflage bag so that he can roll it up. All I have on is my $500 Prada black bikini, and as my butt sinks into the bird poop, I feel it go up the crack of my ass. So much for high-end beach fashion.

"What if they're out there?"

"One is dead and two are injured. Three are left, plus Caballero, and they've stopped looking. They have Trishelle and they're waiting for us to come to them now."

"Now I'm scared."

"Scared is good. It keeps you alive. Just keep your antennae up and head down."

"Where'd you get that line?"

"Carl says it to me when I lose focus. If I'd remembered it back in Los Angeles, we wouldn't even be here."

I can't help smiling.

"What's so funny?"

"Mine is 'keep your mouth shut.' If I'd remembered that earlier, we wouldn't be here either."

"I like you," Steven offers. "You're tougher than I thought."

"I like you too," I say.

He snaps his backpack into place. "You ready?"

"I am." We slip down off the ledge and into the cool water.

"If you have to pee, now's the time to do it." He dunks his head and disappears under the ledge.

CHAPTER 41

STEVEN

Day 11: Sunday

We ease out from under the rock ledge and swim. Ten yards away, the body of the Thin Poker floats face down. The ripples from our swimming rock him gently like a bobbing cork. None of his colleagues cared enough to fish him out, poor guy. Julia stares at him with sad scared eyes.

"Eternal rest grant him, O Lord, and let your perpetual light shine upon him. May he rest in peace," I whisper.

We reach the rock wall and climb it like it's a ladder. Our wet bodies drip water back into the round hole. The drops echo, making too much noise. We pause at the top and peek over. No one is there. I signal that it's okay and we both dart over and dash into the trees. My heart is pounding.

I motion for Julia to wait, sneak back over to the hole, and reach down against the rock and grab something that Julia climbed right past, but didn't see: a foot-long land crab nestled into the rocks so flush that he looks like he's part of the wall. I grab him by a back leg so he can't reach me with either of his claws, and dart back into the trees.

"Did I crawl over that?"

I nod and signal for her to be quiet.

I pick up a rock to smash him, but Julia grabs my arm to stop me. Her eyes are wide and teary. You never know what the last straw will be for someone, and killing this crustacean might be it for her. I drop it. It turns and raises its claws at me.

Julia waves her hands. "I know how you feel. Now shoo. Go away. Live." The crab crawls sideways back into the sun and over the edge of the hole and back down against the rock.

We move back into the trees. I find a hidden spot where our voices won't travel and take off my pack.

"Why are we stopping? We need to get to Carl."

"He's waited five hours. He can wait another five minutes. We need to talk now, because once we get to Carl it's all work and no more talking for a long time."

"So talk."

"We have one Zodiac raft hidden on the next cay north. It can't hold four people. But it can easily hold two. That means you and Carl will take it."

She shakes her head. "I can't leave Trishelle behind."

"Yes, you can. Get away with Carl and then send help back. I'll go and get Trishelle, just like I got you."

"If they know I'm gone, they'll kill her. And that death will be your fault too."

"You'll be no help to me. You have to get in the raft."

"I won't go. I've fought you before, and I'll do it again. We need to get Trishelle."

She sets her jaw and shoots me the same bitchy look I've snapped in a dozen photos. But *bitchy* is the wrong word. She's *determined*.

"I can shoot a gun. I did it for two different movies. You're willing to do what's necessary? Well, so am I."

"Four people won't fit on the raft, get it?"

"You already said that."

"That means that no matter what, I must stay here."

"So for Trishelle to live, you have to stay and die?"

"No. I can survive on this cay with an army looking for me. But can you and Trishelle survive without me on an overloaded Zodiac in the middle of the Bahama Bank and keep Carl alive at the same time?"

"I don't know."

"Then listen to me and remember everything I say."

"I'm listening."

"At some point you and I will separate and you have to find that raft and get on it without me, maybe with Trishelle, maybe not. Maybe with Carl, maybe not. But when it's time to run, you must run. Without me, and without hesitation. Understand?"

She looks scared. I unzip my pack and hand her my T-shirt and shorts, her damp boat shoes and a pair of dry socks.

She pulls the clothes on over her damp bikini, and tugs on the socks and shoes. I lay out the pack's contents—ammunition, tool kit, knife, rations, waterproof matches, water pack—and explain how each item works.

"You'll take both my pack and Carl's on the raft. I'll keep some rations and a canteen. Carl's water bag is full, but mine is almost empty. I'm going to refill mine with water from the blue hole."

"But it's dirty. The man you shot—"

"If you make it off this island you'll be happy with whatever fresh water you have. When you have to drink from mine, remember to drink it through this." I hold up a thick round white piece of plastic with a nipple on the end—the BCB water purifying straw. "This is a safe drinking straw. The filters suck out any toxins and microbes. Understand?"

She nods.

"There's only food in the packs for two days, so we'll gather coconuts now. There is some fishing line and lures on the raft, but there's no bait. I'll kill a land crab. You can eat his meat or use the flesh for bait to catch bigger fish."

She nods again.

"We'll get as much ready as we can now, so when you come back all you need to do is get the raft. It's on the north side of the next cay, hidden in the grass above the beach. It has a small 20-horsepower outboard motor."

"I can work an outboard," she quickly says and I believe her.

"Drive it back across the channel and beach it due west of here. Then you have to get Carl and Trishelle and your supplies into that raft. Then you motor west until you run out of gas. Hopefully, you'll reach the north-flowing current."

"And then what? We just pray someone finds us?"

"Pray if you want, but always do something to survive. Conserve water and energy during the day. Get under a tarp. Rearrange your supplies. At night, row and fish."

"How long will we be out there?"

"I don't know, at least a day, maybe more. But people escaping Cuba do it all the time. There's also a rescue beacon on the raft you can set off, but only when you're far enough away, otherwise Constantinou will pick it up and get to you first. The chief constable from Long Island said he would come looking for Carl if he didn't come back in two days. He'll be looking for you and listening for that beacon."

We come to the first aid kit. She kneels down next to me.

"We left Carl five hours ago. I don't want to give him more morphine unless he's begging for it. I want him to drink a little water, but not much. We won't change his bandages, but if they get waterlogged on the raft you may need to. If the bandages stick to his wound, that's good, don't pull them off. Just let it dry in the sun, and then add more bandages and tape him up again. Keep the bloody bandages on the raft, because the blood will attract sharks. Got it?"

"Yes."

"When we find him today he's going to be dehydrated and no amount of water can fix it because he's lost blood. That means I am going to run an IV into his arm. We need him to be responsive so he can hobble to that raft himself. Watch me carefully so you can do it later without me."

"What if he dies?"

"A soldier who's been shot can live for weeks with his injuries as long as he has decent first aid. He's going to be weak and scared, but we have to stay calm and give him confidence. If he sees any fear in our eyes, it will make it worse for him."

"Why did he come?"

"What do you mean?"

"You took the photos of me, not him. Why did he risk his life for me?" she asks.

"That night in Colombia, Caballero saw Carl's face and remembered him. He knew it was us, and last week he sent men to kill Carl and me. That's like poking a sleeping lion."

"So Carl wants revenge?"

"More like unfinished business. We both need to set things right, from that night and other nights."

"Does he have nightmares like you?"

The question pisses me off. How does this girl know about my nightmares? Then I remember, we were entwined in a survival bag less than an hour ago. She stares at me, completely unembarrassed by the question. She thinks she knows me now. She makes a lot of assumptions, this actress. This isn't one of her Hollywood acting classes where we all discuss our motivation. I wish I hadn't told her I liked her. Then again, she said she has trouble keeping her mouth shut. Maybe that's just her.

"Maybe. We all have regrets," I finally offer. "Even you." Now it's my turn to stare at her, as if I know her deepest secrets. She blinks and nods. Message received. Hell, maybe she needs to know all of our baggage. If our backstory gives her more resolve to help Carl, so be it.

"There's a nursery rhyme—'Run, run, run away, live to fight another day'?" I ask.

"I remember it."

"That's what you should know about me. If we get separated, or if I get shot, or they grab you, you must stay strong because I will stay alive and I'll come back. And when I show up for you, you and Trishelle must get away and do everything I've told you without thinking about me, because I am going to be fine. Okay?"

She seems to shrink inside my clothes.

I roll up the first aid kit, put the pack back together and slip it on.

"Think you can remember all that?"

Julia has her game face on again.

"I can memorize thirty pages of dialogue a night. I'll remember."

We head off into the trees toward Carl.

CHAPTER 42

JULIA

Day 11: Sunday

We find our way back to Carl and when we pull aside the palm fronds, he looks so grey he seems dead. Steven and I get down on our knees and lean close. His eyes are closed and he's breathing very fast and very softly.

Steven pulls out Carl's plastic water pack from inside his backpack. It's three-quarters full. "He drank some."

He paws at the ground and finds another empty goop packet. "And he ate a little. See, the boy is concentrating. He's working on staying alive."

Steven opens his own backpack and unfurls his medical roll. From the last mesh pouch he pulls out a plastic coil with valves on each end, a packet with a small needle that I know is the catheter, and a plastic bag filled with fluid.

"Is that saline?"

"Hextend. It's a hetastarch. It's miracle juice. It's not plasma, but it's like plasma. Hold it over him right there." He hands it to me.

I try not to look at Carl. He's the color of cement and the only thing that tells me he's alive is a slight movement in his nostrils that shows he's breathing. I concentrate on Steven instead.

Steven assembles the coil, attaches it to the bottom of the bag that I'm holding in midair, and then turns a little valve doohickey. He puts on another pair of sterile gloves, wipes alcohol on Carl's arm, then opens the package with the catheter and guides the needle into the vein in Carl's right arm. He then rips off a piece of duct tape and plasters the needle down.

"This stays in his arm until we get rescued." He then attaches the coil to the catheter, turns the valve and removes the plastic brake, and the yellow white fluid flows into Carl's vein.

Steven stands up next to me and pats my back to let me know I'm doing a good job, then scans our surroundings. The wind is the only noise, so he looks back at Carl. We both stare at him for five minutes and slowly his face turns from cement to the color of flesh again. He suddenly breathes deep, like he's sighing in his sleep, and then his eyes flutter.

But his eyes don't open.

Steven pulls out another IV bag from the medical roll—and it's empty and wet.

"Shit," he says. "The saline bag got hit somehow. The Hextend is all we have."

Steven looks worried. He paws through the medical roll and finds the small bullet hole that tore clean through the saline bag.

Steven looks at his watch. The IV bag is almost empty.

"This boy needs to wake up, or we're not going anywhere."

"So what do we do?"

CHAPTER 43

STEVEN

Day 11: Sunday

I should have started this IV earlier. I should have brushed up on my battle trauma protocol along with the books on the flora and fauna of the Bahamas.

My knees shake so bad I bend over and grab them. This is no time freak out. Another bad choice could start a very negative cascade effect.

My brain flashes back to my training—*Fluid Resuscitation in Modern Combat Casualty Care*. Battlefield knowledge from the 90s that we learned firsthand in Mogadishu, Somalia.

Clean the wound. Done.

Stop the bleeding. Use dry fibrin sealant dressing and bandage. Done.

Start an IV with one 500-ml bag of Hextend/Hetastarch. Done.

Once responsive, this plasma extender should increase blood volume enough to last for eight hours, as long as bleeding has stopped. If it doesn't work, use a second bag of Hextend until the wounded is responsive.

Except I don't have another bag of Hextend. And he's not responsive. I'd try the saline next, but that exploded in the pack. I need this guy to hobble to a raft and hold a rifle. I need a full medical trauma kit, but this is what happens when you gamble and go lean and mean.

Think. What can I do?

Should I shoot him up with seawater?

No. That's stupid. Even worse things would happen.

But he needs something. He's eyes flutter more and his breathing is less shallow, but his skin is grey and he can only moan when I poke him. What are my choices?

My eyes close. My head tilts back. Inhale. Exhale.

My eyes open. Coconuts. Coconuts aren't native to the Bahamas, but they tried to grow them here two generations ago. The plantation failed, but enough of the palms grow wild that they are all around us.

In World War II, Americans used coconut water as a plasma substitute when they were trapped and wounded on distant Pacific Islands. The North Vietnamese supposedly used it all the time on their wounded soldiers. It might work—or it could just screw him up worse. I could overload him with too much potassium and calcium and whatever else is in the coconut water and wreck his kidneys.

"You watched me, right? When the bag is completely empty, I want you to put the brake on the tube near the catheter and take the tubing off the IV bag but keep it clean. Can you do that?"

"Why?"

"You'll see. Can you do it?"

She looks at all the tubing and nods.

"I'll be back." I run into the trees, weaving through the brush and looking for palm fronds on the ground. The wind kicks through these low-lying islands hard enough to knock palm fronds and coconuts off the trees, and a green coconut probably has a half a cup of sterile fluid right in its heart.

I retrace my path from last night and find palm fronds again. Two dozen mature trees are lined up, and the ground is scattered with coconuts. I fit five in my arms without dropping the whole pile, set my chin against the one on the top and move back to Julia like Santa carrying too many Christmas presents.

I find Julia and drop all the nuts in front of her. She's already taken the IV gear apart. "Good work."

"What now?"

I hold up the coconut. "We have to put what's inside this inside him."

"Is that going to work?"

"I don't know, but if it doesn't, we're screwed."

CHAPTER 44

JULIA

Day 11: Sunday

Steven rips off his filthy latex gloves and tosses them aside. He picks up a coconut and turns it over in his hand as if it were a puzzle with a hidden lock. His face is full of doubt, and when he looks at me, he sees the doubt on mine.

He unsheathes his knife and wipes it with alcohol, does the same to the coconut, and sets it between his knees. He then twists the tip of his knife into the green flesh and bores a hole. He pulls the knife out and peers into the coconut. "I'm at the shell."

He puts the blade back in the hole and hits the palm of his hand against the butt end of the handle, then changes the angle and does it again. He pulls out the knife, smiles and gestures for me to hand him the free end of the IV tube that I'm holding, and he guides it into the coconut.

He rips off small pieces of the gaffer's tape and glues the tube into place, like a fifth grade science experiment.

"Best item you could have taken."

He gets to his feet and holds up the coconut chest high. A few drops dribble out of the coconut and into the plastic tube, but not much. "You're going to have to siphon it, to get the flow going Have you ever siphoned anything before?"

"Yes." Resentment seeps into my voice. I siphoned gasoline on motorboats on Ontario lakes every summer, but I hold my tongue. It also surprises me that I now care what he thinks.

Instead I exhale sharply so he stops his bossy man lecture. I remove the other end of the tubing from Carl's catheter. I rub my hands with alcohol, run a bit of it in my mouth and spit it out, then suck on the tube leading up into the coconut. A thin line of clear fluid runs down the tube. I take the tube out of my mouth, cover it with my thumb and insert it back into Carl's catheter, then turn the valve.

Coconut water starts flowing into his vein. "How much do we add?"

He shakes his head. "I don't know, I'm just guessing."

We look at each other, then at Carl. He looks asleep—not dead—but he hasn't moved in ten minutes. I touch his face and his eyes flutter lightly but don't open.

I put my mouth next to his ear. "Come on, you need to wake up."

"I need you to stan up and hold this," Steven says, gesturing to the coconut.

"Why? You're doing a fine job."

His face darkens as he narrows his eyes. "What's the next thing we do to stay alive?"

"I don't know."

"Exactly." He holds out the coconut.

I stand up and we trade places. If my comment bugs him, he doesn't let on.

Steven sets another coconut between his knees and bores into it with his knife, this time faster. He gets through the outside, then resets his knife, and pokes a hole through the husk. He peers in the hole and seems satisfied and sets it aside.

Steven yanks out the water container from his own backpack, and it's only one-quarter full. He and I drank a lot in the last few hours. He squeezes it into his empty canteen, filling it. "This is what we'll drink today."

He then squeezes the remaining amount of water in his pack into Carl's water bag. "This is the only clean water for you three on the raft." He grabs his empty water bag and stands up.

"Where are you going?"

"To fill up my empty pack with more water from the blue hole. You'll need two bags of water on the raft, remember?" He runs into the trees without making a noise.

I stand there holding the coconut, watching Carl's face. The rising sun hits my back and the ocean breeze rolls through the trees, shaking their leaves. Sunlight and wind usually make me feel content, but not today. I crouch down. If the sun can see me, so can the whole world.

Carl's eyes flutter again. Maybe hearing us talk helped rouse him, or maybe the coconut water is helping.

I kneel down. Holding the coconut high with one hand, I use my teeth to yank off the latex glove on the other, and then lay my bare hand against his face. Whatever works. Carl is now pink instead of grey.

He opens his eyes. He's conscious for the first time in hours, and he seems confused, scared and in pain. He starts to sit up and I put my hand on his forehead and shush him.

"Hey, handsome. How are you feeling?" I whisper.

"With you here, I feel a lot better."

"Are you in pain? What do you need?"

"You know what I need." He puckers his lips.

He's so bold that I decide he deserves it. I give him a good long kiss on the lips—and he has enough strength to kiss me back. We pull away and smile.

"Not bad. Are you really a movie star?"

"Some people would call me that."

"What about you? Because I need to say I kissed a movie star."

"Yes, I am. I'm a movie star."

"Really? You kiss like a regular beautiful woman. Can I compare again?"

He's a charmer, this guy. I oblige him again.

I hear a cough and look up. Steven is standing there with a full plastic water bag in one hand and a massive dead land crab in the other. He stares at us with eyes that change from surprise to confusion to something that looks like jealousy.

"Feeling better, Sergeant?"

"Getting there. A little more first aid and I'll be fine."

Carl winks at me and Steven rolls his eyes. Steven is jealous of my nursing techniques, which amazes me. It's also clear how their friendship works. Carl is the confident one with the ladies, while Steven is always playing catch up.

Steven kneels next to me. Carl holds out his left hand and Steven takes it, and by the firmness of the grip I can see how strong the bond is between them.

"Thank you," Carl whispers.

"Never doubt," Steven answers.

Steven turns off the valve on the catheter but leaves the IV coil attached. Then he yanks the other end of the IV tube out of the coconut and jams it into the new hole he made on the next one. He nods at the gaffer's tape roll then at me. "Want to lay a couple of strips down here and seal this sucker up?"

I rip off three long pieces and tape the plastic coil flush to the coconut, making a waterproof seal. "Are we giving him this now? He's awake."

"No. Leave the brake on. This is for later, if he needs it."

"Later? Let's just get out of here," Carl says.

Steven and I trade looks. I should do the explaining. I kneel down and touch Carl's face again. "It's not just us three. They have my friend. We have to go get her."

His eyes narrow as he takes it in. "I can concentrate a little while longer. But hurry."

Steven arranges the pack and the water so Carl can reach it, and puts another packet of goop in his hand.

"I need something for the pain."

Steven reaches across Carl and finds the remaining morphine syringes. There are three left.

"I don't want to give you this. Your fluids are messed up right now."

"I need something if you want me to move on my own."

"Just a little bit. But let me get your vest off first." Steven pulls the Velcro straps on Carl's bulletproof vest, at his hips and shoulders. Carl fights to lift himself, and Steven pulls the bottom half out from under him.

He tosses it to me. "Put that on."

I slip it over my shoulders and tighten the straps. It's still loose on me, but it's better than nothing.

Steven injects Carl in the vein of his left arm and pushes the plunger less than halfway. Carl's eyes roll back. Steven pulls out the syringe and whispers in his ear. Carl nods.

Steven unclips the Carl's holster and clips it to his own belt, next to the one he's already wearing. He slides Carl's gun inside. "I'm not giving you his weapon until you need it."

"When you do, I'll be ready."

He puts the water bags back inside the packs, then lays out Carl's rifle, the coconuts and the dead crab in a neat line. "This is what you're taking on the raft, understand?"

"Yes."

"When you come back, if he's not responsive, you turn the valve on the catheter and lift up the coconut and give him more juice until he wakes up again."

"What if he doesn't wake up?"

"You have two choices—leave him here and I'll keep him alive. Or you drag him in his survival bag down to the beach and roll him into the raft if you can."

"How will I know?"

"Make the best decision you can. But don't be a hero and try to save him if it means all three of you end up getting killed."

He then sheathes his knife and snaps the canteen of water in place on his belt. He checks the pistol in the holster on his hip.

"When you come back here, I want you to handle all the supplies, and I want Carl to hold the rifle. You use the gun. Understand?"

Again, I nod.

He stands up and looks at Carl, then looks at me. "You ready?" he asks.

"Aren't we going to cover him?"

"I want to make it easy for you to find him again. And if they're the ones who find him, it means it's too late anyway."

He heads into the trees. I wish Carl's eyes would open, but they don't, so I hurry to catch up. I hope I make it back in time for him.

We reach the beach on the west side of the cay in two hundred yards. Steven stops just inside the trees. The rocky point with the light beacon is about a quarter mile to the north, and past that there's rough water and then sandy land beyond it. That must be the next cay.

"See those rocks in the water in front of us? In a few hours the water will be lower and they will stick out more. Look how they line up. That's how you'll find this exact spot again."

"Got it."

He then points north. "There's a beach on the north side, past these rocks. That's where we saw the boat burning last night. You must swim three hundred yards across to the next cay, which is a half mile long. Find the raft and bring it back here. Carl can walk or hop, with someone helping. He'll hurt like hell, but he has no choice. Get the raft in the water first with all the packs and gear, then make sure it's far enough out in the water. You don't want to dump him in and have the raft hit bottom—then you'd have to haul him out again."

"I understand."

Steven then points straight out to the water. "Then go that way."

"You make it sound easy."

"It won't be." He stares at me. "We still can still leave right now."

"We have to try to get her."

"Okay. We'll get her, I promise."

He then unhooks the transmitter receiver on his belt and flips the top. He points at the small video screen and points at two dots. "See that dot? That's Carl's transmitter. This dot is my transmitter," he says, then hands it to me, "Now it's yours. Use this and the directions I gave you, and you can find Carl and get out of here."

He starts to leave, but I grab his arm. "What did you whisper to Carl before we left?"

Steven stares at me before answering.

"I explained how I wouldn't be back, but that you and Trishelle would be."

He jogs away. I run after him just to keep up.

CHAPTER 45

STEVEN

Day 11: Sunday

We head south, moving through the trees but staying close to the beach. As we get closer to the villa, the sound of people talking and laughing comes through the trees. We round the last point and are now four hundred yards shy of the estate. Constantinou's yacht is parked at the end of the dock with the gangplank down, and a line of people stroll out onto the dock with their rolling suitcases. The movie crew is leaving, and they are as loud and happy as vacationers boarding a cruise ship for a tour of the Caribbean.

Julia bounces on her toes. "That's Bernard, he's leaving!" She points at a guy wearing a seersucker suit, a straw fedora and sunglasses.

"Aren't they all leaving?"

"He's my co-star. We still had one more scene to shoot, the big climax. If he leaves, that means we can't finish the movie."

Her smile lights up her dirty face, but I still don't understand why she's so happy.

"Don't you get it? Xander loses! He's giving up on the movie, it's over!"

It's not just the movie people getting on the boat either. The gardeners, chefs and maids all board the yacht as well. Dressed in their tropical shirts and black slacks and pulling their wheelie bags, they look like flight attendants heading to the next city.

Austrian Arnold and the Watcher stand next to the gangplank, and as the last person boards, they follow up behind them and onto the yacht, leaving the dock empty. A crew member pulls the plank onto the yacht, the captain blows the marine horn and the sleek white yacht pulls away.

There's only one boat left in the tiny bay now—the sleek black cigarette boat. It is fast enough and has enough fuel that it can reach four different Caribbean countries within a few hours.

The only bad guys left are the Angry Poker who guarded the staircases, Caballero himself, and Constantinou. It feels like they're on the run, and that we may even be chasing them now.

"I didn't see Trishelle go on board," Julia says.

"But our odds just got better." I say pull her through the trees.

Constantinou, Caballero and the Angry Poker must be getting on that cigarette boat soon. Maybe They know the authorities are coming. If I give them a bad enough time, they may go faster and leave Trishelle behind.

We reach the estate. I peek over the lowest balustrade and see no one on the patio, then hunker back down next to Julia against the wall.

"Where would she be?"

"Her room was above the kitchen. Mine was the room with the big outdoor balcony. She's in one of those two places."

"We need a way in besides the main entrance."

"I know a way."

We pull ourselves over the balustrade and onto the patio. We dart across the open marble without a sound. We pass empty chairs and tables covered with wine glasses, dirty plates and napkins blown by the wind. It's more proof that everything ended quickly and the island is being abandoned.

We reach the exact spot where I landed on French Smoker and broke his back. Julia keeps going into the bushes. We creep behind a banyan tree next to the villa wall, and she points up at a window that is cracked open a notch.

"This is the bathroom to his office. Boost me up."

I hold her foot in my cupped hand and lift her. She jams her hand in the crack, cranks the window completely open, and pulls herself in. She motions for me to follow.

I pull myself up through the open window and almost land face first on the toilet lid. Julia pulls me the rest of the way in. Thick curtains and plush carpet muffle our noise.

I peek through the bathroom door. His office is empty and the door is closed. We ease into the room. A computer with two screens and a multi-covered keyboard fill one side of the office.

I hit the space bar on the colored keyboard and the sleeping monitors wake up. An image of Julia fills both screens. A silent clip plays. She's sunlit in a beautiful dress, and the wind blows her hair as she stares off into the distance. She sees something and gets scared. It seems like a real movie, but it's what they shot just yesterday on the veranda with the fan blowing, with the crew just six feet away. The clip finishes and her image freezes.

"What are you doing?"

"Is this the whole movie?" I ask.

"Yes. This is the edit system. Now let's go."

I scan the other side of the office. There's a laptop computer, financial newspapers and a pile of investment returns. That's the money side of the room.

The answer to everything is in this office somewhere.

Julia tugs on my arm. "Come on!"

I push through the piles of paper. He has accounts in several countries. He's got stock and bond options at several exchanges. He's probably gambling with big money…but is it his money?

Julia exhales with frustration.

I go back to the edit system and find a stack of paper next to the monitors. It's the script, and the script break down, listed by shoot days. I leaf through it fast and get the basic story.

On the last few pages, the heroine shoots her murdering husband before he can kill the New York cop. That's the scene Julia doesn't have to shoot now, because that actor got on board the ship. It's also crossed out. In the margin in a tiny scribble, is written—Ver2: Risa KIA.

Risa KIA: Killed in Action?

She pokes my shoulder. "We don't have time. Let's go."

I unholster Carl's weapon and hand it to her. She takes correctly, and then does a perfect press check to see if it's loaded.

"You know your stuff."

"Told you."

I open the office door and peek out. There's a back staircase, which must lead directly up to Julia's room. If Trishelle is in her own room, she's twenty-five yards farther down that hall, directly over the kitchen.

We ease up the staircase. It's strange. We've heard and seen nothing, and that eerie absence suddenly makes my antennae stand up very high. I unholster my gun and I push Julia behind me as we get to the top of the stairs.

I reach the second floor and turn left to go to Trishelle's room. Julia joins me at the top of the stairs. The door to her room opens and a man with curly gray hair and wearing a linen suit steps out.

It's Bernard, who boarded the yacht just a few minutes ago. Julia freezes.

He smiles. It's Caballero, with dyed hair and dressed to look like Bernard. He plucks the gun from her hand like he's taking candy from a baby, then yanks her in front of him.

I try to get to her. I raise my weapon but I'm off balance. Someone punches me in the back of the head. I turn fast. It's the Angry Poker. He kicks my gun from my hand, then shoots me in the chest. The bullet hits me so hard that it lifts me off the top step and I fly backwards back down the stairs.

CHAPTER 46

JULIA

Day 11: Sunday

"Is he dead?" Xander asks.

"If he's not he will be soon," Diego says. "And we have his weapon."

The lights click on. All the equipment is still in place, but with two cameras now. Black duvateen is draped over the windows, blocking out the daylight. The room is bright with tungsten light, ready to shoot some kind of scene.

"Welcome back, Julia," Xander says, stepping into the light. "We were going to improvise something with your friend, but since you made it back, we can finish the actual movie with you now."

In the folds of the curtains, a woman sits staring at the floor, her hair hiding her face. My heart sinks—it's Trishelle. She's in the torn sundress with the blood splatters that I've been wearing the last few days, and she has long blue bruises on her arms and legs. A blonde wig that matches my hair is on the floor next to her.

She stares at me, her face dirty and streaked with tears, then smiles sadly.

Rolando grabs my arm and twists it until I fall to my knees. Xander grabs a chair and sits directly in front of me. He takes my chin and tilts my face up so I must stare into his eyes. "We have just a little bit more work to do."

I fight to look brave. "I will never do it. People are on their way here now. Just let us go and disappear while you can."

Xander smirks, like he has a huge secret that he's been dying to share. "The last scene is almost completely shot. We shot the last dialogue with Bernard and Trevor last night while you were dashing around in the trees. We even did all the insert shots with the guns and knives. Trishelle was your body double. All we need are a few close-up shots with you."

Caballero steps behind one camera and adjusts the focus. Diego yanks Trishelle to her feet, drags her behind him and hits her in the face.

"No!" I jump to my feet. "Stop it!"

Diego grins and hits her again. The red tally light starts flashing. Rolando is running the camera and he has me in a close up.

"Don't hurt her, please."

"Now just say 'him' instead," whispers Xander.

"Don't hurt him. Please."

Diego twists her arm. Trishelle cries out.

"Again," Xander says.

"Please. Don't hurt him."

"Now shoot him," Xander hands me a pistol. A prop pistol. I raise it and shoot it at Diego, and the blast from the blank echoes in the room. There's a long pause before Rolando turns off the camera. Diego pushes Trishelle back into the curtains where she falls to her knees.

"Scene done. That wasn't so hard, was it?"

"Now let us go."

"Sorry. You made your choice last night."

"No one will watch it. You won't make a dime."

314

"It doesn't matter to me whether anyone sees it. It's just a distraction. It's the second version that's going to be a hit."

"Second version."

"Call it the producer's cut. The alternate ending."

"No. You can kill me, and I won't do it."

Xander laughs and then leans in close. "Killing you IS the scene, Julia."

The truth hits me. He grins, and the light behind him frames his head like a halo, sitting on top of a real-life Satan. The rest of the room darkens as my heart drops.

His face softens with a fake look of pity. "Oh? So now you finally understand? That's been the plan all along."

"Why?"

He grabs my chin again, hurting me. "I almost lost everything the year you left. After all I did for you, it was a nail through my heart. Then I had to watch you rise in Hollywood and become a good actress while all I had for my efforts was a half-finished film. It gnawed at me," he says. "I'd relive our last afternoon together, the words you wrote burning into me. Then I'd stare at the footage we shot and imagine all the ways I wish you were dead."

"Please, Xander." He covers my mouth with his hand.

"Then an idea came to me—what if you died in the climax of our film? Really died? That would be a surprise ending. And how much would people pay to see it, if they could watch a well-known Hollywood actress, a real celebrity bitch, being killed in the final scene of a real Hollywood movie? I'd pay a lot. It turns out, many other wealthy people want to see my producer's cut too. Who needs a studio when we live in the digital age?"

"I hate you."

"Well, I love you. Your fans have already signed up for an exclusive Internet download. It's a select audience—only two hundred people. But they pay well. A million dollars each. I'll make two hundred million dollars within a week. I wanted last night to be my wonderful final memory of you, but when the money arrives, that regret will disappear."

Rolando yanks my arm, tugging me to my feet. Trishelle sobs. Rolando's outfit and makeup make sick sense now. Rolando now plays my murdering husband instead of Bernard, and now he will kill my character Risa—and me.

"You'll never get away with it. People will find out."

"No, they won't. They want to believe the story in the tabloids, a story that's still being written. Our dream project wraps today. Next, we will vacation together on my yacht, but you will drown in a tragic accident that will leave me heartbroken. More tabloid covers will publicize your untimely death and my pain. It's all novelty promotion that will make the producer's cut that much more valuable."

Diego puts his gun to Trishelle's head and gestures for her to stand, cooing and whistling as if he were coaxing a small, scared animal out of a hole. She rises and rocks on her heels, catatonic.

"Your perceptive photographer is the only one who figured it out, but he and his friend aren't leaving the island. Everyone else will write the story I pay them to write."

"Not everyone will believe it."

"Enough will. And I can live comfortably in many places in the world where no one cares. And eventually, everyone will stop caring."

"What about Trishelle?"

"No one is looking for her. She's obedient now and does what she's told. I will let her live as long as her good work continues— and you finish yours."

Diego motions for Trishelle to undress. Trishelle unbuttons the sundress, letting it drop to the floor. She's naked except for a pair of panties, and she instinctively covers her bruised breasts with her arms and hunches over, trying to disappear.

"Get dressed, Julia," Xander says, as if I was a daughter late for school.

Trishelle can't look at me. I unbutton Steven's shorts and let them drop, and then pull his T-shirt over my head and kick off the oversize shoes. I stand there in my filthy black bikini.

This is the moment I've been trying to avoid for the last two weeks, and I walked right into it. My heart beats so fast that it hurts inside my chest.

Diego kicks the dress toward me. He pushes the gun hard against Trishelle's temple and then uses the same disgusting cooing noises and finger gestures to get me to put the dress on. I want to kick him in the face and knock all his teeth out, but Trishelle would die in front of me. I step into the sundress, pull it on, and button up the front.

Diego sits behind the second camera. Rolando steps forward.

"This is your final scene, but one of Rolando's first. I promised him a showcase for his unique talents, and he's been very patient. He brings such passion to his work, I know he'll be the true breakaway star of this production."

Xander clicks the "on" button. Diego clicks on his camera as well.

"Shall we get started?"

I have seconds to live. In the face of my hopelessness, I do what comes most naturally to me. "Hey Xander, you getting excited back there? I bet it's the first time you haven't needed a blue pill in years."

He doesn't answer. I can't see his face past the hot white lights, but his silhouette shifts.

317

"You've nothing to say? Everything I wrote on that mirror is still true."

"Time to die, my love. Rolando, enjoy."

Rolando kicks me hard in the back and I land face first on the bed. I spin and try to kick him, but he blocks my leg with his arm, punches me in the gut and then jumps my chest with both knees, knocking the wind out of me. Xander laughs behind the camera. Before I can gasp and get air in my lungs, Rolando sits on my stomach and grabs my throat hard, crushing my windpipe.

"Slow down, take your time. I want choices for the edit bay."

Rolando lets go with one hand while still crushing my throat into the mattress with his other. I feel my face grow huge with the trapped blood pumping in my brain. Then he lets go just enough so that I get a gasp of air, then tightens it again. The tingling in my legs fades away as I lose feeling below the waist.

Rolando pulls out a switchblade. The metal gleams in the light. I watch his face change. He's in a zone of deep pleasure...his bliss.

CHAPTER 47

STEVEN

Day 11: Sunday

My head hits the ground floor and bounces hard off the marble. My chest aches. My lungs won't inflate.

At the top of the landing, the Angry Poker aims my own gun at me. I roll fast. Bullets hit my vest in front and back, and then one hits a soft spot right above my right hip.

I roll into a downstairs hallway and the door slams above me. I prop myself onto my knees and elbows and suck hard, but I still can't get them to work.

Something catches and my lungs re-inflate again. Pain shoots through my body. I pant, forcing my lungs to push past the pain. I touch my hip and blood rushes through my fingers. The bullet went straight through the meat of my love handle. I press on it trying to get the blood to stop, but it doesn't do much.

I look around. I need a weapon, a plan, a bandage. Something....

I push on my knees and get to my feet. I limp down the hall and into the main entrance. What's here that I can use? A plant, a footstool, a rug and a mirror. Nothing. I limp down the main hallway and spot the kitchen. There must be something in there.

I limp inside. Serving trays half full of eggs, bacon, fruit and pastries are strewn across the metal countertops. I rifle through drawers and cabinets. There are cooking utensils, and pots and pans. I yank out the carving and cooking knives from their blocks. Nothing I can use.

I find dishtowels and jam them in the top of my pants to sop up the blood. There's an industrial roll of plastic wrap for sealing up leftovers. I tear off long strips and wrap them around my mid-section to hold the dishtowels in place. It will be enough to stop the bleeding for now. On the next counter are three boxes full of blue metal water canisters with black plastic twist tops. The name *Betrayed in Paradise* is printed on the side with a drawing of a palm tree and a gun. There must be thirty of them, most of them still half full of water.

I find the walk-in freezer. I open an ice chest on the bottom metal shelf and find two whole mahi mahi fish. Their dead eyes stare up at me through the cloud of carbon dioxide hovering in the bottom of their coffin.

And idea comes to me.

I toss the fish out and tug the chest out of the freezer and into the kitchen. Pain shoots through me, but I push it into the back of my mind. I find a hammer in a utility drawer and I whack at the ice slabs at the bottom of the ice chest, making smaller pieces—small enough to fit inside the mouth of a metal drinking canister.

Four kitchen aprons are on the counter. I tie them together and make a sling that fits across my shoulders. I find ten canisters still filled with some water, twist off their tops and line them up on the counter, just like it's high school chemistry class. I drop in as many pieces of dry ice into each of them until gas vapors rise from each open top. Once I twist the tops on, the frozen CO_2 will expand from solid to gas. In minutes the cannisters will explode like hand grenades.

I move down the line and twist them closed, then stack them in my makeshift sling. I slip it over my shoulder and across my back. I tighten it, and the metal canisters shift and hiss against each other.

I run out the main entrance and around the villa to below Julia's room. I run and kick up into the tree, grab its lowest branch and start my climb. The Kevlar vest and the tight plastic wrap around my gut hold my diaphragm and ribs in place, but I still hurt like I've been in a head-on car accident. I push through and keep climbing. The canisters move against my back like jumping beans. The hissing is louder. The gas is forcing the black twist tops out of their narrow metal openings. When that happens, ten bombs will go off.

My only strategy comes from high school chemistry. If I throw these bombs hard enough, they will pop their tops on impact and turn into rockets—and hopefully hit them instead of me.

I get to a branch that is four feet below the balcony wall. I bounce on the tree limb like I'm on a three-meter diving board, and leap.

My hands grab the edge, but my body slams hard into the outside wall. The cans clang on my back and hiss like angry snakes. That was a big noise. Someone is coming out on the balcony, so I better get on that patio.

I vault over the edge, swing the satchel off my shoulder and pick out my first canister. The sliding glass door in front of me is open a crack, but a thick black curtain covers everything.

Someone's hand parts the black curtain and a shaft of light comes from inside the room. I heave my first canister toward the target and it goes right in. I roll to my right as bullets from Mr. Angry Poker's gun burst past me.

The first canister hits a wall inside and explodes. Glass shatters, someone shouts and the lights go off.

My sling falls apart and canisters roll around the patio. Another canister explodes and it flies right into the sliding glass window. The window splinters and all the glass falls to the ground, pulling half the black curtain down with it.

I pick up two canisters and throw them inside. One explodes, and then the other. There's more shouting. I'm glad that it's dark in there now. The remaining six canisters spin on the tile like misguided rockets. Another goes off and flies right into my shoulder, knocking me to the ground. That thing hit me half as hard as the bullet I took ten minutes ago.

Five hissing spinning canisters are left, ready to pop. I run over and hike them hard between my legs, one after the other, like a center heaving footballs at the quarterback, one-two-three-four-five straight at the hole in the glass. Each of them explodes and rockets around the room.

I run to the broken window, grab the rest of the black curtain with both hands and yank it down, flooding the room with light.

Caballero is face down on the bed. I got lucky; he got hit. I step inside, and see the Angry Poker writhing on the floor next to a camera. He clutches his head with both hands, my gun next to him. I kick him in the head, then pick up my gun and shoot out the guts of the camera.

I scan the room. Where's Julia?

Trishelle stands against the wall in her underwear, staring at me with dead eyes. Julia then gets up from behind the bed, coughing and clutching at her throat.

There's a pile of clothes in the middle of the room, some of them mine. I grab Trishelle's wrist and pull her toward the door, kicking the clothes at the same time. "Grab these and go! Now!"

Trishelle stares at the pile, catatonic. Julia dashes over and scoops up clothes, then grabs Trishelle's wrist and tugs her. She's still got the will to live, thank God.

A noise comes from the back of the room. I spin and raise my gun—it's Constantinou, behind another camera and a shattered light. He's wearing the same confused look that he had last night when I caught him naked in the same room. I shoot out the guts of that camera too.

Julia and Trishelle rush out the door. I turn to follow them, but Caballero rises off the bed and lunges at me with a switchblade. The knife goes into my right thigh.

I howl in pain and my knees buckle, but I hang onto my pistol. I can't lose my weapon, not for a third time. I throw myself toward the door. Caballero rolls off the bed. A bullet hits me in the back and knocks me to my knees, but I get one foot under me and dive out the open door. Julia yanks it shut as gunfire rips into the heavy wood. We all tumble down the staircase in a spinning ball of clothes.

We land at the bottom. I get on my back, aim my gun up the stairs and wait. When the door opens a crack, I send a bullet back up the staircase, and it slams shut again.

Julia and Trishelle scramble away. I push myself up against the wall and prop my one good leg against the metal banister to keep from sliding back down. I'm shot, stabbed, and may have a broken rib, but my adrenaline is pumping. I can do this.

I hiss through my teeth. "Get your clothes and go."

Julia kisses me on the forehead. "Thank you." She slides a torn T-shirt in the long pocket of my pants to stop the bleeding, they gather up the armful of clothes from the room, and then they are gone. Their bare feet echo across the patio.

From here I can guard the staircase and keep them in their room. Soon they will find a way down from the outside, but the island is quiet enough to hear them coming.

The sticky puddle of blood under my legs is growing larger. I grit my teeth and push my leg harder against the staircase railing. There's no movement, no noise.

Minutes pass. How long?

The door opens again, and I send another bullet up into the wood. The door slams. Soft voices are talking. They're on the outside balcony and will be coming down that way.

More minutes pass. How long?

The door opens once more, I fire again and the door slams. They're trying to distract me now. They're coming at me from the other side. I can hear them.

Constantinou's office is still open, so I roll away from the staircase and scamper on my hands and knees inside and slam the door shut with my foot. I get to my knees and lock it just as the doorknob twists frantically. I crawl into the bathroom and twist the window shut and lock it too.

There are windows behind the thick curtains, so I stay low as I crawl back into the office. I roll onto my back and my body sinks into the plush carpet. Nice rug. Comfortable. A good place to bleed to death. I hear banging on the door and the outside windows, but the noises seem far away. I feel warm all of a sudden and I don't hurt so much, which is also pleasant.

Once I close my eyes I probably won't open them again, so I look around one last time. The walls are dark wood. Cozy. There's a cobweb under the table. It reflects silver. Pretty.

I notice the monitors. They're dark. It makes me want to see Julia again. I haul myself up to a sitting position. I almost faint, but

I grab onto the editor's chair, reach up and hit the space bar on the computer.

Julia's face fills the two screens. She stares in the distance, her hair blowing in the wind. She looks strong, determined and scared all at the same time. Most of all, she looks beautiful.

It makes me regret all the photos I took of her. I've done all I can. I hope she makes it.

Then I remember—the *why* behind everything Constantinou did is somewhere in this room. It's in the papers, the filing cabinets or on the laptop. One last twinge of anger and regret pokes at me, and it energizes me.

They are old friends, my anger and regret. They've been my driving force for the last five years. They must give me a bit more energy for this last push.

CHAPTER 48

JULIA

Day 11: Sunday

We run down the patio stairs, out to the beach and into the trees. We stop. I make Trishelle put on Steven's shorts and T-shirt that I was wearing before. I yank on the oversized deck shoes.

"Follow me."

We're running again. My muscles feel like lead, and my lungs ache. My body wants me to stop, but I remember Rolando's face and his hand on my throat, and a new burst of adrenaline kicks into my veins.

We run on the hard sand just at the beginning of the tree line. Branches and twigs whip my face.

Trishelle is falling behind. "Come on!"

"I'm barefoot!"

I let her catch up. Reaching me, Trishelle falls to her knees and gasps, sucking air into her lungs. She's had too little exercise and too many nights bumming cigarettes in nightclubs.

My hands go to my throat. I'm breathing fine, but every muscle and bone in it aches, like something inside is bent. My head even tilts to one side. Fear instantly goes into my legs. We got to keep going.

I grab her wrist, but Trishelle pulls it back. "I can't."

I come close and grab her face with both hands. "It's my turn to help you now. You can do this."

A tear comes to her eye and she nods. I pull her.

We run on the hard sand heading north—one mile, then another. The taste of blood and metal fills my mouth, I'm running so hard.

The three rocks appear and we slow down. Steven was right. They're sticking out of the water more than they were two hours ago. I line myself up with the three rocks, then turn and run inland through the trees.

"Where are we going?"

"Just keep up! You'll see!"

I dart left and right, green whipping past me. The palm trees look familiar. The packs come into view and we reach Carl.

I stop and Trishelle plows into me. She gets her balance and stare at him, lying there on the ground. His right leg is bare from the thigh down and his skin is seeping red from under the gaffer's tape. He's bleeding again. His face is as grey as when we found him this morning.

"Who's he?"

Instead of answering I take the brake off the IV coil and lift the coconut up high, and watch the coconut water dribble into his vein. Is this working? Or making it worse?

"Is he dead?"

"Not yet."

After five minutes his right eye opens. I fall to my knees and grab his face. "You okay?"

Carl nods, his eyes closed.

"Will you tell me who he is now?"

Carl opens both eyes and smiles.

"Trishelle, this is Carl. Carl, this is Trishelle."

"Hello," he breathes.

"Hello," Trishelle says.

"Water." His mouth moves, but no noise comes out.

I lay down the coconut, then cup his neck up so he can sip from the straw to his pack. "I'm going to get us out of here."

"You better hurry." He tries to smile, but looks scared.

I hand Trishelle the coconut. "Hold this up for until it's empty, then take out the tube but leave the needle in his arm. Then carry all this gear to the beach." I point to all our supplies on the ground.

"Where are you going?" Her eyes are so wide, there's a circle of white around each iris.

"To get the raft. You'll be fine."

"You can't leave. What if they come?"

"If they're coming then we don't have much time, so I have to go now."

Then I look at Carl. "And when I come back you have to be strong enough to move, because I'm not carrying you."

"I'll crawl if I have to."

I grab Steven's pack, unzip the bottom and pull out the swim fins. "See you on the beach, Trishelle." She blinks and nods.

I dart through the trees, ducking branches and jumping over roots that are now familiar.

I reach the beach and kick off the dumb deck shoes. I dart across the soft hot sand and reach the hard sand at the water's edge where I can run faster. The breeze hits my face and cools my skin, giving me my second wind.

I pass the beacon and the rocky point, then run over the berm and reach the north end of the island. I rush into the water, pull my fins on and start swimming. I'm still wearing the sundress I was supposed to die in and it drags and slows me down, but I'll need it on the raft to protect me from the sun. The fins make up for it though, and I kick harder. I aim for the beach on the other side, which is about three hundred yards away now. I put my head down and I do the crawl stroke, but the warm current is pushing me sideways faster than I can move forward. I lose my strength and I turn over on my back and just kick. With both ears in the water all I hear is my breathing and my own heartbeat as I stare at the blue sky above me.

I flip over and plunge my face under the water and see that the shallow sandy bottom is farther to my right. I slow down and let the current carry me there. Four more strokes and I reach down with my feet and my fins touch sand.

I pull off my fins and wade out of the water. Four, three, two feet deep, and I'm on the beach again but on a brand new island.

My legs are cramping, so I grab my knees and suck air into my lungs. The trade wind blows against my wet skin, making me shiver.

There are white clouds on the blue horizon. A gorgeous sight, worth seeing a second time. I hope I see it tomorrow.

Time to run again. There are barely any trees on this flat island, which is like an overturned dish that popped out of the sea with nothing to block the strong wind. I lean into the breeze, and it blows sand granules into my eyes and mouth. I spit and blink it away. The other other side of the cay comes into view.

I run past debris on the beach and the black torched hull of the boat that was burning last night. Almost nothing is left.

I reach the other end of the island. There's nothing but crusted sand hills and grass blowing in the wind. I run into the tall grass and zig zag back and forth, searching, until the thin stiff blades cut my feet.

It's not here. Someone took it. Maybe Carl moved the raft. I'm screwed—

There it is. It's a small black Zodiac, seven feet long, with a Coleman 5-horsepower outboard motor. I motored around on a Zodiac on Lake Shebandowan back in Ontario when I was a kid, zooming with my friends between lake houses on long summer nights.

I find the bowline and drag the Zodiac out of the grass. I get it over the berm and down into the water, then step inside and push off from the beach.

The boat drifts as I pump the bolus bulb on the metal gas tank. It sends a shot of fuel into the engine. I flip the switch and yank the cord and it starts up right away. I plop down in the stern and twist the throttle.

The engine whines to life. People will hear it over a mile away, this is the only option. I have to get to Carl and Trishelle and all our gear inside the boat before they get to us. I steer the Zodiac into the shallow water next to the small island and twist the throttle more. The nose of the Zodiac rises up as it picks up speed.

Inside the raft, there's rope, a survival kit, two oars, and that red rescue beacon. We must get far away from shore before I can hit that thing. That's the goal.

I reach the southern end of the small island and cross the hundred yards back to Elysian Cay. My new speed gives me confidence. I am almost there. In front of me is the fifty-foot-high remote tower with the red beacon that pulses at night, and a long line of dangerous rocks jutting out of the water. I must go west four hundred yards to find a way past them. Just under the water are huge limestone rocks covered with coral and surrounded by fish—a miniature mountain range just under the surface.

I slow down and find a break between the sharp rocks shallow enough to ease the raft through, and the bottom brushes the top of a boulder. I twist the throttle and zoom forward, making the nose rise again.

Trishelle is waving on the beach, surrounded by all the gear. I run the Zodiac right up on the sand, cutting off the power and lifting the propeller just in time. I've beached these at many lake parties before, at even higher speeds.

Trishelle is already throwing in the gear, weighing down the raft too soon. I jump out, run to the front, grab the bowline and pull the raft out of the water onto higher ground. We load the two packs, the extra water, the coconuts, the dead crab, and Carl's rifle, which I slide in carefully.

"Let's get him." We run back into the trees.

When we reach him, Carl is already on his one good leg and hugging a palm tree. "I heard you coming, so they did too. We've got to go."

I position myself under one arm and Trishelle slides herself under the other, and we all hobble together like a broken tricycle with square wheels. Carl winces with pain on every step, but we make it to the beach.

I let him go and grab the bowline and drag the Zodiac back into the water. They hop into the water right behind me.

"Wait! Let me get it deeper!"

The raft has to be in almost three feet of water and pointed the right way before it can take all our weight, otherwise we risk hitting bottom and we will have to climb out again. I get it lined up and wave that it's okay, and they tumble in.

Carl screams in pain as he falls back into the raft, and Trishelle bounces off the rubber and ends up with her butt in the air—but they're in, with me right behind. We barely fit, and the rubber sides of the Zodiac are only a foot out of the water.

I yank the cord. The engine sputters but doesn't catch.

I yank the cord. Again, the engine sputters but doesn't catch.

I yank the cord one more time, and the engine sputters to life. I twist the throttle and the Zodiac putters forward. The engine whines, but we are only moving two miles an hour, tops. I move my hips and my head, as if jerking my whole body will somehow make the tiny boat pick up speed.

Behind us, the island is so close it's like we can touch it, and in front of us the Bahama Bank is a painting that's too far away to ever reach.

The water below us finally gets deeper, and the trees behind us lose their distinct shapes.

We are one hundred yards out, then two hundred…

I feel something hot zoom past my cheek and I hear a gunshot from the beach an instant later. It's Diego, aiming his gun. We all duck and bullets hit the water around us.

"If he hits the Zodiac, we're screwed."

"Hand me my rifle." Carl sits up on one of the benches.

Trishelle hands him the rifle like her hands are burning, she can't get rid of it fast enough. Carl clicks and moves things on it. Another two bullets zip into the water, their long white rocket trails zooming under the raft.

"Stay down and keep the throttle open."

I drop down even lower in the boat. He aims and shoots three times, then stops.

I don't look back. Carl lowers his rifle, slides it into his sheath on his pack, and then collapses against the rubber side of the Zodiac.

The water underneath us changes color to dark blue, and we leave the sheltering protection of the island and we are in open water. The wind hits us and sends choppy small waves splashing into the boat.

"Just keep going, girl, as long as you can." Carl closes his eyes.

I smile at Trishelle and she blinks at me. She's still terrified. I flash her the A-OK sign, and she manages a sad smile.

CHAPTER 49

STEVEN

Day 11: Sunday

S omeone is trying to get in. It's just one person. Whoever it is, he won't give up. He smashes windows with rocks, then pries at the door, then tries to enter through the window again.

I pull myself into an Aeron chair and I feel the wound in my hip squirt blood all over the carpet. Pain shoots down my leg and up my spine, making me so dizzy that the room spins around me. I squint my eyes until the desk in front settles and comes into focus again.

I aim random shots through the thick curtains and out the broken glass. It works to keep him out, but soon I will run out of ammunition.

I jiggle the mouse on the computer and the screen flashes to life.

The pounding starts again, and the thick wood door heaves in its frame and splinters on the other side. In moments the wood will split around the metal bolt, and the door will collapse and he'll kill me. I want to die knowing the answer.

A dozen folders appear on the desktop—travel itineraries, production costs, budgets for the film—and then I see the last folder. Investors. I click on it.

Inside the folder are hundreds of documents, all with names. I click on the top document—Somchai Khunpluem. It's a one page dossier. Thai businessman and politician. Multimillionaire. Addresses in Bangkok and Dubai. Invested one million. Final payment on September 30th upon delivery.

I click on the second document—Ali Khalif Galeydh. The name is familar—a Somali warlord who escaped Ethiopia and disappeared. Address in Madagascar. He also invested one million.

I click on the third document—Semion Mogilevich. Ukrainian Exporter. Addresses in Kiev, St. Petersburg and London. Russian Mafia? He also invested one million.

I glance at the bottom of the folder. There are two hundred and five documents in this folder, all men who are rich enough and sick enough to pay one million dollars each to see a famous actress die in their own private version of a real Hollywood film.

The banging starts again, and the door heaves. Whoever is on the other side has an axe or a sledgehammer and he'll be inside in less than a minute.

I open the drawer and push aside paper, pens and coins and spot a flash drive.

The door heaves again.

I push in the flash drive in the side slot and it lights up. On the screen an icon appears and I drag and drop the investor folder onto the flash drive.

The bar appears on screen that shows that it is copying.

The door splinters. I don't have time. I yank out the flash drive and pop it into my mouth, fight my own gag reflex and swallow. My only hope is that some Bahamian coroner opens me up and finds it so they'll know what happened here.

The door falls off its frame into the room. I aim my pistol and pull the trigger, but nothing happens. No more bullets. Caballero steps in. He has a massive bruise on the right side of his face, and his eye is closed shut and bleeding.

"You look terrible. What happened to your face?"

He kicks my chair over and I land hard on my back. He leans over me and punches my face, then stares at me with his one good eye.

"Who are you?"

"Colombia. I was there."

Caballero smirks. "US Army Ranger."

"I saw you kill a boy in an Arhuaco village. You shot him in the chest."

"I don't remember," he spits with disgust and pushes down hard on my bleeding hip, sending an electric bolt of pain through my body.

He pats me down. He pulls out the bloody rag that Julia pushed inside my pocket. He unwraps it and finds something black, as small as a cell phone.

Caballero holds it up, clicks it open, and smiles. He shows me the screen. "What do you say we take a trip and find her? If we can't finish the movie, you should at least watch her die."

He grabs my throat and pushes down against my windpipe. I have no strength left. Constantinou steps into the room and leans over me. Both his face and Caballero's fade into a white light.

CHAPTER 50

Day 11: Sunday Afternoon

We drift, out of fuel. It's been three hours since the motor sputtered and died and we've been baking in the hot sun. Our skin burns.

I unwrapped a thin blue tarp from the survival kit and now we're trying to hide under it, but the sun heats it up hotter than an oven. Trishelle and I pop our heads out every minute, trying to breathe, then we flutter and fan ourselves with the tarp, trying to create a breeze. Nothing works.

Carl is bleeding again, and he hasn't moved in an hour. His soaked bandages need to be changed, but I'm scared.

Time to do it. I open the first aid kit and find the scissors. I cut away the rest of his pant leg and expose the blood-soaked bandages. Some of them have come loose, so I cut them away and toss them into the water.

The gobs of blood dissolve away from the sinking bandage and I remember what Steven said—"Don't take them off, don't dump them in the sea. If there's blood the sharks will come."

I find the fresh gauze and the duct tape. I make Trishelle hold the gauze in place while I rip off a long piece of tape and wrap yet another twisting roll around his leg. Carl still doesn't move. I cover him with the tarp and gently flap its edge to get some kind of air moving across him.

The hot sun burns the back of my neck and bakes my skin under my dress. I need shade too, so I crawl in next to him. Trishelle is on his other side holding up her end of the tarp with her arm, and I do the same on my side.

"A-OK?"

"A-OK," she answers, but neither of us smile.

There's nothing we can do except to stay under the tarp, sip water and conserve energy. Only when it's dark can we use our precious energy to move around, try to fish, and use the oars to row.

I stare at the red button on the survival beacon. I want to hit it now. Maybe that police chief from the island is looking for us. Then again, maybe Xander is too. He has that fancy black speedboat, so he must have radar. He may be watching for us right now. It's too soon to hit the button. I have to wait until nightfall.

We float in an endless bathtub of flat water that stretches forever under a dome sky, and the two worlds meet in a straight line right at the horizon.

I peek over the edge of the raft and look down into the water. I can see the bottom. How is that possible? It's less than twenty feet deep, and the water is so clear I can see the pink sand with its tiny ridges. A few silvery fish dart in and out of the shade of the Zodiac.

I lean my head back against the Zodiac and close my eyes.

There's a whining noise. It's a speedboat, coming closer.

"Someone's coming! We'll be rescued!" Trishelle shouts.

We push the tarp down and look around. The sound seems to be coming from everywhere, but there's no boat near us.

My eyes find it—Xander's black speedboat is coming at us full speed, and the whine from the engine gets louder as he pushes it into a higher speed.

He's going to ram us.

CHAPTER 51

STEVEN

Day 11: Sunday Afternoon

My body is vibrating. Someone stabs me with a knife in the palm of my hand. The pain shakes me awake. I am on a speedboat going top speed, and we are bouncing along blue water in the hot sun. Constantinou is driving and Caballero stands in front of me. He smiles.

"I wanted you to be awake for this."

He holds my GPS locator up to my face and then points out in front of the speeding boat. There's a dot of the horizon, getting larger. It's the Zodiac and Constantinou is going to ram them.

"Still glad you came?" Caballero grabs the gunwale and sets his feet to prepare for impact.

My eyes catch little flicker on the water's surface. It's the same little ripple that I saw yesterday morning in the early predawn light.

I heave myself backward over the gunwale and put my arms up to protect my head. It's like hitting wet cement, and I feel salt water shoot up my nose, into my ears and even up my ass as I skip over the surface of the water.

My body finally stops and I sink, then kick to the surface and look. The boat plows into the sandbar at full speed. Metal and wood explode as the hull slams to a stop, but Constantinou and Caballero keep going and their bodies smash through the tiny front windshield. The boat then flips stern over bow, and for a moment there is a mass of destruction in midair—a motor, broken glass and huge chunks of boat—before it lands upside down right on top of them.

Past the debris, Julia and Trishelle sit up in their raft, completely untouched.

"Hey! Over here!"

She waves back as the two women scramble around their tippy little craft. They get oars into place and row away from the flipped speedboat.

I go under and unlace my boots and kick them off. I swim fifty strokes and lift my head. Julia angles the raft toward me. My toes touch the bottom and I crawl to the top of the sandbar. Again, I'm in a foot of water in the middle of a vast sea. I pause for a moment of thanks, then splash over into the deeper water on the other side. I reach Julia and the raft.

"Are you okay?" she asks.

"No. But I'm doing a lot better than a minute ago."

Trishelle grabs my arm and pulls me into the already overloaded raft. I land on Carl, who grunts with pain but doesn't move. My extra weight almost swamps the raft and water spills around until we distribute my weight.

I push aside the bags and coconuts and find his rifle. Julia yanks on one oar and gets the raft turned around, while I spin and look at the wreck.

Caballero crawls from the wreckage and staggers through the water to the top of the sandbar. He is bleeding and his right arm hangs broken at the shoulder. I spot Constantinou floating face down. Caballero staggers toward us.

He lifts his left hand and aims his gun. I can't get the rifle up fast enough.

He pulls the trigger, but it backfires and he drops it in the water. He plops down in the shallow water of the sand bar like a rag doll and stares at us.

Julia yanks on the oars and with each blade in the water we move another five yards farther away. Caballero gets smaller and smaller as we move one hundred, and then two hundred yards distant. Soon he is just a dot on the horizon next to a larger black bump.

"You can hit that beacon now," Julia says.

I reach over, flip open the rescue transmitter and hit the red switch. It pulses. I breathe deeply, sucking air into my lungs.

"Can you believe that?" Julia says.

"Did that just happen?" Trishelle says.

I stare at the straight blue line of the horizon. I can't believe it. I'm alive.

Something flicks the water's surface to my right. A black fin descends under the water. I peer over the edge and see a familiar black shape that disappears under us.

It nudges the raft from below, spooking everyone aboard.

"What was that?" Trishelle asks.

The black shape moves out from under the Zodiac and its fin breaks the surface. It's a bull shark, maybe the same one, and it circles us.

"Oh shit, we're going to die," Trishelle says.

But then it flicks its tail and swims toward the black dots on the horizon. Ten seconds later another black fin cruises by, and then another.

"What's going to happen?" Julia asks.

"Predator meets predator," I answer, "While the gazelles get away."

"Are we going to make it?"

"Just keep doing what you're doing."

I lie back next to Carl and feel overwhelming permission to pass out. I grab the edge of the tarp, yank it over our faces and close my eyes.

CHAPTER 52

JULIA

A bright light appears in the middle of the night. It's a helicopter, or a boat. Or two boats.

Men shout. An engine comes close. Someone shines a light in my face and yells louder. Salt water splashes me and soothes my burnt skin, but stings the open blisters on my hands. I cry out.

Hands carry me, then I feel solid wood under my feet. I try to stand but my knees buckle. Someone grabs my arm and another person wraps me in a blanket, and they carry me inside the boat.

It's a big boat, big enough that I can't feel the water moving under me anymore.

They put me on a cot. My eyes open and I see a man—a boy really—in some kind of uniform. "Close your eyes and rest, you're fine now."

"Is everyone okay?"

"Everyone is okay."

"Good," I lay my head back and exhale.

The boy keeps smiling at me. His face is strange. "What's wrong?"

"I thought you were great in *Junk Conspiracy*. I'm a big fan."

"Thanks. I'll give you an autograph later."

My eyes close.

CHAPTER 53

STEVEN

Sixty Days Later

After a month in a Bahamian hospital and another month limping around Carl's house, recuperating, I'm headed home. My nest egg is gone. It went to repairing Carl's house, replacing his fishing boat, my hospital bills and my rehab. Retirement is a distant horizon.

Carl will walk with a cane for at least six months, but he never mentions it. I'm welcome back any time.

The boy still visits my dreams. So does the tall man who I killed, floating in the blue hole. The dreams come every night, and they may come forever. I don't know.

One thing has changed, however. I accept them now. When they wake me up, I can close my eyes and sleep again, sometimes until morning. Sleep is what my mind and body need, and I'm thankful.

I look out the window. The Grand Canyon is far below. We're almost to my Golden State.

My landlord didn't mind that I stopped paying rent for two months, and with one call he said I could go back. Maybe my surfboard will still be there. I'm not sure if I'll keep living there. All I know is that I'll always live somewhere in California.

I flip the tiny flash drive in my hand. I haven't plugged it in yet to examine what's there, but when the time is right, I will.

The plane lands at LAX. My motorcycle is still in the parking lot, in the exact spot I left it two and a half months ago, covered in dust and grime. The parking bill is $800. I hand the cashier my credit card and she runs the charge without blinking.

"My motorcycle isn't even worth eight hundred bucks."

"It happens all the time. Have a nice day."

I drive up PCH and watch the warm autumn sun glinting silver off the ocean. It's a Saturday and the coast road is crowded with beach goers. Gladstone's restaurant patio is full of college kids drinking. The surfers are out near Malibu Beach Pier, and Pepperdine University looks pristine. The cool salt air feels different than the Atlantic that I left on the other side. I'm home.

I turn onto the road to Tivoli Cove and pull up to the tilted 1970s beach house where I live. It looks the same.

There's a town car by the staircase to my bachelor unit, with a driver behind the wheel. He looks up from his book, smiles and goes back to reading. That's odd.

I walk down the leaning wooden staircase and reach the landing. With one yank on the rope cord, the wood gate to my patio unlatches—and I find Julia is sitting on my hammock, swinging between my surfboard on one side and my Weber BBQ on the other.

She smiles. "Your place is a dump, but the deck is great."

"My thoughts exactly. Is that your car up top?"

"I thought I'd take you out to dinner. You like Thai food?"

"Sounds good. Mind if I have a beer first?" I unlock my sliding glass door.

"Go right ahead. Can you bring me one too?"

The room smells like warm stale socks after being closed up for so long. I toss down my backpack, go to the fridge and find two Coronas inside. I pop off the caps and sip one. It tastes fine to me, so I walk through the glass doors and hand Julia the other. She takes hers, sips and then moves over on the hammock to make a spot for me. I sit next to her.

She holds up her beer. "Welcome home."

"Thanks." We clink bottles.

We lie back, and she kicks the hammock into a slow rocking motion.

We sip our beers and watch the sun sink into the sea.

ACKNOWLEDGMENTS

Special thanks to my wife, Robin, and my daughter, Lily.

And thank you to: Mom aka Carol Tutu, Douglas Gorney, Paul Marshall, Aletha Rodgers, Jeanne Epstein, Aileen the Bean, the Dark Sisters, Lisa Cerasoli, Dr. Ken Atchity, and Derek Murphy for the stunning cover design.

The Picture Kills and *Six Passengers, Five Parachutes* are the first two books in The Quintana Adventures. *The Danger Game,* book three, is out now.

Ian Bull is also the author of the romantic thrillers *Liars in Love* and *Facing Reality*. He also writes nonfiction under his full name, Donald Ian Bull.

If you're interested in reading more of his work, email him at:

IanBullAuthor@gmail.com

Or visit:

www.IanBullAuthor.com

And, please, write a review of this book!

.

CHAPTER 1

STEVEN QUINTANA

Day 1: Saturday Night
Los Angeles, California

"**H**old up your Oscars!" the Academy publicist shouts. Everyone who just won an Academy Award for Science and Technology lifts their gold statuettes, grinning and blinking into a lightning shower of camera flashes. Only their host, actress Julia Travers, holds her gaze into the camera lens. She knows how to work it, of course. Her thick, blonde, flowing hair, and designer dress makes her look like a shimmering red ribbon against a black and white checkerboard of mostly men in tuxedos.

A week from tomorrow, she will walk out on stage at the main Oscar broadcast and announce the winners from tonight with a billion people watching. There's no denying it. Julia Travers, a woman from a small city in Canada, has overcome obstacles that would have killed most men...and she is now a movie star.

Julia has been famous for a while. First, she was famous for being a beautiful ingénue. Then she became infamous for having a "bad attitude" in public, a persona that I inflated when I worked as a paparazzo, selling her photos to the tabloids. Then she became even more famous for surviving a kidnapping and a murder attempt, which I survived as well. Now she is famous for the right reasons: for her talent and her hard work.

I'm not famous at all. I'm still just Steven Quintana, ex-Army Ranger, ex-tabloid paparazzo, ex-boyfriend to Julia, current nobody. I'm dressed in this monkey suit because Julia asked me to come. We're still close, despite our love affair imploding. I wished her luck in her dressing room before the show, then watched the ceremony from the farthest table back in the International Ballroom of the Beverly Hilton Hotel. She's been getting more crazy fan threats, which is the real reason she wants me here. There's plenty of security, but she feels safer when I'm close by. Saving someone's life does that to a person.

David, an actor friend and her official "date" tonight, talks to a bigwig in the corner. We make eye contact. He nods. He's the only one who recognizes me. Eighteen months ago, the gossip about Julia and me was so big it was in the tabloids and on the cover of *People*. But the buzz has faded since we broke up. Now, she grows more famous while I grow more anonymous.

Julia spots me from the stage and smiles. Smiling back, I realize that I love her…but ruined everything. "I'm an idiot," I say out loud.

"I won't fight you on that." It's Rikki Lassen, Julia's powerhouse manager. She's short, round, and dressed in a purple business suit that makes her look like a grape. "You're riding with me. I don't want photographers seeing you. Once Julia leaves with David, I'll call for my car."

I wish Julia's best friend Trishelle was still her manager, but she's living in Canada now with problems of her own. Still, Rikki is damn good at her job.

"Where are they going?" I ask.

"That's not your concern. Just stay out of sight."

Julia hired Rikki a year ago to revamp her image, and it worked. Rikki got Julia this gig tonight, and Julia's coming off one hit movie and starts work on another next week. Rikki's right—I'm bad press and don't help Julia's image. But I can still make sure Julia is safe.

"I'm going to make another loop and check security, if you don't mind."

"Chill, soldier. Sarah Hammond's security team doesn't need your help." She jabs her finger into my stiff tuxedo shirt before walking away.

As I head into the main lobby, all the guards touch their ears and speak into their lapels. They're tired of me checking on them. There aren't many limos and cars in the hotel turnaround yet, but ticket stubs are coming out of jacket pockets and valets are grabbing them and dashing off to the parking structure.

I sense someone behind me. It's Sarah Hammond herself, the boss of Hammond Security.

"Hello, Steven. I haven't seen you in months."

"I've been out of town. Sorry I quit on you like that."

"You were great for the six months you worked for me, so I can't complain."

She hires a lot of guys with Spanish surnames. Some are ex-military, some ex-sheriff's deputies, and some are ex-gang members who found religion. I thought the work might suit me, so I asked her for a job. The guys called me Güero, which means "white-washed," because I pass for Anglo. But people would recognize me, so I had to quit.

"You and Julia still having paparazzi problems?"

"Not since we broke up. But Julia has the jitters. She's been getting threats again."

"Stay safe, Steven." While she's close, she pushes on my left armpit.

"Are you checking to see if I'm packing a gun? I know that trick."

"No gun, but you're wearing a Kevlar vest. Why? Are you expecting trouble?"

"I haven't been in public in a while. PTSD residue is all."

"Just let us handle things." Sarah nods and leaves me.

I exit the hotel and stand behind the valet stand. A line of Lincoln Town Cars for the studio executives and sedans for the nominees inch forward to pick up their passengers. Burning gasoline hangs in a pungent cloud. The sound of vibrating engines mixes with the sound of doors shutting, and shouts goodbye. Ten paparazzi stand outside the drive around, just off hotel property. They'll snap photos with their long lenses as David and Julia come out, then surround her car as it leaves. But once in traffic, she'll be safe and I can go home.

A black Audi makes my antennae perk up. Two big guys are inside, and neither of them is in a suit. All the windows are tinted except the front windshield, which isn't right. I stare at one of Sarah Hammond's security guys, willing him to look at me. He scans the crowd, then we lock eyes. I nod at the black Audi. He looks over, touches his lapel, and starts speaking.

A shout goes up as David and Julia exit the hotel. Julia spots me and smiles. I just made her feel better, which is why I'm here. A driver stands ready to open the door of a black Porsche Cayenne. David and Julia pose in front of the car for a last set of photos. The paparazzi snap their pictures and move into the circular garden in the middle of the drive around. They're now on hotel property, and Sarah's guys motion for them to step back.

"That's it, people, they're leaving," Rikki says, voice booming from her small purple body. David and Julia and the driver get in. The doors close, but their car can't move because there's a line of cars in front of it. The paparazzi move toward the trapped Cayenne, like Komodo dragons descending upon a staked goat. Rikki looks worried, but Sarah's team is already working on it. Three of her guys block the paparazzi, while another three clear the traffic in front of Julia's car.

Except no one is paying attention to the black Audi now. It inches forward, sneaks past one car, and is now driving right up against the Cayenne's bumper.

Coming from behind the valet, I step off the curb into the car's path. The Audi lurches forward, but I hold my ground, hoping it will stop...but it doesn't. I dive forward and tuck into a roll. My left shoulder hits the hood first. There's a thump as I dent the metal and a screech of brakes as the car stops. I roll onto the pavement feet first. No windshield in the face, thank God.

Shouts go up from the crowd. Sarah's two biggest guys step in front of the Audi, blocking it from moving. I try to open the driver's door, but it's locked, so I peer through the windshield. The driver has straight black hair, light eyes, and bad acne scars, and his passenger has curly brown hair, white skin, and wears sunglasses. Both stare ahead, refusing to look at me.

Julia's car gets clear and peels off toward traffic. The meathead driving the Audi hits the gas. His car lurches as he tries to get past the guards, but Sarah's guys put their hands on the hood and hold their ground.

Sarah is by the valet on her cellphone. "They're gone, all clear!"

Her guards step back and the Audi screeches away, zooming up the driveway and into traffic on Wilshire Boulevard. They'll try to find Julia's car, but the Cayenne is long gone.

"Hey! He's that Steven Quintana guy!" someone shouts. The paparazzi spot me and plow through the garden in the middle of the circular drive, lenses up, shouting my name.

"Steven! Are you still dating Julia?"

"Is it true that she's supporting you?"

I'm bathed in a thousand camera flashes. Up on the curb, men in tuxedos and women in dresses hold their cellphones aloft and record my humiliation. The paparazzi push their cameras right into my face, hoping I go off on one of them again. I recognize a few of them, like Simon Le Clerq, a heavyset guy in a USC cap, who I knew when I was working as a paparazzo.

"You think you're better than us now, prick?" Le Clerq asks.

"How does it feel to have a camera in your face now?" asks another one.

"You gonna swing on us again, Soldier Boy?" asks a third.

The hotel cops arrive. "You're on hotel property, please leave!" one shouts, but they won't push through the Komodo dragons and pull me to safety.

A lens hits me in the back of my head. When I don't react, another hits me in the head from the other side. They want me to go off. Another story about me losing it, backed up with some photos of my yelling face, would make another perfect tabloid cover about Julia and me.

A car screeches behind me, followed by a long honk that doesn't stop. We all look—it's Rikki Lassen behind the wheel of her green BMW SUV. She revs her engine and lurches forward, hitting six of the paparazzi below the knees. They all clear away.

"Hey!" one shouts. "You hit me! I'm going to sue you, bitch!"

Rikki lowers her window and howls at them. "Tell the cops you got hit by Rikki Lassen, asshole, and see how far it gets you! I will have you tortured and killed!"

The six wounded paparazzi limp away. They know that she's the great white shark in their scummy ocean, and she really can hurt them if she wants.

"Get in the car, you stupid cowboy," she says as I rush to the other side. As I buckle in, the purple wrecking ball lets me have it. "What the hell? You think you're Simone Biles now? I told you to stay back and instead you're flipping over car hoods!"

"There were bad guys in that black Audi."

She's too busy screaming to hear me. "I said stay away...showoff...ruin my work...can't get a job...riding her coattails...."

I lower the car seat and close my eyes. Her screaming has a lilting rhythm to it. If you don't concentrate on the words, you can actually zone out to it. I actually like Rikki, but I'm not going to tell her that. She tears past the high-rise apartments in the Wilshire Boulevard corridor.

"Where are we going?" I ask when she finally stops yelling.

"To my place in Malibu."

Rikki's place is a mile from my tiny bachelor apartment in Tivoli Cove, where I pay rent but haven't lived in months. Rikki's beach house is nicer. She and her husband used it as a family getaway for years until they got divorced. She hates the place now, so she leases it to Julia.

"Just leave me at my place, I don't want to go there."

"Hey, I don't want you staining my sheets either. Julia wants you there, not me."

"Julia and I aren't together anymore, Rikki."

"And I'm praying it stays that way." We pass under the 405 Freeway, headed into Brentwood. "So, what do you do all day now that you're not mooching off her?"

"I've been working on my own projects."

"Projects? Have you gone Hollywood now, too? That's hilarious."

"I've been digging into the names on the flash drive from the Bahamas."

Rikki yanks the car over three lanes and takes the exit ramp for the Veterans Administration Hospital. She stops the car in the bus zone at the bottom.

"Want a tour of the VA?" I point toward a sandstone building that looks like a high school. "That's where I go for rehab on my shoulder and to talk to my shrink. Past that is Serenity Park, where veterans help abandoned parrots. Julia and I used to volunteer there."

"Julia doesn't care about that.".

"Julia loves those birds. We have a favorite, a little biter named Malo."

"I mean the flash drive!" Rikki wags her finger an inch from my face.

"I was shot and bleeding when I transferred those names and numbers to that flash drive. And then I swallowed it and carried it around in my gut for a week."

"Yuck. TMI. That was almost two years ago. Get over it."

"Get over it? Julia and Trishelle would have died in Xander Constantinou's snuff film if Carl and I hadn't rescued them. And that file lists all the rich men around the world who invested in that fiasco."

"What about earning a living?" she asks.

"I still have a little money from my paparazzo days. Julia hasn't given me a dime."

We fall into a silent truce as the car flies down San Vicente Boulevard toward Pacific Coast Highway. Then, in the side view mirror, I spot a black Audi following us. Rikki turns right onto 7th Street and goes down into the Santa Monica Canyon. The black Audi does, too.

"We're being followed by a black Audi Q5 SUV."

"Are you shopping for a car?"

"Remember my somersault? That was the car."

Rikki looks in her rearview mirror. "What do they want?"

They want me, I realize. They used Julia to lure me into the open. I suddenly regret the flash drive "research" I've been doing. The Audi is right on our tail now.

"Run the red light at the bottom of the hill."

The Audi pulls into the oncoming lane, then swerves and bumps her on the driver side. Her side airbag deploys and a pillow-size balloon explodes next to her face. She screams.

"Don't stop!" I grab the steering wheel.

Rikki's eyes beg me for help as light glints off the metal of a gun in the Audi's open passenger window. A white flash fills the car as her window shatters with a sonic boom.

She hits the brakes. I duck down with my whole body, pushing her legs away so I can hit the accelerator. I'm blind but I can hear the Audi's engine alongside. I peek up, hoping to steer my way out of trouble—

—and smash into a light pole. The front airbags inflate, knocking me back.

An invisible boxer punches me in the body four times as glass explodes around me.

THE PICTURE
KILLS

Made in the USA
Middletown, DE
30 September 2020

20376979R00224